A mewling drew
Kaa's attention

One of the muties was giving birth. The piebald lord knelt and picked up the newborn one. For a moment he dangled the blood-bathed infant by its umbilical cord.

Kaa pressed the baby to its mother's breast, and it began to nurse at once. After a few hours of steady feeding, the creature would uncouple from the nipple. The little mutant would be able to run and hunt the moment its feet touched the earth.

By the time they reached the ville, many hundreds more would have been birthed, nursed, fattened and ready.

Soon Kaa's army would number in the thousands— and it was only the beginning.

**Other titles in the
Deathlands saga:**

JAMES AXLER

DEATH LANDS®

Skydark

A GOLD EAGLE BOOK FROM
WORLDWIDE®

TORONTO • NEW YORK • LONDON
AMSTERDAM • PARIS • SYDNEY • HAMBURG
STOCKHOLM • ATHENS • TOKYO • MILAN
MADRID • WARSAW • BUDAPEST • AUCKLAND

First edition March 1997

ISBN 0-373-62536-7

SKYDARK

Printed in U.S.A.

"Iron covered the fields and roads: iron points reflected the rays of the sun. This iron, so hard, was borne by a people whose hearts were harder still."
—From *Bullfinch's Mythology*,
    "Legends of Charlemagne,"
    attributed to Ogier the Dane, circa 800 A.D.

"From what same clay are both heroes and tyrants made?"
—From *Relativism and Reality in Modern
    Political Thought* by Dr. Donn Tretheway, D.D.,
    Patti Party Press, Sandpoint, Idaho, 1999

THE DEATHLANDS SAGA

This world is their legacy, a world born in the violent nuclear spasm of 2001 that was the bitter outcome of a struggle for global dominance.

There is no real escape from this shockscape where life always hangs in the balance, vulnerable to newly demonic nature, barbarism, lawlessness.

But they are the warrior survivalists, and they endure—in the way of the lion, the hawk and the tiger, true to nature's heart despite its ruination.

Ryan Cawdor: The privileged son of an East Coast baron. Acquainted with betrayal from a tender age, he is a master of the hard realities.

Krysty Wroth: Harmony ville's own Titian-haired beauty, a woman with the strength of tempered steel. Her premonitions and Gaia powers have been fostered by her Mother Sonja.

J. B. Dix, the Armorer: Weapons master and Ryan's close ally, he, too, honed his skills traversing the Deathlands with the legendary Trader.

Doctor Theophilus Tanner: Torn from his family and a gentler life in 1896, Doc has been thrown into a future he couldn't have imagined.

Dr. Mildred Wyeth: Her father was killed by the Ku Klux Klan, but her fate is not much lighter. Restored from predark cryogenic suspension, she brings twentieth-century healing skills to a nightmare.

Jak Lauren: A true child of the wastelands, reared on adversity, loss and danger, the albino teenager is a fierce fighter and loyal friend.

Dean Cawdor: Ryan's young son by Sharona accepts the only world he knows, and yet he is the seedling bearing the promise of tomorrow.

In a world where all was lost, they are humanity's last hope....

Prologue

There was no escape from the nightmare of Deathlands after the nuclear holocaust in 2001. Ryan Cawdor understood that, take it or leave it, this was his world. He never forgot that no court of law, no army of deliverance, no rescue squad would be there to put things to right—ever.

What population was left existed without laws or moral guidance, other than to obey the savage rules of survival. Nature lay waste, ruined, contaminated, the tragic price humanity paid for the blind worship of science. And there was hardly a steeper price than the kind of severe genetic scrambling that created those mutated humans who were monstrous in body and mind.

Life always meant peril in the Deathlands, but the mutants seemed to symbolize the unconscious dread of the disintegration of the species. So they were often targeted for summary execution by the norms, and those mutants who were able and of a like mind energetically returned the favor.

Through this world Ryan Cawdor and his warrior survivalists roamed, with predark wags if a lucky find provided scarce fuel. But even with the wags travel was a high risk enterprise, and increasingly the mat-trans units in the redoubts offered the best option for a change of scene or quick exit from a hotspot.

Built before skydark, the redoubts and their mat-trans gateways had endured the nuke barrage because they were entirely self-contained, blast-proofed and powered by their own nuclear reactors.

In the course of dozens of locational jumps with the units, they had come across only a very few people who had discovered the secret of the gateways.

All that was about to change.

And not for the better.

Chapter One

A whisper of chill, stale air crept along the mat-trans chamber's armaglass walls, and with it came a whiff of something sharp and electric. As the raised metallic floor plates began to glow brighter, Ryan Cawdor scanned the faces of his five friends.

Only Krysty returned his gaze, her green eyes steady. Though she held her head high and her long-limbed, statuesque body defiantly erect, he could tell that deep down she was anxious about the jump: her prehensile, mutant red hair had drawn close to her nape, retracting in response to danger.

The woman's anxiety was understandable. The danger was very real, and close enough to taste.

Mildred Wyeth sat beside Krysty with her eyes shut and her head bowed. The multiple beaded plaits of Mildred's hair swayed slightly as she clenched her hands into fists at her sides, her stocky form tensed as if to absorb a body blow. Whip-lean Jak Lauren stared blankly off in the middle distance; though the expression in his ruby-colored eyes was unreadable, the tendons of his jaws flexed like steel cables under the waxy white of his scarred cheeks. J. B. Dix gripped the brim of his beloved fedora with both hands, twisting it down to seat it more firmly on his head. Behind the Armorer's round, steel-rimmed spectacles, Ryan caught the glimmer of a sardonic smile. What was that old predark saying? When the crapfall really got heavy, it was time to screw on your hat.

Ryan turned to Doc Tanner last. The old man's eyes were tightly closed, his lips moving as he muttered softly to himself. He repeated a short phrase over and over. Under the present circumstances, on the verge of molecular disassembly, any whisper might have been taken for a prayer. Though the phrase Doc was repeating sounded vaguely like a plea for mercy or salvation, it wasn't.

The one-eyed man recognized the strange words. Doc, a fountainhead of obscure, dated and often arcane knowledge, had taught Ryan the phrase and its meaning.

Morituri te salutamus.

As Doc had explained, the words were in Latin—one of many human languages long dead before the nuke shit hit the fan. *Morituri te salutamus* was a Roman gladiator's oath to his emperor before entering mortal combat, which signified submission and allegiance to a higher power and an acceptance of one's own fate.

"We who are about to die salute you."

Ryan figured the part about accepting fate was a flat-out given; what the rest meant was a mystery to him. He had no idea who or what Doc thought he was saluting, or if the old man even knew. The experience of having been time-trawled into the future had done something to the old man's mind. He didn't always talk rationally.

A swirling gray mist appeared near the chamber's ceiling. Tendrils of the mist drifted down, obscuring everything.

A curious person caught in the same situation might have wondered if the fog really existed or if it was an illusion, a figment of a mind already being systematically deconstructed, cell by cell. Ryan Cawdor wasn't a man to linger over questions that served no immediate purpose. He was a stone-hard pragmatist, a bottom liner, which was why he and his friends used the mat-trans units. Having journeyed across post-Armageddon America on foot and in the Trader's war wags for many years, he knew how dangerous those alternate modes of transportation were. The odds were heavily stacked against the long-term survival of conventional travelers, no matter how well armed they were. Of the many thousands of human fatalities he had seen in Deathlands, few had been quick and painless.

Ryan fell through the space where the floor should have been, spiraling downward, faster and faster through black emptiness. Somewhere in the middle of his windmilling fall, he completely lost consciousness. Mercifully everything went blank. But not for long. The mind dreamed in transit, and the dreams were always bad.

The instant of deathlike oblivion was shattered by a

surge of color, sound and the full range of physical sensations; the jump dream had begun.

It was night.

He hit the ground running. His bare feet slapped against moist soil as he raced toward a distant tower of flames. And as he ran, he knew it wasn't his own body that carried him. It was too light, too quick, too strong for its size. The differences—the raw speed and the agility—amazed him.

Effortlessly he closed the gap between himself and a crude defensive wall of skinny, unpeeled logs seated in heaped, tamped earth. A narrow section of the tree-trunk barrier was smoking, the ax-sharpened tops of its logs shattered into fans of splinters as if by a lightning strike. He slipped through a break in the wall and into the midst of a tiny, triple-poor ville. Ryan knew he had never been there before, but he had seen many outposts just like it, clinging for life at the edges of Deathlands. The nameless ville's packed-dirt courtyard was surrounded by a jumble of thatched-roof shanties. Most of its two dozen mud-and-stick huts were already burning. Beyond their steeply peaked roofs, at the rear of the compound, he could just make out the sawtooth top of the log wall.

All around him the humid darkness echoed with animal shrieks of pleasure and cries of pain. The air hung heavy with a maddening perfume: the metallic scent of freshly spilled blood and the sour smell of wood smoke. He caught the dim shapes of white limbs moving frantically at the edges of the firelight—the arms and legs of others like him, gleefully killing with bare hands and feet.

His kin had already found their prey.

He caught himself gasping, not from the exertion of the full-out run, but from the intensity of the excitement he felt. Heat radiated from his very core, surging through his limbs and his face. It was the heat of desire, of an unquenchable hunger. Not a hunger for sex; this lust wasn't focused in his loins, but in the center of his torso, between heart and stomach. Even as the heat billowed outward, it seemed to compress his lungs in hoops of steel, forcing him to sip greedily for air. And from his own throat came a strange mewling sound, liquid, plaintive, sinuous. The vibrations of the soft cry cascaded over his chest like a caress.

He turned slowly, taking in every detail of the grim scene: the fires, the brutal murders of the ville's people and their livestock, the wanton destruction. Everything he saw as he turned, everything he felt was new—and fascinating.

A staccato crackle of gunfire froze him. It was from a single blaster, inside the ville's perimeter. There was still at least one survivor. He crossed the courtyard, homing in on the source of the sound.

When he tried the front door of the shabby hut, it wouldn't open, even to a full-force kick. It was heavily barred from the inside. Without a thought he climbed the hut's front wall, as quick as a lizard, scampering up onto the thatched roof. He peered down through the ragged hole that had been torn in the thatch. The room below him was lit by rows of guttering candles, illuminating several corpses around a long table.

Ryan dropped twenty-five feet, landing softly on the killing floor.

Three adults and four children lay facedown in the middle of their evening meal. He sniffed at one of the crude wooden bowls, recognizing boiled mashed roots, boiled mashed beans, boiled prickly leaves. It was a gray-green, tasteless last supper. The rough-hewn table was puddled with the blood of the seven diners. From the eye sockets up, the tops of their skulls had been ripped off, the contents plundered, splattered and smeared over the clay-colored interior walls. Their arms and legs were cracked and twisted into impossible positions, their necks grotesquely bent.

The sweet stench of gore suffused the warm, moist air, and made it even harder for Ryan to breathe. A surge of internal heat, more powerful than anything he had yet felt, slammed him. And he had the sudden urge to throw himself into the pool of blood spreading across the tamped earth floor, the urge to roll and wallow in it. At some deeply submerged level of mind, Ryan recognized the alien nature of the thought and recoiled. Though he tried, he couldn't stop himself from kneeling and touching the spilled blood. Nor could he stop himself from feeling disappointment when he realized it had already gone cold.

He examined the floor. Multiple bloody footprints led away from the red pool. And then he caught a faint whiff of a familiar, fishy odor: kin on the hunt.

His strange new body's response was automatic. Once more the strangely pleasurable mewling sound erupted from his throat. As it did, a horrendous, sustained burst of gunfire rang out, this time so close it seemed to shake the hut's walls. Ryan leaped over the blood and through the yawning doorway beyond. It opened onto a cramped, dark room where rude straw pallets were spread out on the ground. At one end of the room a door to the outside stood ajar. He peered cautiously around the jamb. The doorway looked onto a small lane that separated the ragged line of huts. Lit by the nearby burning rooftops, the dirt track lay heaped with still-thrashing white bodies: his kin tangled up in yards of their own spilled bowels.

Only one creature remained standing in the narrow lane.

The enemy.

A tall, rangy and powerfully built man bent over a fresh corpse, trying to pry the first six inches of a long-bladed knife from the center of its bony chest. With his back to Ryan, the black-haired foe braced the sole of his boot on the dead face while he savagely levered the knife handle back and forth.

The sight sent a wave of righteous hatred and rage coursing through Ryan's blood. Under the hate and the rage—and more terrible than either—he felt a surge of pure delight, delight in what he knew to be his own vastly superior physical strength, delight in the destruction he was about to visit upon the unwary man.

In a single, catlike bound, he crossed the space be-

tween the doorway and his target. He launched himself
with his arms outstretched, and when he slammed onto
the enemy's back, he caught hold and drove him forward, but not down as he had planned. With a combination of balance and strength, the man managed to
keep his feet despite the sudden impact. Ryan's arms
whipped in a blur, hands tearing at the broad shoulders.
Cloth gave way, presenting him with bare, warm skin.
Ryan snatched hold and pulled as hard as he could.
The skin stretched and stretched until it could stretch
no more, and then it began to rip loose from the dense
layers of muscle underneath.

The man screamed and whirled, punching, kicking,
trying to throw him off.

Ryan held on, riding his enemy like a wild horse,
and when the man paused for breath, he repositioned
his grip. As he moved his hands, he saw the torn strips
of skin, the bright, slick blood and the rows of round
red welts he had left behind. Suddenly everything made
sense. The speed. The uncanny climbing ability. The
animal urges. Even as Ryan realized with a pang of
horror what the welts meant, what kind of subhuman,
mutated body he possessed, his body slapped a hand
against the side of the man's face. The tiny suckers that
lined his fingers and palms seized the flesh of cheek,
nose and forehead. Bracing a knee in the middle of his
enemy's back, he used all his power to twist the strain-
ing, corded neck and draw the chin toward him over
top of the bleeding shoulder.

The dark-haired man had a single eye, blue and full

of hate. The empty socket on the other side of his face was covered by a patch, which only partly concealed the old blade scar that split eyebrow and cheek.

It was like looking into a mirror.

The life Ryan Cawdor was about to take was his own.

Then something even stranger began to happen: it started to hurt.

Bad.

For a terrible instant Ryan floundered in a jumble of conflicting viewpoints and sensations. His world blurred as two different sets of images, from two different sets of eyes—murderer's and victim's—were superimposed on one another. His consciousness inhabited both of the struggling dream-bodies at once, but he couldn't control either. Though he ordered the aggressor to let go, it wouldn't obey; though he commanded the victim to break free, the attacker on his back was too strong. Ryan simultaneously felt exquisite pleasure and unendurable pain as the tendons that anchored face to bone snapped, and the brutally drawn flesh tore free from the front of his skull. Victim Ryan's head wrenched back with such force that his neck vertebrae shattered, severing his spinal cord.

Blackness cut through Ryan's consciousness like a sword slash, dividing him from the slumping human form.

And once more there was only one creature standing in the narrow, corpse-littered lane.

Straddling the broken human body, Ryan the victor

clutched in his suckered fist a bloody rag of muscle and sinew and, dangling by its torn nerve bundle, one intensely blue eye.

THE HUGE BONFIRE BEAT against Mildred's bare back in scorching waves. Of their own accord, her legs responded to the erratic rhythm of the heat, propelling her around the edge of the blaze in a jittery, jerky, arm-waving dance. Between her toes the earth was gooey soft, churned to muck by the footsteps of the dozens of others who circled the fire with her. Numbed by the pleasure she felt, Mildred danced through roiling clouds of rank smoke, through showers of golden sparks. Beside her the fire roared like an engine from hell.

It hissed and whistled, squealed and screamed.

As Mildred jigged and hopped, her arms pumping overhead, something in the heart of the pyre exploded. The soft *whump* hurled chunks of flaming wood, like miniature comets, across the courtyard. Wood wasn't the only thing burning—or flying. Hot, wet gobbets of flesh spattered her bare breasts, stomach and thighs.

For the first time Mildred looked down and took note of her dream-body. Its stark whiteness stunned her. She stopped dancing, letting the other celebrants brush past her. Her limbs weren't dark brown as they should have been, but pale as ash. And they were the wrong shape, too. Not muscular and heavy boned, but slender, almost fragile.

When she turned over her hands, she saw the rows

of tiny suckers that lined their mutated palms. A chill of horror crept up the back of her neck.

A wall of blast-furnace heat rolled over Mildred. It was so intense that she had to jump away or have her skin blistered. As she whirled, the burst of heat penetrated her from head to foot, and like an exotic drug, lubricated her joints, her belly, and made her brain bubble and froth. Instantly her concern over what she had become vanished—and the lithe, pale body resumed its erratic dance.

At the edge of the firelight she could make out the smoldering ruins of the little ville. A group of scrawny, white-limbed figures rushed from the deep shadows, bearing more fuel for the pyre. Some carried great armloads of thatch, broken pieces of furniture, piles of the pathetic personal belongings of the ville's inhabitants— lice-infested straw beds, flea-ridden furs and coarsely woven blankets. Others ran forward in pairs, dragging limp human bodies between them by the heels or wrists. Four of the pale firebugs carried a struggling, screaming, dismembered hog. With all its legs torn off, it looked like an enormous, grotesquely bloated, pink grub.

Into the great fire went the thatch, the people and the pig. Fountains of sparks shot into the black sky, then the night echoed with overlapping shrieks of agony—the great sow wasn't the only still-living thing that had been tossed into the blaze. Trembling charred hands reached out through the curtain of fire, clutched at nothingness and fell back.

Mildred's human spirit retreated in horror from the sight, even as her strange new body delighted in it, spinning and capering in ecstasy. In her wild exuberance she collided with a fellow reveler. The impact bounced her from the dance track at the edge of the bonfire. She stumbled and slipped on the muddy ground. As she caught herself with a hand, she looked up.

Fifty feet away, at the edge of the light, stood another figure, impossibly tall and as still as a statue. Obviously, enormously male, its gleaming, oiled body was hairless and naked, but for a knotted loincloth and combat boots.

"Kaaa…" she said automatically, the sound rippling up from her throat like the purr of a cat.

What the cry meant, Mildred didn't know.

But it felt delicious.

The giant had odd, piebaldlike markings on his skin: brown cloud shadows crawling over his snowy whiteness. A bandolier of black-tipped cartridges hung across his massive chest and shoulders—ammo for his weapon, the mother of all shoulder-fired blasters. In his hands the M-60 machine gun looked like a child's toy.

He didn't have the look of kin, nor the familiar, rank-sour smell.

He looked and smelled like the god he was.

Mildred prostrated herself before him, pressing her face deep into the mud. Kill or die—there was nothing she wouldn't do for him. When she raised her face, he gestured sharply with the machine gun, acknowledging her supplication and releasing her from it.

"Kaaa..." Mildred purred, crawling backward on her belly.

When she rose and turned again to the pyre, a great plume of sparks shot skyward. Her kin had just fed it more fuel. Fresh screams cut through the throbbing roar. Mildred's body responded to the sudden surge in heat with an instant jerk-dance. Then something bounced out of the fire, landing almost on top of her feet.

A baby.

It writhed in its own miniature ball of flame, screeching like a teakettle.

A pang of human conscience pierced her mat-trans dream state. For a second Dr. Mildred Wyeth, the trained physician, the care giver, fought for control. Though she felt the baby's pain and wanted to save its life, she also felt an opposing and even more powerful need: to kill all those not kin, to burn the corpses and stomp the dry bones to powder. The woman struggled to make the alien body respond to her will, but it was as if her true, human self was stuck to flypaper—she could only drag herself a short distance before she was pulled back, exhausted. And before she could reach the dying baby and put out the fire, another pale and scrawny figure stepped up and kicked it back into the heart of the blaze.

Mildred tried desperately to wake up, to end the nightmare, but to no avail. Buffeted by the heat, she continued to dance like a automaton, drool sliding down her chin and throat and glistening between her rock-hard breasts.

KRYSTY DREAMED she was climbing, hand over foot, up an incredibly steep incline. She moved joyously, as light and quick as a spider across a great, mist-shrouded, gray cliff. As she scaled the face, reality began to shift and skew. The incline's sheer, vertical surface started to sway and ripple under her weight. It felt more like a net ladder woven from rope than a mountain of rock. As she continued upward through the blinding fog, she realized that it wasn't made of rope, either. The hand-and footholds she climbed were warm and smooth, and electric to the touch.

Then the wall she climbed but couldn't see began to sing.

The sound of a thousand flutes surrounded and enfolded her. They chirped, they tweeted, they trilled up and down three octaves. If any of the flutes played a melody, it was lost amid the chaos of random notes. The volume pulsed louder, reaching a mighty crescendo like a cheering crowd, then it trailed off to near-silence. It roared again, and again faded. Louder, then softer, over and over. The sawing, atonal music stirred something inside Krysty, sending a tickle of excitement rushing from the base of her skull to the base of her spine. Without warning, the fog around her lifted, and everything came into sharp, startling focus.

Not only was the cliff, the net, the wall beneath her alive, but it was in constant, undulating motion.

It was made up of thousands of creatures, their arms and legs laced together, interlinked chains of pale, naked beings. Krysty raised her bare foot to a shoulder and gripped the front of the thigh above, pulling herself higher. She smelled sour sweat from the bald head of the creature upon whose back she climbed, felt the seething animal heat. The brush of skin against skin told her that she, too, was naked. She looked up to see that the tapestry of bodies hung from some indistinct point out of sight overhead. And it wasn't made of a single sheet of living beings, but many sheets, laid one on top of another, and layers of individual creatures locked as she was now, chest to back, chest to back, chest to back.

From below, a hand closed around her ankle and yanked. Krysty braced herself and lashed out with a savage mule kick. Her heel made solid contact with a face, and the hand released her foot. She glanced over her shoulder and saw a white body pinwheeling away from the living wall, and as it did, it crashed into the climbers below, creating a chain reaction, an avalanche. Dozens of white forms were knocked free and sent tumbling thousands of feet before they disappeared into the mist. Their deaths panicked and momentarily froze the hundreds of other pursuers swarming up the web.

Krysty felt a delirious exaltation. No one could stop her. As she climbed higher and higher, the interlinked creatures she passed over became noticeably larger and stronger—they had to be in order to maintain their position in the chain of bodies.

The strongest of all were at the very top.

They were the most desirable mates.

Mates!

Even as Krysty understood the purpose of her dream-body's superhuman effort, she felt a strange pull, an arching ache in her groin. She looked down at herself in astonishment. She had no breasts, and she was most definitely a male. A sexually excited male.

Her initial impulse was to laugh aloud.

Prior to her first sexual experience—with Carl Lanning, the son of Harmony ville's blacksmith—Krysty had wondered what it would feel like to have masculine apparatus. Predark shrinks might have diagnosed her as suffering from a mild case of penis envy. After that first time with Carl, she was no longer envious—or even curious. Her body had told her, had shown her, that the Gaia power she possessed, the mutant abilities passed down to her by her mother, Sonja, dwarfed anything that male physiology could ever hope to do.

The man thing jerked upward, seemingly with a will of its own.

Watching it, she felt a tangible sense of loss. Whoever, whatever she was now, she was no longer Krysty Wroth, no longer connected to a long line of highly evolved females. Her Earth Mother power had been replaced by the more obvious—and much less imposing—prod between her legs.

Even as she grieved for her femininity, a passion, an

animal need, swept over her. It was like nothing she'd ever felt before. The body she inhabited knew what it wanted. The body would not be denied.

The body climbed.

She could see a creature moving above her, with small breasts and sturdy thighs and hams. Waves of heat washed over Krysty's face and down her chest. Unable to control the body, she retreated into herself, drawing as far away from the alien sensations as she could.

Though her body tried to overtake the creature, it couldn't; its quarry had too great a lead. The creature reached the top of the chain, and once there, clasped itself onto the back of what looked to be a huge male. Despite her attempt to curl up and hide, Krysty found herself experiencing everything her body felt. She was a helpless passenger as it moved into position on the creature's back, as with a suckered hand it guided its upstanding member under the unprotected buttocks, nosing it into the warm, moist crevice it found there.

Trapped inside the male body, swept away in its hormone storm, Krysty momentarily lost touch with her real-world identity: she wanted only what the body wanted. A chirping sound erupted from her throat as she thrust deep into the clinging softness.

Ecstasy swallowed her up.

As her body's hips fell into a rocking rhythm, a hand from below gripped her foot, then her hip. Krysty felt the weight of another creature on her back. It was enormous. The vibration deep in her belly became an earthquake as a rough hand reached under her buttocks, as something thick and hard nudged against her.

Pleasure—very familiar, very feminine—exploded between her legs; it brought her back to herself in a headlong rush. The unmistakable sensation told her that her dream-body had two sets of sex organs, one male, the other female, both fully operational.

As did all the creatures in the living web.

As her hips reared back for another jab, the huge creature hanging on her shoulders thrust, and she was penetrated. As her body lunged forward, the creature she rode turned its head and opened its wet mouth in a gasp. Krysty stared into a white, flabby face framed by a bald pate. The eyes were unreadable, flat, as dead as a doll's. The teeth like yellow nail points.

Stickie!

Krysty's spirit fought with all its strength, but there was no escaping the predicament. Unable to break free of the grip of the creature that had mounted her, wedged in, front and back, lost in the tweeting chant, the lubricious, thrusting pleasure, Krysty panicked, flailing in the darkness of the alien skull. Her real self wasn't just lost and adrift; it was drowning. It was dying. There was no Gaia power in this feverish universe, nothing and no one to come to her aid.

As more and more stickies added links and layers to the chain, the mass humping built to a frenzy. Krysty knew with a terrible certainty that she would be impregnated by the great thing on her back, that her belly would swell and swell until she staggered under its weight, and that soon she would give birth to a gaggle of needle-toothed, dead-eyed monsters.

That's what this elaborately choreographed exercise was all about.

The birthing of monsters.

As that realization sank home, at the edge of consciousness she sensed an onlooker, a shadowy presence lurking beyond her field of view. A presence of pure and perfect evil—which stepped forward, into the light of her mind.

Not just a bystander, this, or a mere watcher.

This was a laughing ringmaster.

With steel eyes.

RYAN AWAKENED on his hands and knees on the gateway floor. As he clung to it, the gleaming surface seemed to dip and swirl, and the chamber's violet-tinted armaglass walls spun wildly around him. Strands of acrid bile dangled from his parted lips. His mind reeled with more than the usual postjump confusion. He had suffered an awful defilement, a rape of soul that not even a lifetime of Deathlands' horrors had prepared him for.

Against his will he had been forced to share space, breath, heartbeat with the mutated and inhuman.

The gateway chamber reeked of vomit. Ryan dry-heaved from the stench, his stomach threatening to invert itself and climb out his throat. All around him, amid the groans of his companions, he heard what sounded like dozens of tiny lips blowing soft, wet kisses. Slowly, like a curtain rising, the mat-trans haze lifted from his brain.

It was then he realized there were too many legs, arms and bodies inside the sealed chamber.

With an effort he focused his eye.

Inches away two huge eyes looked back at him from a pale, hairless face, black eyes, alive but dead to feeling, to sympathy, to mercy. Below the eyes were tiny nostrils centered in moist flab, and its mouth was lined with rows of pointed, vulpine teeth.

Before Ryan could make his body react, the stickie lashed out. A cold, sucker-lined hand slapped against his face, covering mouth, nose and cheek. But the suckers failed to attach themselves to the man's flesh.

As he bounced the back of the stickie's head onto the floor, Ryan glimpsed other muties sprawled and tangled in the hexagonal-shaped chamber. His companions were outnumbered two to one.

He started to reach for the handblaster on his hip, a 9 mm SIG-Sauer semiautomatic, but thought better of it. At point-blank range, in the close confines of the chamber, the high-velocity, full-metal-jacket slugs would undoubtedly drill through the stickies and hit either his companions or the armaglass walls. Hopping into a low crouch, Ryan drew his panga from its sheath. The stickie screamed up in his face as it, too, started to rise.

Instead of using the razor edge of the eighteen-inch knife to behead the mutie—there wasn't enough clearance behind him for a sideways swing—Ryan brought the knurled steel pommel of the handle down on the hairless head in a full-power arc. The top of the skull crunched under the impact and caved in, punching bone shards deep into the brain cavity. The stickie's screaming stopped as if cut off by a switch; the huge black pupils of its shark eyes floated on seas of bright red. Blood jetted from the tiny nostrils as it slumped, twitching feebly, back to the gateway floor.

Even as it fell, the other stickies began to rouse themselves, sitting up and blinking in the harsh, artificial light.

Ryan gripped the shoulder of Doc's frock coat and gave him a hard shake. "Rad-blast it, Doc, get up!" he shouted. Jak and J.B., though obviously still dazed, pushed themselves to their knees. Ryan stepped to Mildred's side and shook her, too. "Get up and fight!" he told her. "Fight now or we all die!"

Krysty was the only one who didn't respond to his war cry. She lay curled in a fetal position, her back against the violet armaglass, separated from Ryan and the others by a knot of stickies.

The band of killer muties screamed in unison and hurled themselves across the slippery floor, charging their enemies.

Discarding the ebony sheath of his swordstick, Doc set to work in a frenzy that more than matched his inhuman opposition. Fearless in the face of the stickies' fury, his narrow, straight, double-edged blade flicked like a steel serpent's tongue, driving in and out of the pale bodies in a red-tinged blur. Doc avoided the blade-seizing trap of the bony sternums, and sought out the soft and tender parts, piercing bowels, stomachs, hearts.

Ryan pivoted around the stickie charge, skating on the nasty, slick floor to get between Krysty and the pair of muties who had turned to attack her. Bracing himself, he made a mighty, two-handed slash with his panga. The keen blade clipped through both of them at waist height, cutting off their arms at the elbows, dropping their coiled guts to the floor.

As Mildred tried to stand to meet the attack, she, too, slipped in the slimy mess underfoot. Her faltering step made the onrushing stickie lose its target. The suckered hand missed her head by less than an inch and slapped against the armaglass wall. It stuck there, trapped by its own suckers for a second—long enough for Mildred to unholster her ZKR 551 pistol. The Czech-made blaster was a precision target weapon and chambered for the relatively light .38-caliber Smith & Wesson round.

Light was just what the doctor ordered.

Without worrying about the possibility of a through-and-through, Mildred pressed the muzzle of the blaster against her attacker's breastbone and fired. The tiny gateway chamber rocked with the boom and flash. The stickie's arms flew back, opening wide as if to better display the blackened, starburst hole burned into the center of its chest. As the creature hurtled like a rag doll toward the far wall, it knocked down four of its comrades.

Ryan moved in on them with his panga. He gripped

it like a baseball bat, hacking at the heads and necks of the flopping muties. The deaths he gave them were neither quick nor clean. Still infected by the dream, Ryan exorcised his loathing for the debased species, making these few pay dearly for his nightmare. The stickies shrieked under the rain of heavy but indifferently aimed blows.

While the one-eyed man worked off his fury, Jak ducked under the crazed rush of a trio of muties. The teenager spun and struck like a poison-spitting cobra, with perfect aim. Too fast for a human eye to follow, leaf-bladed throwing knives leaped from his hand to the unguarded necks of the stickies. The metal handles of his deadly blades appeared as if by magic in the sides of their throats, slicing through the clustered arteries and sending bright blood spurting. The sudden, complete loss of blood pressure to their brains dropped the stickies where they stood.

There was a loud hiss behind Ryan, and a blast of fresh, cool air hit his back. As he whirled, he saw the last surviving stickie. Screaming in rage, it clung to J.B.'s back, riding him out of the open chamber doorway.

Fighting to keep his balance, the Armorer tripped over the portal and crashed to the floor of the brightly lit room outside. The stickie's weight came down on top of him, but J.B. already had the slim, polished steel of his Tekna knife clutched in his fist. He thumbed the button in the butt of the knife's handle, and the metal sheath flicked back, exposing a bright scalpel blade.

As the stickie ripped off his hat and glasses, J.B. reached back and slashed at the join of the mutie's hip and thigh, deftly slitting the femoral artery. Though its blood pulsed out in great gouts, the stickie refused to die. It grabbed hold of its enemy with both hands and started tearing at his neck.

Ryan jumped from the gateway chamber and with a downward slash of his panga cleaved the creature's right arm off at the shoulder. Before the massive wound could even begin to bleed, he brought the long knife swinging around in a tight horizontal arc. The stickie's head fell from its neck and skittered across the floor, rolling under a gunmetal gray desk.

With Mildred's help, Ryan managed to pry the dead but still-strangling fingers from their friend's throat.

"Scab-ass bastard," J.B. croaked, massaging his neck, "wanted to take me to hell with him."

"Hey, somebody, need hand here," Jak said from the mat-trans chamber's entry. He held Krysty draped against his hip. Her head lolled loose on her shoulders, and her prehensile red hair hung in limp strands. Her long, slender legs wouldn't support her weight.

"I got her, Jak," Ryan said, scooping Krysty into his arms.

There had been a time in Ryan's life when he would have thought twice about stepping forward. As a wild, young coldheart riding shotgun on the Trader's War Wag One, under the same circumstances he might even have turned his back. Before he'd met Krysty, his only concern had been for his own survival, and for improving the odds for the same. Now he couldn't deny the powerful feelings he had for the red-haired beauty. As he carried her over to a desktop, he could feel the shallow and rapid rise and fall of her breathing, and he was grateful for it.

Ryan gently laid her down on the desk, then stepped back so Mildred could give her an immediate examination. Standing idly by and watching the procedure served no purpose, except to make the one-eyed man feel helpless and impatient, so while the doctor worked he and Jak reentered the chamber and retrieved the weapons and gear they had dropped during the close-quarters battle.

Doc leaned against the edge of a desktop, his brow furrowed, lost in a troubled reverie until Jak prodded him with the tip of his swordstick's ebony sheath. The old man jerked violently at the unexpected touch. "By the Three Kennedys!" He pointed his rapier at the headless body on the floor. "Foul incubus! Phantasm of the dunghill! What cruel joke Morpheus has played and made me its clefted fundament!"

His companions stared at him, waiting for a translation of the archaic syntax and references.

"Though I am loath to admit it," Doc said, "during our recent journey I dreamed I was one of those unspeakable creatures."

"That's very odd," Mildred said as she completed testing the light response of Krysty's pupils, "because the same thing happened to me. And it was the most awful jump nightmare I've ever had. Makes my skin crawl to remember it."

When the doctor looked at Jak, the ruby-eyed teenager scowled back unpleasantly but said nothing. J.B. was more forthcoming about his experience.

"I had a dream like that, too. And my dream stunk almost as bad as what's in there." He jerked a thumb at the pale corpses heaped inside the mat-trans chamber.

"Can fix," Jak said. As quick as a cat, he moved to close the door.

"Fireblast!" Ryan swore. "You know better, Jak! If you close the door, more of the earless bastards can come through the gateway!"

The truth of his words hung in the air, as cold and certain as death.

As far as the six travelers knew, the race of homicidal mutants known as stickies had never used a gateway before. Now that the stickies had apparently taken their first mat-trans leap, and arrived as Ryan and company lay on the floor recovering, they had to face the possibility that they had done it on purpose; if indeed that was the case, the dead-eyed whirlwinds of slaughter and destruction could pop up anywhere, anytime.

"Mebbe they just stumbled in," J.B. suggested, trying hard to offer another explanation for the muties' presence in the gateway chamber. "Wandered in like stupes and accidently tripped the unit. Or mebbe they didn't jump at all. Mebbe they found the entrance to this redoubt open and were poking around inside the chamber when we arrived."

"No," Jak said with conviction. "More come through here." He pointed at the floor, which gleamed under banks of fluorescent lights. Tracks in the yellow vomit on the light gray linoleum led away from the mat-trans chamber in uncountable numbers, growing fainter as they crossed the broad, windowless room. Jak crouched and touched a footprint with his index finger, then rubbed it with his thumb. "Still wet," he said.

For a second, above the riot of nauseating odors in the room, Ryan could smell them.

Not their puke, *Them.*

In his life the one-eyed warrior had killed many stickies hand-to-hand, face-to-face, but never before had he noticed that particular smell. Then he remembered the source of the olfactory cue: it had come from the nightmare. Trapped in a mutant dream-body, he had recognized his fellow stickies by the distinctive scent they left behind. Now that he was wide-awake and fully rematerialized, the telltale stench shouted at him like a pile of fish guts left three days in the sun.

Not possible, Ryan told himself. Dreams, mat-trans or otherwise, weren't real. He shook his head to clear it of still-lingering jump ghosts.

"Stickies are rad-blasted triple stupe," J.B. protested, firmly seating his fedora back on his head. "No way could they have jumped on purpose. Dark night, most of the time they can't even find their own pricks!"

"J.B.'s right," Mildred agreed. "None of the stickies

we've ever crossed paths with has shown much in the way of practical intelligence. Nine times out of ten they don't even use simple weapons, like clubs and rocks, for their killing. I find it hard to believe that a bunch of gibbering idiots could organize themselves to do anything like this. Think about it. How could they possibly understand the process of matter transfer well enough to use it?"

"Mebbe they're getting smarter," Ryan replied.

"Morituri te salutamus," Doc muttered to himself, but loud enough for all to hear and be chilled by any lingering stickies.

"Can it, you old fool!" Mildred barked.

Ryan shot the physician a warning glance. Now wasn't the time to reopen a personal squabble. He looked past Mildred, to the desktop where Krysty lay. Her breathing had deepened and slowed. Her prehensile hair no longer dangled limp and lank over her shoulders—it twitched and coiled around her face like a nest of irritated red snakes. "How's she doing?" he asked.

"She's severely disoriented from the jump," Mildred told him. "I can't find anything else physically wrong with her. Of course, that doesn't mean too much, considering the tools I have to work with. If I haven't missed something critical, I'd say she should snap out of it in a few minutes."

"Can she be moved?"

"Sure."

"Where goin'?" Jak asked Ryan.

Before the one-eyed warrior could answer, Doc spoke up.

"Ryan, dear fellow, loath as I am to propose it, might we not risk embarking on another jump?"

"I'm afraid it's not an option in Krysty's case," Mildred said. "In her present condition there's no telling what damage a second jump would do to her."

Ryan addressed the old man's suggestion. "At this point, Doc, we aren't sure what the stickies know about the gateway system. They could use it to follow us, and we could find ourselves fighting an army of the dead-eyed bastards wherever we end up."

"Oh, wow!" Mildred said, her eyes widening with a sudden realization. "Wait a minute! There's a basic problem here that I think you're all missing. It's a matter of logic—"

"Dark night!" J.B. interrupted her. "Our basic problem isn't logic, it's stickies."

Mildred didn't appreciate being contradicted, and especially before she had been allowed to make her case. "But—"

Ryan put up a hand. "No, Mildred. Save whatever it is for later. We don't have time to discuss it now. We're not safe here. The stickies we just chilled might be missed by the others."

He moved the still-unconscious Krysty into a sitting position and eased her over his left shoulder in a fireman's carry. With his Steyr SSG-70 rifle in his right hand, he headed for the elevators on the other side of the control complex.

Chapter Two

Bolted to the wall beside the pair of elevators was a level-by-level map of the entire complex. From the schematic they could tell they were five stories down from the redoubt's vanadium-steel exit doors.

"Place big," Jak commented.

"One of the biggest we've come across," J.B. agreed.

Ryan scanned the index, row upon row of color-coded numbers and names that corresponded to points marked on the map. It was more than big; it was a small city. According to the map, the redoubt had its own hospital, residential areas, several theaters, four dining halls, two sports centers, various automated labs, machine shops, hydroponics gardens—all bunkered underground. In addition to the nuke fuel source that powered the complex, the map showed a fossil-fuel storage cell and an armory.

"Behold the promised Elysium," Doc intoned. "Sanctuary for predark potentates. Snug harbor for big-wig whitecoats and military, for well-heeled politicians and corporate CEOs."

Mildred took a careful look at the room behind them. The steady, whistling breeze of a high-tech air-filtration system kept the floors and elevated surfaces clean, but the corners, where the ceiling met the walls, were hung with funereal drapes of thick, gray cobwebs. "Doc, I think your VIPs got caught with their pants down on Doomsday. They never arrived at their own party."

Ryan adjusted Krysty's weight on his shoulder, then warned the others to stand back from the elevator doors. "Be ready," he said. "We're on triple red." He poked the elevator's button with the muzzle of his rifle. As he moved to the side of the left-hand pair of doors, he slung the rifle over his shoulder and seized his SIG-Sauer P-226 with his free hand.

From above came the mechanical whir of the car's descent. The light went on behind the plastic arrow over the doors, and an electronic tone sounded. Some sixth sense told Ryan that danger was very close. As the doors jerked apart with a whoosh, his finger was already pressing the trigger.

The four stickies inside the elevator reacted to the sight of humans with amazing speed. Howling, in a blur of intentionally confusing, arm-waving motion, they attacked.

Standing rock steady, Ryan fired the SIG-Sauer.

Blown onto their backs on the floor, the quartet of muties thrashed their arms as they tried desperately to get up. But they couldn't move their legs or hips because Ryan had blasted great chunks from their spines.

J.B. stepped forward with his Uzi and quickly gave each of the snapping dead-eyes a full-metal-jacket 9 mm round in the head.

The elevator doors started to close. Jak reached out and stopped them. "Where to?" he asked. "Out?"

"Before we leave, we'd better check out the armory," Ryan said. "Mebbe we'll get lucky this time and find something we can use. We're getting low on ammo."

He got in the elevator and gently set Krysty against the rear wall. She was lost in a deep and troubled sleep. As Ryan straightened, Jak poked the illuminated button for the fourth floor.

When the doors opened on the next level, all of the companions stood with their blasters drawn, ready to defend themselves. They were greeted not by kill-crazed mutants, but by pitch-darkness. The light from the elevator penetrated only a few feet into the gloom. Then, one after another, the banks of ceiling lights flickered and started to come on. Some of the fluorescent tubes continued to flicker annoyingly; others remained dark. Enough of them lit up for Ryan and friends to be able to see there was no opposition down the long, windowless corridor.

"Those are some long-life bulbs," Mildred said appreciatively.

"Probably keyed to movement or sound," Ryan replied. "Don't come on until someone triggers them. Saves wear and tear that way."

He turned to the Armorer and said, "J.B., give Jak your scattergun. He can sit and watch on the elevator and Krysty while we recce."

The Armorer unslung his Smith & Wesson M-4000

12-gauge and handed it to Jak. The white-haired teen automatically checked the breech for a live round, then found and tripped the car's control-panel switch that locked the doors open and held the elevator in place.

Ryan and the others leapfrogged down the hallway, kick-entering every room, making sure no muties were lying in wait, and that their backs—and line of retreat—were protected.

They were closing in on the armory when J.B. stuck his head out of a doorway and shouted down the passage to his friends. "Hey, I found somebody in here," he said. "It looks like one of your predark whitecoats, Doc. Don't get your hopes up, though. He's already well chilled."

Ryan, Mildred and Doc followed J.B. into the room. It was a scientific laboratory, with its own mainframe computer and a row of automated chemical-analysis machines. The walls were lined with metal shelves, bearing hundreds of stacked, labeled, sealed glass jars. Similar jars rested on the workstation counters and the floor.

Ryan scanned some of the labels. The dates printed at the tops went all the way back to the days immediately after the nuclear holocaust.

The room contained thousands of jars. Some were packed with what looked like wads of human hair and fingernail clippings. Others were filled with cloudy liquid in different shades of yellow and amber. Still others contained brown, segmented coils of excrement suspended in clear fluid.

A broad, white writing surface on one wall displayed a hand-drawn graph in red. Numerous points on the parabola were marked with blue dots, and above the dots were numerical values and Greek letters. Five-foot-high stacks of computer spreadsheets stood beside the writing panel.

"He's over here," J.B. said, waving them to a big, wall-mounted freezer unit with smoked-glass doors.

Inside the freezer a man-shape sat facing out, cross-legged, its arms folded over its chest. It was wearing a white lab coat. Ryan could just make out the round lenses of its eyeglasses under the hoary growth of frost. From the dates on the jars, the whitecoat had lived in the redoubt for decades before pulling his own plug. While he had waited in the freezer to die, he had written something in the frost on the inside of the door with a fingertip. He'd written it backward so anyone looking in at him could read it.

Ryan read the two words aloud: "'Science rules.'"

Laughter exploded from Doc's throat. He hooted so hard, it sent him into a fit of coughing. He doubled over, gasping for air, while he continued to laugh.

Ryan clapped the old man on the back. "Easy, Doc," he said, "or you're gonna bust something important. We don't have time for this. Let's get out of here."

The armory entrance they sought stood near the dead end of the corridor. It had a heavy, double-wide, tempered steel door and a massive and still-operational computer card lock.

"Get us in, J.B." Ryan said.

"No problem," the Armorer replied. He dug around in the capacious side pockets of his pants and took out two wads of homemade C-4 plastique, a blasting cap, some scraps of electrical wire and a hand-twist, mechanically powered detonator. He bracketed the card-lock with flattened gobs of C-4, linked the charges, then fused them. "Out of the hall," he ordered the others as he unrolled the detonator's wire and backed into an open doorway.

J.B. twisted the handle, and the corridor rocked with a mighty boom and a bright white flash. Though a section of the overhead lights was extinguished by the blast, when Ryan looked out from cover, he could see the massive door no longer had a lock and that it had slid back on its hidden floor tracks, thrown away from the jamb by a good foot and a half.

Then an alarm started to wail, and red lights concealed in the ceiling began to flash on and off.

"Fireblasted sec system!" Ryan snarled. "Ears or no ears, that's going to bring stickies down on us."

It was a shame they had to hurry because the redoubt armory was like an unguarded candy store. Nearly all of the century-old complexes they'd jumped to had been stripped bare as the redoubts' former occupants had evacuated the place or had been looted by people who had broken into the upper levels. Usually nothing of value remained.

This one had never been touched.

"Look at all the ammo!" Mildred breathed. "Unopened factory cans of 9 mm and 5.56 mm."

"Grenades," Doc said. He used a scrap of rag he found to wipe the protective layer of grease from a flip-top antipersonnel device. "High explosive," he announced, reading the weapon's color code.

"Ryan," J.B. said, "there's reloads for caseless G-12 assault rifles. The air-sealed packs look in good shape."

"I got LAWs over here," Ryan said. "Check all the gun crates, J.B. If there's caseless ammo, there might also be G-12s. We could use the additional firepower."

The Armorer poked around for a few seconds, removing box lids, then said, "There's an open crate with three G-12s inside. They looked unfired."

"Take them," Ryan said. "Their reloading units weigh about two pounds each. Take two dozen, six for each of us to carry out."

Weight was always a problem for them and, as much as supply, limited their traveling arsenal. When you had to lug all your armament on your back, you had to be selective: being slow in Deathlands was just as dangerous as being undergunned.

KRYSTY HUNG SUSPENDED in blackness, ensnared by sticky webs of the lingering jump nightmare. She couldn't move so much as a fingertip. The prolonged, futile struggle to break free had drained her spirit's strength. The dream was in complete control of all she thought and felt. Like a spider's victim, first paralyzed by a toxic bite, then wrapped head to foot in wet silk, she believed that she had been seeded with alien life, dozens of baby monsters that would soon hatch in her belly and eat their way out of her.

Then, from what seemed to be hundreds of miles away, at the furthest, dimmest limits of her perception, a man spoke. His tone was quick, decisive, commanding.

And familiar.

The sound of her lover's voice was a lifeline, pulling her back toward his world.

Their world.

The wraps of psychic silk loosened slightly, and Krysty could feel the hard floor under her legs, the wall at her back. The insistent pull of gravity reconnected her to the source of all her mutie powers, Gaia, the Earth Mother. She called on that feminine force, drawing it into herself. Her strength returned in a rush. She used it to drag herself from the clinging vestiges of the dream.

Krysty opened her eyes.

At first she couldn't figure out where she was, but she sensed a rapid upward movement and the presence of her comrades close at hand. Her eyes quickly adjusted to the light of the single, caged bulb beside her. Beneath the light unit, a motor hummed and heavily greased cables slid around a spinning flywheel. Encircling gray walls slipped past. She blinked up at a rectangular shaft made of reinforced concrete, realizing she was on the roof of an elevator. Then the movement stopped and an electronic tone sounded. With a whoosh, the doors below jerked open.

Krysty started to speak, but before she could make a sound, a hand was clamped firmly over her mouth. She looked up at Ryan. When she nodded that she understood, he removed his hand and tenderly brushed her cheek with his fingertips in a quick welcome-back caress. There wasn't time for anything more.

J.B. had the lid of the emergency-exit hatch slightly ajar and stood crouched over it, waiting.

The car swayed and creaked beneath them as it took on passengers. Lots of passengers. Krysty heard soft, moist kissing sounds through the open hatch. Holding her breath, she quietly rose to her feet. From under her fur coat, she drew her Smith & Wesson Model 640 handblaster.

Ryan reached over and tapped J.B. lightly on the arm.

The Armorer pulled the pin on the frag gren, silently counted to three, then dropped it through the gap. As it clunked on the floor below, he whirled away from the hatch.

The car jolted sharply as the grenade detonated. The hatch lid jumped out of its frame, flipping off to one side. Heat and cordite smoke billowed through the opening, up into the concrete shaft. The caustic fumes burned Krysty's throat and made her choke.

Then the elevator's automatic doors slid closed.

With a screech the car started up to the next floor. Steel scraped against concrete, raining showers of sparks on top of them. The high-explosive grenade had bulged out the sides of the car so it no longer quite fit the shaft.

"Don't like the sound of that," J.B. stated.

"Me, neither," Ryan agreed. "No more grens. Better chill them with blasters next stop."

Then they all noticed another change, this one even more distressing: the damaged elevator was climbing at about half its previous speed.

"We can always take the other car," Mildred suggested. After a pause she added, "Assuming this one gets us to the next floor."

Krysty caught a quick movement at the very edge of her vision, near her feet. She reacted and had her blaster up and tracking before she realized what it was. Despite her quick reflexes, the stickie was halfway out of the hatch by the time her brain-to-finger message was received, and the weapon barked and bucked in her fist. Angling her shots down and away from her friends, she punched a pair of slugs through the stickie's smooth forehead. It dropped back through the opening, out of sight.

"Good one," Ryan said.

The doors to the next floor loomed just overhead.

"My turn," Jak said, picking up one of the new G-12s. He rotated the cocking knob, a round circle set flush in the stock behind the pistol grip. "Hold legs so don't fall."

The teenager positioned himself over the hatch opening, then with J.B. and Ryan securing his ankles, he eased through it, hooking the backs of his knees over the edge of the frame. He hung upside down from the roof of the elevator like a white-haired bat. The car stopped with a jerk, the electronic bell chimed and the doors whooshed apart.

Strobe-light flashes from inside the car accompanied the canvas-ripping sound of full-auto blaster-fire. Shrieks of animal rage and pain echoed through the shaft.

It was over in less than a minute.

Krysty understood Ryan's strategy, why he wasn't making a nonstop run for the surface, why he was hitting every floor on the way up. Like moths to a flame, the homicidal crazies lurking around the complex seemed to be drawn to the elevators. Even though they couldn't chill all of the stickies in the redoubt, the companions could make a serious dent in their numbers. Each one they chilled now was one less they would have to deal with when they returned by this same route to jump out.

Jak raised himself partway up, and J.B. and Ryan pulled him to his feet.

"Bastard prime," the teenager said, grinning. He wiped the spatters of blood and tissue from the sides of his face with the tail of his T-shirt.

"Are we going to switch elevators now?" Mildred asked.

It was already too late for that. Somewhere far below, an electric motor came to life.

"We got trouble," Krysty said. The set of lift cables on the other side of the shaft began to move.

As they all looked down, they could see the second elevator coming up from the bottom level. Even in the dim light it was obvious that the roof of the car was loaded with stickies.

"Dark night!" J.B. exclaimed. "Where'd they come from?"

"Must have transported in with the chamber open," Ryan said. "The ones closest to the doorway probably got torn to shreds, but the rest of them made it through."

Their own elevator started up with a lurch, but slowly. With each second that passed, the other car gained ground. It was clear that it would overtake them before they reached the top floor. No one had to spell out the danger: if the stickies got above them, the creatures had the tactical advantage. They could jump down and overwhelm Ryan and company by sheer force of numbers.

"Gren time," J.B. stated. It was an announcement, not a question. And even as he made it, he had the frag in hand and was separating the explosive from its grip safety. He lobbed the bomb into the midst of the stickies below.

The solid thud of detonation was followed by the clatter of metal shards hurtling through the shaft.

The companions looked down to see the car still rushing at them, rising up through the smoke. And as it climbed, more stickies poured up through the open hatch onto the roof, scrambling over the blast-ripped bodies of their fellow muties.

"Get down!" Ryan ordered, unslinging a LAW from his shoulder. His hands moved in a blur as he jerked the pull pin, rotated the rear cover out of the way, then extended and shouldered the launcher. There wasn't time for him to elevate the weapon's sighting system, but nor was there any need. The target was close and getting closer. Moving the safety handle to Arm, Ryan took a trap lead on the flywheel and pressed the trigger bar.

The 66 mm antitank rocket launched with a roar, its HEAT warhead exploding a split second later. The top of the oncoming elevator's roof vanished in a blinding flash of orange light, then its supporting cables snapped, jerking up as if they were made of rubber, coiling and slashing, sizzling through the air. The car dropped away, slowly at first, then faster and faster as it gathered momentum. The crash when it hit the bottom of the shaft made the walls tremble and sent a cloud of dust billowing up and sweeping over them.

Ryan tossed the spent launcher down into the pit as their elevator crept hesitantly toward the closed doors of the top floor. "Everybody down in the car," he said, "except you, J.B. Fix the elevator so no one but us can use it."

Krysty followed Ryan, dropping down through the hatch. The heels of her boots squished into something soft and wet as her full weight hit the floor of the car. The inside of the elevator was a charnel house, the walls scorched and concave from the gren explosion, and dripping with fresh splatters of stickie blood. They booted the knot of corpses aside and prepared to open fire the instant the doors parted.

There was nothing alive to shoot at, just an enormous, low-ceilinged, concrete-floored room lit by tracks of overhead fluorescents. To the left, along the wall, were a dozen camouflage-painted armor-plated wags parked there generations before.

"We're clear," Ryan shouted up at J.B.

The Armorer yanked the motor's power coupling, freezing the car on the redoubt's top floor. Then, he hopped down to join his companions.

They crossed the broad room in spread single file, on triple red alert, blasters up and ready, heading for the row of APCs and Hummers. With the precision that comes from much practice, Ryan, Krysty and the others moved around the stored vehicles, sweeping for stickies in hiding. They found none.

"These wags look operational," J.B. said. He opened the door of a Hummer and stuck in his head. "The nuke batteries are showing full charge. I think this redoubt's antirad bunkering held up."

Ryan was admiring one of the two-track APCs. Its gun turret was set well forward on its squat, blocky body. The turret had four cannon barrels and, concealed in an armored bubble beside its top hatch, what looked to be a sophisticated electronic aiming system. Above the driver's ob slit was an unfamiliar emblem: a solid red circle on a pale blue field.

"It's a Mitsuki Meteor fighting vehicle," Mildred said. "Also known as the Mitsuki Meatball. I remember seeing a lot of news footage on it maybe six months before I went in for my surgery. The Asian Alliance started manufacturing them in 1998. They first saw combat in the conventional-force battle of Hong Kong in the summer of 1999. The Meteor's missile-defense system worked well against Taiwanese air-to-ground and ground-to-ground heat-seekers. Produces a pulse of EM rad that throws a protective dome over it. Makes incoming missiles veer off target at sixty or more degrees, which gives the Meteor's laser-guided 20 mm cannons time to lock on the enemy."

"There aren't any more heat-seekers to worry about," Ryan said, using the hand- and footholds to climb up to the turret. "But if this Meatball runs, we could sure ride out of here in style." He opened the hatch and looked around inside. "This thing is big enough for all of us. Mildred, do you remember anything about the fuel range?"

"I remember it was excellent," she said. "Notice anything unusual about the hull?"

He put his hand on it. "It's not cold."

She nodded. "That's because the armoring isn't steel. It's some kind of high-temp, Kevlar-armaglass composite. It's very light for its strength, which adds to the fuel efficiency. I seem to recall that in the Hong Kong campaign the Meteor was averaging a couple of hundred miles per tankful over mixed terrain."

"Let's see if she'll start," Ryan said, dropping down through the hatch.

While Doc and Mildred stood guard, Jak, J.B. and

Krysty picked up their gear and followed him into the dark, cramped space. They had to climb around the gunner's chair, which was suspended in a metal cage from the inside of the turret. The Meteor's interior was cluttered with a latticework of structural braces, and with conduits and cables wound in dull silver tape. At the front of the compartment were the driver's and co-pilot chairs; at the rear was a storage area that housed the power cells for the electronic systems. Rows of jump seats lined the rear side walls.

Ryan slipped into the driver's seat and opened the ob slit. It provided enough light so he could read the dials on the compact dash. He found the interior-light switch. When he turned it on, red light bathed the compartment.

"Trader had himself a war wag kind of like this once," he said after a quick review of the control system. "Two levers, one for steering and braking each track. An automatic tranny with four forward speeds, neutral and reverse." When he punched the starter button, it whined ferociously, but the 750-horsepower engine failed to turn over.

"Dark night, maybe the whitecoats mothballed it," J.B. said over his shoulder. "Have you got oil pressure?"

"Yeah." Ryan tapped the accelerator twice and hit the button again. The engine growled to life.

"Let it run awhile," J.B. suggested. "Get the engine temp up and melt that hundred-year-old grease. I'm going to check out the weapons system." He hauled himself up into the caged gunner's chair, removed his fedora and pulled the target-acquisition helmet over his head. After flipping down the VR visor, he reached out for the dual joystick fire controls.

The instant he touched the sticks, the weapons system came on. A powerful electric motor whirred, and there was a flutter of movement along both side walls of the rear compartment. The movement caught Krysty's eye and made her look more closely. Under the clutter of braces and conduit, she could see the chains of linked, 20 mm antitank cannon rounds that fed up from the magazine under the floor.

J.B. turned his head to the left, and the turret followed suit. He twisted right, and the turret moved with him. Pleased with himself, he juked the joysticks, and to everyone's surprise, including his own, the quartet of cannons roared thunderously. Almost in the same instant there was an explosion that jarred the vehicle on its suspension. J.B. opened his hands at once, releasing the fire controls, but it was too late for the third Hummer down the line. The accidental 8-round burst of HE rounds had already blown it in two.

Mildred and Doc pounded on the outside of the hull and yelled at him to cut it out.

"J.B.," Ryan said, "are you sure you know what you're doing?

"I wasn't," the Armorer admitted sheepishly, "but now I am."

"Doc! Mildred!" Ryan called over his shoulder. "Get in here. We're rolling!"

When they were safely inside and J.B. had dogged the turret hatch, Ryan shifted the APC into forward gear and pulled both steering-braking levers toward him. The Meteor's tracks spun on the slick concrete, then caught hold.

"That looks like the only way out," Ryan said, heading for an opening at the far end of the room. He braked to a spot at the entrance to a rectangular tunnel.

"Dark in there," Jak commented, trying to squint ahead through the copilot's ob slit.

Ryan searched the dash until he found the switch that controlled the halogen headlights. When he flicked them on, he could see that the tunnel sloped up and that it appeared to end in a solid wall after about fifty yards. He drove the Meteor into the passage anyway. About a third of the way along, the APC's headlights illuminated a hard right turn, one of many tight switchbacks designed to deflect ground and air-burst radiation.

It was slow going to the exit because of all the turns.

The vanadium-steel doors had just swung into sight, reflecting the glare of the headlights at the end of a long, straight section of tunnel, when Jak nudged Ryan with an elbow, pointed at the control panel and said, "What mean?"

A single gauge light flashed on and off.

"Don't know."

They had traveled only a few more yards when the dash squealed a shrill warning and all the gauges started to blink. The Meteor bucked and chugged, then died one hundred feet from the steel doors. It wouldn't restart.

"Fireblast!" Ryan swore as he set the brakes. "We're going to have to walk, after all."

Chapter Three

It was night and the weather was unsettled. Ryan and the others turned their backs to the wind that whipped across the barren mountaintop. A bank of storm clouds raced east, away from them. Chains of lightning flashed at the storm's core, lighting up the ominous purple mass with bursts of sickly yellow. The ground at their feet still sizzled and popped as the weak acids from a recent chem rain percolated into the soil. Overhead, between the scattered, straggler clouds, the stars were bright and the bone white moon half-full.

Ryan, Mildred, Doc and Krysty fanned out and took up defensive positions around the doorway, guarding Jak's back while he tapped the redoubt's exit code into the keypad beside the double doors. The entrance closed with a hollow clang, and its internal bolts shot home.

Meanwhile, J.B. had his minisextant out and in the gauzy light was trying to figure out where they were.

"Well?" Ryan asked him softly.

"From the position of the moon, I'd say we're somewhere east of the Shens, not far from the Lantic. Mebbe the Linas."

"The lovely Carolinas," Doc said. "That's far from

the less than jolly England we'd just survived, and by the skin of our teeth. And it's not all done with yet, I wager. But what a bittersweet trove of memories this part of the world brings to mind! Emily, Rachel, Jolyon and I had the pleasure of taking a brief holiday on the shore there one summer. So very long ago. I recall most clearly its distinctive, serene beauty, genteel folk and most gracious hospitality."

"Well, now it's just another rad-blasted hellhole," Mildred said. "Smell the smoke?"

"How could I miss it?" the old man replied. "A stench to greet the nostrils of neophytes to hell."

Ryan narrowed his gaze. Something else was in the wind, something more subtle: the scent of blood.

Human blood.

Though he knew it had to be an illusion, another flashback from the mat-trans nightmare, Ryan snorted to clear the rusty, metallic odor from the inside of his nose.

"Fires this way," Jak said, heading into the wind. He climbed the mound of bare rock that framed one side of the ruin of a road.

Ryan and the others followed him to the crest, and from there they looked down over a wide valley. A dozen miles away, on the far side of the basin, a tight cluster of orange lights danced.

"A ville," Krysty said.

"Yeah," Ryan agreed. "My guess is it'll take us until nearly daylight to get over there."

"Night march?" Jak asked.

"The stickies aren't going to stop because of the dark," Ryan answered. "They like the night for hunting. We've got to stay with them. We better get going."

"At least the stickies are going to be easy to track," J.B. stated as he started down the rubble mound. "Like walking in the wake of a tornado."

"Come on, Mildred," Ryan said when he realized the woman wasn't moving from the crest. "Mildred?"

She didn't respond. She stood perfectly still, staring intently at the distant flames.

When Ryan touched her arm, she started violently. "You okay?"

Mildred blinked at him. "Uh, yeah, I think so." With a troubled expression on her face, she forced herself to turn away from the vista. "I'm fine. Let's go."

Moving single file, on triple red alert, they followed the vague remnants of a road down the flanks of the broad, low mountain. Ryan had no doubt that the road, overgrown as it was with grass shoots as sharp as steel needles, pierced and cracked by stunted, thorny trees tough enough to survive the acid fall, had been unrecognizable before the stickies had taken that route. After they had passed, as J.B. had predicted, it was like walking in the tracks of a whirlwind. In the moonlight, curving down the slope ahead, Ryan could see the swathe of freshly trampled earth and crushed foliage.

He and the others took care to give the broken branches a wide berth. A gummy sap dripped from the wounds in the tree limbs and pooled in white puddles on the ground. The corrosive sap could strip the flesh from bone in a matter of seconds. Once it entered the bloodstream, the milky juice burned like wildfire, destroying everything it touched.

Death, when it came, was never soon enough.

A SULFUROUS DAWN STARTED to leak through blue-black cloudbanks on the horizon as the travelers neared the valley floor. It had been a hard march, with few stops, but otherwise uneventful. They had encountered no stickies en route and had seen no sign of human refugees, either.

Ryan halted the column behind an outcrop and, while his companions rested, he cautiously surveyed the terrain below. The middle of the valley was split by a great predark highway. Though his distant view was obscured to the right by air rank with low-hanging smoke, the road appeared to run the entire length of the basin. It was six lanes wide and had a crumbling median strip that had once separated a two-way flow of traffic.

The road had been built to last. From his elevated position, Ryan could see the slip-joints that crossed the roadway at regular intervals, engineered to compensate for seasonal expansion and contraction of the substrate on which the highway sat. So on doomsday, when nuke-blast earthquakes rippled through the valley, instead of fracturing into a billion fragments, the enormous blocks of pavement tipped either up or down, absorbing the shock waves. That left the plates of roadway jutting at angles that would have burst the tires and shattered the axles of predark fossil-fuel-powered vehicles moving at high speed. But the foot traffic and animal carts of the post-Apocalypse, industrial devolution could easily pick their way over or around the obstacles.

No one was moving on the highway now, and beyond it, on Ryan's left, their immediate goal was no longer visible.

The raging fires that had acted like a beacon during the long night's trek had burned down, leaving behind a dense pall of smoke that concealed whatever remained of the ville.

Ryan and his companions trotted down to the road and, once there, turned into the cloud of swirling smoke. Visibility dropped to fifteen or twenty feet. They had to slow their pace and close ranks. It was very hard to breathe without coughing. Then a sudden breeze shifted the haze. Looming up in front of them was a massive barrier of concrete rubble—a highway overpass that hadn't survived the nuke-quakes. It had collapsed a century before, blocking all six lanes. Ryan led them to the left, off the road, following a two-rut track that diverted traffic around the barrier.

As they rounded the end of the fallen overpass, they came upon a series of neat piles of concrete chunks that had been reduced to pebbles. Some pathetic soul had been chipping it away, trying to salvage the rusty steel reinforcement that interlaced the concrete.

When they returned to the pavement, they caught a glimpse of the dead ville. What they saw on the other side of the median strip, to the right of the highway, was a red-orange glow pulsing in the depths of the swirling smoke. Ryan took them over the median, then across the three paved lanes. Before they reached the other side, they could feel the heat from the banks of live embers. Another two-rut lane led from the side of the highway to the center of the glowing mass.

"Slow and careful," the one-eyed warrior said as he pointed out the deep, two-foot-wide holes in the ground where the ville's stockade wall had once stood. Leg-breakers, for sure. The stickies had pulled out all the defensive perimeter's sharpened logs and fed them to the blaze. Inside the broad circle of holes, the monsters had burned everything to the ground.

The roofs and walls of the huts had been torn apart, and what couldn't be moved to the central pyre had been burned where it stood. Ash piles marked the foundations of the clustered, crude dwellings. Smoke still rose from scattered hot spots among the ashes, and fingers of fire licked up from a great pile of coals in the middle of the ring.

Mildred walked quickly ahead of the others, moving toward the center of the inferno in a straight line, kicking up puffs of ash from the heaps that drifted around her ankles. She seemed distracted and disoriented, oblivious to the blast-furnace heat.

Krysty started after her.

As Ryan moved to follow, something crunched under his boot heel. He knelt and brushed the blanket of warm ash away. He saw the fire-blackened teeth of a child, scattered like tiny seeds in the dirt. Pushing more of the ash aside, he found a little jawbone, part of the cheek crushed by stamping feet. He could see the prints of bare soles in the soft ground. There were other bones pounded into the soil, as well, the bones of livestock and adult humans. All of them had the flesh burned off, all of them broken into small pieces.

Ryan hadn't seen such systematic and total destruction in a long time.

Apparently these stickies were no longer content with the hit-and-run slaughter that until now had been their trademark. They had, with considerable expenditure of time and energy, erased not only these poor humans, but all traces of their presence. When the next round of chem storms swept past, the broken bones would dissolve in the downpour of dilute hydrochloric acid, the cinder piles would sizzle and froth and melt away. Nothing would be left but the ring of holes.

As Ryan stood, his head was flooded with a vision of the horror that had been done here only hours before: the screams, the pain, the blood. In the pit of his stomach, something dark and malevolent stirred.

"Wickedness and misery, my dear Ryan," Doc said sadly, as if reading his mind. The old man had knelt, too, and was sieving warm ash and bone chips through his fingers. He wiped the white powder on the lapels of his frock coat. "Wickedness and misery. What we have spread before us is a deed of uncommon evil."

"You're right, Doc," Ryan said. "This one's triple mean." He looked up to see Krysty returning from the center of the ville with Mildred. She held a sheltering arm around the doctor's shoulders. When the two women got closer, he realized that Mildred's clothes had caught on fire; the legs of her camouflage fatigue pants were charred at the cuffs and knees and still spilling puffs of smoke. Her face bathed in sweat, Mildred seemed to be coming out of some kind of a shuddering fit. Her arms and legs twitched so violently that she could barely walk without Krysty's help.

"What happened?" he asked.

"She got too close to the coals," Krysty said. "I think something's wrong with her, Ryan. If I hadn't stopped her, she would've walked right into fire. This place is doing something to her mind. We've got to get away from here."

He nodded. It was doing something to his mind, too.

Jak was waiting for them on the far side of the ring of devastation. He seemed unusually agitated and impatient to move on.

"How many do you figure we're tracking?" Ryan asked him.

"Thousands," Jak replied, brushing strands of the lank, shoulder-length, white hair from his face.

"Thousands?"

"Yeah."

"Dark night, a hundred is the biggest colony I've ever come across," J.B. said. "And that was deep in the heavily nuked zone."

"This isn't a colony, J.B.," Ryan said "This is an army."

There was no denying the truth of his words. In the depopulated, largely disarmed, postnukecaust world, it didn't take many troops to make a formidable force. Wars had been fought—and won—with a few dozen mercies or sec men carrying blasters; with much less, an enterprising baron could take slaves and extort tribute from a wide area.

"Fielding an army takes organization," Ryan went on, "and planning. Something stickies haven't shown us before. Every other time we've run into a large group of them outside the nuke zones, they've always been working under a coldheart human or a nonstickie mutant, someone intelligent enough to plan battle strategy."

"So you think that's what's happening here?" Krysty said.

"Mebbe."

"Some say stickies are norms. Genes just rad melted," Jak said.

"Another popular hypothesis," Doc added, "is that their perverse physiology is the result of prolonged exposure to nitrate-contaminated water."

"You're all just guessing," J.B. argued. "Face it, we don't know shit about stickies, except that they're crazy mean and hard to kill."

Krysty uttered a soft, startled gasp.

When Ryan turned and looked at her, a pang of concern shot through him. Her face had gone deathly pale, and her sentient hair was retracting, coiling tight to the sides and back of her head. Before he could ask her if

she was all right, a rustling sound came to him through
the smoke.

Multiple footsteps were moving quickly away.

With a quick hand signal, Ryan split and spread his
force. Then they all slipped into the haze. As they followed the footfalls away from the ruined ville, up a
slight incline, the layer of smoke thinned a little. Not
thirty feet away they could see a raggedy man and
woman moving low and fast along a shallow cleft in
the earth. The man was carrying a small bundle in his
arms.

Ryan caught Jak's wrist as he prepared to throw a
leaf-bladed knife.

"No," the one-eyed warrior said. "They're not stickies and they're not armed."

At the sound of Ryan's voice, the refugees stopped
running and huddled together in the ditch.

As the companions ringed their position, the man put
the bundle on the ground. It turned out to be a small,
dirty child wrapped in rags. He and the woman took
up a back-to-back defensive stance, and from the scabbard at his waist he drew a long, curving saber tinged
with rust. The woman wielded a cudgel made of
gnarled wood and spiked with sharpened prongs of re-
bar.

"Come on, you stickie bastards!" the man shouted
up at them. "We'll show you how chillings done!"

"Take a closer look, you stupe," Ryan told him.
"We're not stickies. We're not going to hurt you."

"Keep your distance!" the woman shrilled back.

"Husband, be careful. Don't let your guard down. They're not stickies, but they could be cannies wanting to eat our little girl."

"We're not cannies, either," Ryan said, waving for the others to move in closer. "We're travelers, from a long way off.

"Everybody sit," Ryan told his friends, "and lower your weapons."

When they had done what he'd asked, he addressed the refugee couple. "Are you from the ville?"

"Nothing left of it now but smoke," the man said bitterly.

"What happened?"

"We were overrun by stickies. They attacked in waves. One after another. It wasn't long before we used up all the ammo for the few blasters we had between us. The stickies kept on coming. Like there was no end to them. When they finally broke through the barricade, me and Margee took the babe and ducked down a hidey-hole I made for us. Stayed there until the stickies started tearing down the huts and burning them. Then there was so much smoke blowing around we sneaked away without getting caught."

"Did your ville have a name?" Krysty asked.

"Naw. It wasn't much of a place. Sort of popped up along Baron Elijah's toll road, so's travelers could be safe after dark."

"Baron Willie Elijah?" Ryan asked.

"Of course," the man said. He gave the one-eyed

man a suspicious look. "Where'd you say you come from?"

Ryan didn't reply.

"Everybody's heard of Elijah," J.B. said. "He led the other barons in the Mutie War, about twenty years back. Got them to combine their sec men and mercies to crush the mutie slave rebellion. They killed every mother's son they could get their hands on."

"Old Elijah's always had a thing about keepin' muties in their place," the man said. "He's real picky about the purity of his bloodline, too. Doesn't want them mutie traits creeping in."

"Is he still riding his own daughters?" Ryan asked.

"Daughters!" the woman exclaimed. "He's probably humping his granddaughters' brats by now. He's a nasty old goat and he starts in on them before they've grown a full curl."

"Gonna git what's comin' to him, though," her husband said.

"How's that?" said Ryan.

"The stickies're all headin' his way. Like hungry locust bugs to Willie ville. And in the front of them all is one mutie he sure should of chilled when he had the chance."

"A mutie is leading them?" Krysty said.

"Biggest, ugliest bastard you ever saw. I recognized him right off. I seen him lots of times before. In a cage. Baron had him in his zoo for years. Raised him up from a little bitty squirmer. Old baron likes to gather things, and he doesn't like to let them go. Got this particular specimen from some mercies after the Mutie War. I reckon it's come payback time for old Elijah."

"How far is Willie ville from here?" Ryan asked.

"Twenty-one miles," the man replied, pointing to the road north.

"Whoa!" J.B. said. "You're not thinking about going there, are you?"

Ryan looked into his old friend's face. "Might go for a look-see."

"If we don't get there before the stickies do," Mildred said, "everyone in that ville is going to die, too."

"We'll have to try to get the eastern barons organized for mutual defense, or nobody's going to stand a chance—including us," Ryan stated.

"That's a tall order," J.B. replied. "The barons haven't worked together since the Mutie War."

"There's something else," Ryan added. "I think you should all know about it before you each decide what you're going to do."

"What is that, dear fellow?" Doc queried.

"I've got a history with Willie Elijah that goes back to the war. I wasn't much older than Jak when I hired on with him as a mercie. He and I parted on bad terms and he might still remember and hold a grudge. What I'm saying is, because of that he might not listen to anything I have to say. Worse, he might kill me and whoever's traveling with me."

"You think this is worth the risk?" Krysty asked.

"You saw what the stickies did here. If we don't do something to stop them, they'll hunt down and erase our kind from Deathlands, mebbe from the whole world. I'm going on alone, if I have to. Mebbe that would be best, anyway."

"Count me in," J.B. said.

"Me, too," Krysty stated.

The other companions likewise threw in their lots with their leader.

He turned to the refugee couple and said, "Do you want to come with us?"

"To Willie ville?" the woman said, aghast. She scowled at Ryan as if he were a triple stupe droolie.

"No, thankee, if it's all the same to you," the man told him. "That's the wrong direction for me and Margee. We've seen enough stickies to last us. We'd rather take our chances in the bush." He dipped his fingers inside the slash pocket of his raggedy coat and took out a battered semiauto blaster. The rusted slide was locked back, the action open.

"Got no more bullets for it," the man said. He dumped the magazine of the Brazilian knockoff of a Colt Government Model onto his palm. "Can you spare us three 9 mm slugs, just in case we don't make it?"

Ryan took some loose cartridges from his pocket. As he set them on the ground, he said, "Don't touch them until we're out of sight."

Chapter Four

As Ryan flicked the sweat from his brow, he marveled at the way Doc could run. For two hours they had been jogging on the highway's fractured surface, laboring under the weight of the extra ammo. For two hours the academic had been at the front of the file, pounding out the pace in easy, loping strides. It wasn't fast, but it was gruelingly steady.

As Doc jogged along, he mumbled to himself. Ryan could hear his constant muttering over the in-sync tramp of their footfalls and the rattle of their gear. As was usually the case, the old man was holding a conversation with someone he had conjured up from long ago. His words were so indistinct it was hard to tell if the departed was someone dear to him or someone he despised. Ryan understood the general nature of Doc's ghosts, though. He knew that in everyone's life, specters accumulated, hovering until the moment of death. They were memories of things that should have been said and done that were not, or things that were done and said that should not have been. Doc had been ripped from the bosom of his family, and had much unfinished business to reconcile.

Ryan held up his hand to shield his single eye from

the glare of the noonday sun. Ahead the baron's toll road stretched into the flat distance. At the horizon it vanished into a heat mirage, a shimmering lake of mercury. On the right side of the highway, the valley floor sloped to a barren expanse of silt plain, through which a brown river moved sluggishly. The deeply eroded hills that framed the six-lane road were patched with clumps of stunted trees and spike grass, and scrubby, knee-high colonies of orange-and-white, rad-mutated lichen.

He had decided to use the highway because it was the fastest and most direct route to Willie ville. He wasn't concerned about the lack of defensive cover along the way. If it left them somewhat vulnerable, it also meant that the stickies would be visible from a long way off. He wasn't worried about stumbling into an ambush, either. The army of monsters was after much bigger game than a few stragglers. And he didn't think some part of the enemy force would be lying in wait along the road. Everything the stickies had done so far indicated that they were moving in a single, cohesive unit, for some well-defined purpose.

The idea that one mutie could lead and control that many stickies was as puzzling to Ryan as it was disturbing. Stickies usually had no external ears, which made it hard to communicate with them using speech. Orders had to be shouted at top volume and at the same time, spoken very slowly and distinctly. It made complex operational control of large groups of stickies virtually impossible; the monsters in the back rows never got the message. And on top of that, stickies seemed to have unusually short attention spans.

Something appeared in the middle of the mercury-lake mirage. A black form was headed their way. Ryan strained against the glare to keep the shape in focus. When the dark form cleared the mirage, its head flashed glacier white in the sun.

Jak was returning from a long-range recce.

"Doc," Ryan said, "hold up."

The old man craned his head around and nodded.

"Jak's coming back," Ryan explained as they all slowed to a walk. "Let's take a breather."

They dropped their loads and sat in the meager shade of the median strip's wall. Taking the opportunity to drink from their water bags, they let Jak come to them.

Doc's Adam's apple bobbed mightily as he gulped down the tepid liquid.

"Easy on that water, Doc," Mildred warned, "or you're just going to puke it all back up."

The old man lowered the bag. "I bow to your expertise on such matters, dear Doctor," he said, puffing.

Ryan was glad to see that Mildred had recovered from the odd turn she had taken back at the burned ville. She had never acted like that before, and it worried him. Like Doc, she wasn't a native of this time and place and didn't possess the psychic armor to protect her from the shocking violence, the unspeakable monstrosities that were part of day-to-day existence in Deathlands. When he had seen her come stumbling back from the heart of the ville's holocaust, her clothes scorched, her eyes wide and staring, her ash-streaked face streaked by tears, he had feared for her sanity.

He knew that Mildred's difficulties might well have been due to the aftereffects of the mat-trans leap. And the truth of the matter was, being born in the hellscape had never provided much of a defense against the mind-bending power of the jump dream. The most recent nightmare was a case in point. It had been particularly unpleasant for him, and it had rendered Krysty unconscious for many minutes after the transfer was complete. Though Ryan's lover had apparently recovered from her experience, he felt a distance between them that hadn't been there before.

Perhaps it was his fault and not hers, he thought. His own jump dream had, it seemed, uncovered a side of his nature, a hunger that he had never recognized nor fully faced—and therefore had never shared with Krysty. The hunger was for the blood and suffering of others, and it repelled and shamed him.

"Found them," Jak said when he finally trotted up to his friends. All the white-haired teen carried was a G-12 caseless rifle and a 50-round reloading unit. Ryan hadn't wanted the youth's recce slowed by a heavy pack, so he and J.B. had taken turns strapping on and hauling Jak's load of gear. "All stopped at overpass," Jak said. "Mile and half ahead, around bend."

"Why are they stopped?" Ryan asked. "What are they up to?"

"Not get close enough," Jak told him. "No cover.

Didn't want risk seen, mebbe lead them here. What they doing smelled bad. Wind right in face."

"What about the leader?" Ryan asked. "Did you see him?"

"All saw was a pile of stickies blocking road."

"We going to make a wide swing around them?" J.B. asked.

"Not too wide," Ryan replied. "If the refugee man was right and a nonstickie is running the show, he's got to be with them up ahead. We're going to creep to within mebbe six hundred yards of their position. Inside the chilling range for the SSG-70. If there's a clean shot on this leader of theirs, I'll take it. With any luck maybe we can end this thing here and now."

"Cut off the head, and the body will die," Doc said.

"But the body isn't going to die," Mildred protested. "There'll still be thousands of stickies on the loose around here."

"Yeah, but without a leader, they'll break up into small hunting packs and spread out, the way they always do," Ryan said. "The baron's sec men can track them down and deal with them."

After they had all pulled their gear back on, Ryan led his friends off the highway, to the left. He took them into the sun because he wanted it at his back for the chill shot. They crossed a flat area of soft, moist, alluvial dirt. It was tough going, and they sank in up to their knees. The ground got harder the higher they climbed. When they reached the first patch of thorn trees, Ryan turned them parallel to the highway. They kept well below the ridge line, to avoid being silhouetted against the sky.

Their route hopped from tree patch to tree patch, zigzagging around the bright fields of lichen. Though the frilly colonies looked harmless, looks were almost always deceiving in Deathlands. The fleshy fronds had no armor or poison sap to protect them; indeed, they were very fragile and crumbled to bits at the slightest touch. Which was, in fact, their defense. When the microscopic creatures broke apart, many became airborne. When inhaled by a passing animal, these individuals thrived inside the lungs. In a matter of days they reproduced into a new colony there, which by sheer bulk suffocated the hapless victim.

When the companions reached a spot above the bend in the highway, Ryan paused behind a clump of thorn trees and scanned the road ahead. He could see the overpass, but even with minibinocs he couldn't make out much detail because of the distortion of the heat waves rising off the roadway, just a vague, whitish mound spread across six lanes.

Then all of them heard a noise, faint but clear. It was a roaring pulse that rode on the gusting wind. It came from the north, from the direction of the white mound.

"Gaia!" Krysty exclaimed. "What's that?"

"Stickies making some kind noise," Jak said. "All at once. Heard when snuck up before."

"Let's get closer," Ryan said.

They trotted one hundred feet below the ridge line, working their way to a large patch of trees about six hundred yards up from the overpass. The closer they got to the mass of stickies, the clearer the strange sound became. When they stopped at the cover of the thorn trees, they could make it out quite distinctly.

"Kaaa!" the stickies yelled with all their might. Then they paused for breath and shouted again.

"They're shouting the same thing over and over," J.B. said. "What's it mean?"

"His name," Mildred blurted out. "It's his name."

Ryan stared at her in amazement. "Whose name?"

"Their leader," she said. "They're calling for him to come forward. That's what they're doing."

"How the fireblast do you know that?"

When she didn't answer, J.B. nudged him with an elbow. "Have a look down there, Ryan," he said, passing over the binocs.

The whitish mound they had seen in the distance was made of bodies, living bodies in constant motion. Stickies completely covered the overpass. They were heaped on top of the concrete bridge; they clung to the side railing, hanging off one another, spilling like a nubby carpet down over the roadway. The entire mass rippled and flexed as those on the tarmac climbed over their fellows, attempting to reach the top.

Then a lone figure appeared in the middle of the overpass.

He clambered on top of the piles of prostrated bodies and stood on their necks and heads. He was Ryan's intended target; there was no doubt about that. And he was huge. Though the mutie leader towered over the stickies, a better gauge of scale for Ryan was the M-60 machine gun he held easily in one fist, like a handblaster. The weapon had a strange paint job: blotches of hot pink, green, orange and red, a sort of anticamouflage, as if it were intended to draw notice and hostile fire. If the big man was saying anything to his troops, it was drowned out by their pulsing cry. Waving his arms, he ran back and forth over the backs of their piled bodies.

"He's in range," J.B. said. "Chill him."

Ryan passed the binocs to Krysty. As he unslung the Steyr SSG-70 bolt-action sniper rifle and uncapped the six-power scope, she lowered the binocs and said, "They're mating, Ryan. The stickies are mating down there, making more stickies."

The one-eyed man looked at her doubtfully. He knew they were too far away to see that kind of detail. "How do you know that?" he asked.

"I've seen them doing it before."

"Seen stickies humping?" he asked. "When did you see them? Where?"

"In my jump dream."

He shook his head. "Krysty, you're making about as much sense as Mildred."

"Dark night, Ryan," J.B. said, "take the shot. Or give me the gun and I will."

"No, this one's mine. I'll do it."

He chose a shooting position at the far end of the line of cover, where the trees were thin enough for him to crawl between their trunks without risking a snapped branch and sap poisoning, but where the leaves were thick enough to hide his scope and muzzle-flashes from the enemy. Poking the barrel through the foliage, he quickly acquired the target in the telescope's view field. The SSG-70's scope was a little less powerful than the binocs, but its optics were of better quality. Through the heat mirage, he could see the big bald mutie, his white skin blotched with patches of brown, or vice versa. Ryan couldn't tell if the patches were painted on or a permanent feature.

The mutie wasn't just tall, but had huge muscles and no body fat. For his size, he was amazingly quick on his feet. As he darted from side to side on the overpass, Ryan couldn't hold the cross hairs on him for more than a couple of seconds. The one-eyed warrior knew that if he squeezed off a shot, chances were the big mutie would be a couple of feet one way or the other by the time the bullet reached the intended point of impact.

It was a no-go.

Watching the mutie general exhort his army, Ryan felt a surge of blind fury. It occurred to him that he didn't want to chill the bastard with a long-distance bullet, anyway. He wanted to kill him up close, hand to hand. He wanted to cut off his massive bald head and wash his hands in the blood that jetted from the neck stump, to drink from it like a mountain spring.

Ryan grit his teeth and shook off the hideous image. It wasn't his, he told himself. It was alien, intrusive, vile. He lowered the Steyr from his shoulder and crawled back to join the others.

"It can't be done," he told them. "The shot's clear, but he's moving around too much. I'll never hit him at this distance. And when I miss, all those stickies down there are going to be chasing after us. They'll run us down, too. You can count on that."

"You've got to chill the bastard," Mildred hissed. "We may never get another chance."

The look on her face said she was deadly serious.

"No, it's too risky," Ryan said. "And we can't wait around here for a better opportunity. It's going to be hard enough to get around them and then stay ahead of them all the way to the ville. We've got to go now, while they're stopped. It's our only chance."

He could see that Mildred wanted to argue, but she didn't say another word. They moved in silence behind the line of mutated trees, following the curve of the hillside past the legion of homicidal monsters.

FOUR HOURS LATER, when they were halfway to Willie ville, Ryan called for a much-needed rest break. He led them up a ramp and onto a still-standing overpass. From that vantage point they watched the highway behind them while they shared a few cold MREs—military ready eats—J.B. had picked up in the redoubt's armory.

After a few minutes Mildred moved beside Ryan and said, "That problem I mentioned back in the redoubt..."

"Uh-huh."

"This seems as good a time as any to explain what I meant." She waved for the others to come closer. "Everyone better hear this. It's important."

Ryan screwed the cap back on his water bag. "Go ahead," he said.

"Was there anything different about our last jump?" Mildred asked them all.

"You mean the bad dreams?" J.B. said.

"Partly."

"The stickies using the mat-trans system?" Krysty said.

"Partly."

"My dear Dr. Wyeth, is this some manner of guessing game?" Doc asked. "I do love a turn at charades."

Mildred scowled at the old man. "Let me put it another way," she said. "Whenever we make a jump, our destination is usually fixed by the network's preset controls. Say we use a mat-trans chamber in Idaho. We assume it always takes us to Louisiana. The Louisiana chamber will always take us back to Idaho if we use the LD button. To jump somewhere else, we have to find another redoubt and another gateway, and then we can only go forward and back between two predetermined points. We have no control over where the gateways send us."

"If that's supposed to be news," Ryan said, "it isn't."

"Hear me out. I believe the system wasn't meant to work that way. The designers were a lot of things, but they weren't stupid. Think about it. They wouldn't make a mat-trans traveler in New York City jump to Brazil, then search the jungle for another redoubt, in order to go to Boston. There has to be a way to program the individual gateways for multiple destinations."

"So what's your point, Millie?" J.B. asked.

"So, my friend," Mildred said, "the stickies have done just that. Don't ask me how, but they have. How else could they end up in the same chamber with us? We know they came from a different starting point."

"Couldn't two gateways be autoprogrammed to transfer matter to the same destination?" Ryan suggested.

"In all the jumps we've made," Mildred said, "we've hardly ever gone from a new gateway to a place we've been before."

"She's right," J.B. agreed.

"You're saying the stickies know something we don't about mat-trans," Ryan said.

"Or their leader does," Krysty suggested.

"That's what it looks like it to me," Mildred replied.

"What do you think, Doc?" Ryan asked. "You've had more experience with mat-trans units than any of us. You saw the whitecoats actually running the system. Could she be right?"

The old man screwed up his face as he tried to remember. The act was painful for him. He had endured too many dematerializations, too many rematerializations, not just from one point in space to another, but from one time to another. Connections between facts and ideas, and between fantasy and reality, blurred as they all swirled around in the muddle of his mind. Did he know the answer? Had he known it once?

"I fear I cannot say for certain," he admitted finally. "What the whitecoats did to me in the time before Armageddon, I recall only vaguely and in scattered bits and pieces. I believe they transported me hither and yon just to test their ability to puzzle my atoms back together again. How and where they traveled themselves is beyond my ken. In truth I was nothing more than their prisoner. However, I can tell you this—what the good Dr. Wyeth has postulated is grounded in the logic of Aristotle and the geometry of Pythagoras. To build a conveyance that could only take the most circuitous of routes makes no sense whatsoever. The shortest distance between two points is invariably a straight line."

"If the stickies can run the system and we can't," Ryan said, "it's a disaster."

"It gets worse," Mildred told him.

"Go on."

"I'm worried about the nightmares we had when we jumped this time," she said. "In my dream I bowed down to a mutant who looked exactly like the guy back there on the highway. I recognized his name because I was yelling it in the dream."

"Like I knew the stickies were mating from my dream," Krysty stated.

"That's right," Mildred said. "Look, we've all had

nightmares during jumps before, but never, ever have we had the same kind of nightmares. The coincidence seems unlikely. There has to be a causal factor."

"Have you formed any conclusions as to what it might be?" Doc asked.

"My understanding of the scientific principles of matter transfer is weak," Mildred said, "but I know one thing for sure—the system has never had any trouble telling us apart before. I mean, I've never ended up with Krysty's hair or Jak's red eyes or J.B.'s memories. I think that's because we always start out together, in the same chamber. If things happened the way I think they did, if reassembly instructions and source atoms arrived simultaneously from another gateway, there could be a serious problem."

"You're going to have to make it simpler than that," J.B. said.

"Okay, listen. A very long time ago I saw a film. It was about a scientist who invented a kind of crude mattrans machine. Everything was working fine until a house fly slipped into the machine with him. When he transported, his body parts got confused with the fly's. He ended up with a fly head, and the fly ended up with his. It's a tragic story that might apply to us."

"Are you saying we could have traded something with the stickies during the transfer?" Krysty said.

"I'm saying it's possible. If not something visible, then something on a molecular level."

"We mebbe turn stickie?" Jak said.

"Before I'd let that happen," J.B. stated grimly, "I'd eat the blaster."

"Jak, J.B., it doesn't work that way," Mildred said. "We're fully reformed by the mat-trans system. Whatever stickie traits we received would already be integrated into us. Pointy little teeth aren't going to pop out of our gums without warning. And whatever we received, if anything, it wasn't lethal or we'd already be chilled.

"Even if our physical structures weren't compromised," she continued, "a mix-up in the chamber could explain our similar dreams, which, I remind you, appear to carry some element of truth. At the very least we might have exchanged memories of real experiences with the stickies."

"Memories that aren't going away," Krysty said. "I keep having flashbacks."

"What can we do about it?" Ryan asked Mildred.

"I don't know," she replied. "Maybe I'm completely wrong and there's nothing to worry about. I sure hope so. But I think we should be aware of the possibility that some or all of us might have been changed by the jump."

"I just lost my appetite," J.B. said, glaring at his food. "Anybody want this?" When no one claimed the half-eaten MRE, he cocked back an arm and sailed it off the overpass.

"It's time for us to move on," Ryan said, breaking the stony silence. "Stay alert. Stay alive."

Chapter Five

Five thousand stickies opened their throats and howled for his pleasure. It was a hurricane of homage, of duty, of self-sacrifice.

"Kaaa!"

It wasn't his birth name. If he had been given one by his mother, he didn't know it. As he had no memories of the female who gave him life, he felt free to invent her. It had always pleased him to think that she had died trying to protect her baby, on the day he was stolen by the baron's mercies.

"Kaaa!"

Over the years he had been called many things by the norms—Blotch, Zit, Three Eyes—but this was the name he had chosen for himself. He hadn't taken it from some long-dead hero he admired. It had no literal or translational meaning, yet its symbolic power was undeniable. It was the one sound that all Deathlands' diversely mutated humanoid creatures could make, the only sound they could all chant in unison—a fact he had learned growing up as a specimen in Baron Willie Elijah's elaborate and extensive mutie zoo.

"Kaaa!"

It was a name and a call to battle combined.

The piebald lord raised his arms for silence. He was naked but for a knotted loincloth and jungle boots. He closed the wide-set, yellow-brown eyes socketed above his heavy cheekbones, and with his fingertips pried open the single eye set in the center of his forehead. Blood-encrusted, lashless lids peeled back, exposing a moist white orb, like the newly laid egg of a small bird.

It had no pupil.

No iris.

Yet it could see.

And seeing was the least of what the rad-mutated organ could do.

As he parted the protective flaps of skin, a tremor, like five thousand rattraps snapping shut, passed through the army of stickies. And when it was over, they were one with their leader, one with each other. What each individual soldier felt, they all felt. What each knew, they all knew. The stickies accessed every neuron in their leader's mind, saw what he saw and understood what he understood.

Lord Kaa addressed his troops, not in the inexact spoken words of the norms, but in the stickies' own language, in an oration of image and sensation. He showed them that they weren't debased and despicable, not degenerate subhumans as their oppressors claimed. They were, in fact, demonstrably advanced beings, beautiful to behold, superior in strength and adaptation, in procreative ability. Therefore, they were a terrifying threat to the last dregs of the old genetic order, which sought through force of predark arms to maintain its control over the much larger and rapidly expanding mutie population.

He showed them that their struggle against the injustice and domination of the norms was glorious and that their ultimate victory was assured. Deathlands was their world. They had been touched by it, changed by it in secret ways, and they, not the slave masters, were its true offspring—and rightful rulers.

Summoning all the power of his mind, Lord Kaa spilled forth a torrent of images that proved an even higher case, that there was no division between stickie and scalie, cannie and zombie, doomie and swampie, save what the norms had invented to keep them all apart. He told them that the mutie peoples of Deathlands were, in fact, the scattered tribes of the nuke wind, destined one day to unite and rebuild the world in their image.

With his glistening white eye, the piebald man showed his army of maniacs what they couldn't otherwise see: their delicate and precious communal soul. And as he did this, his mutant pineal eye wept tears of watery blood that rolled down the sides of his nose and onto his lips.

"Kaaa!" the stickies shrieked.

The overpass began to shake.

With careful fingertips he closed the nerveless flaps of skin that hid his third eye. As he opened his norm eyes, the rank, sweet-sour scent of the stickies' mass coupling wafted up at him. Energized by the psychic networking, they set to rutting in a frenzy. Soon the excess of their seed would flow down onto the broiling hot roadway, where it would erupt into pungent steam.

Watching the stickies mate, Kaa felt something stir between his thighs—his own need for sexual release. Though he could have used any or all of the mutants beneath him to achieve a climax, he did not. He was celibate and had been all his life. Control of self was the most important thing he had learned in his long imprisonment. Control of self was the founding power, the basis of all else.

His meticulously constructed conception of himself, of his future, didn't include premature fulfillment with either mutie or norm. He had turned down the advances of all of the baron's discarded daughter-wives, as well as several of his current granddaughter-wives. More than once, the jewels of Elijah's inbred harem had hiked their long skirts over their hips and, bending over, offered up their blond mounds for a quick poke between the iron bars of his cage. Because Kaa had bided his time, waited for his main chance, in the end he had stolen something infinitely more valuable than a few moments of pleasure in the company of the baron's halfwit concubines, something even more delightful than the planting of a three-eyed baby in the belly of every one of Elijah's pure-norm bitches.

It had taken decades of subservience and humiliation, decades of pain, for Kaa to gain the baron's complete trust. And the pain wasn't merely his own. Kaa had acted as Elijah's headsman, executing his fellow muties for crimes, real and imagined, against the royal personage. Once he had gained the man's confidence, he wasted no time using it to get what he'd always wanted. From the moment he'd understood what it was, he'd craved access to the tyrant's vast collection of pre-dark memorabilia, known as the Apocalypticon. He was the first and only mutie Willie Elijah had allowed to see his treasure, which he kept in a bank vault near his twenty-five-story palace.

On that initial visit to the Apocalypticon, Kaa had realized that the baron had no idea what all he had collected and no particular interest in finding out. Possessing it was enough for Elijah, until Kaa had explained that if the baron wanted to keep everything, it was vital to catalog it all. Otherwise, how would he know if anything had been stolen?

In point of fact, the archive had already been plundered by Kaa himself. When the baron's back was turned, he had taken a fragment of text from a broken book he found on the floor, which he had rolled up and stuffed inside his shirt in case he never got a chance to return. It was a dangerous and impulsive act. If he had been caught stealing from his master, his death would have been agonizing and stretched out over many days, perhaps even weeks.

He later came to believe that he had been fated to pick up that particular book. Of all the pieces of forgotten knowledge in the storeroom, he couldn't have chosen anything better to carry back to his cage than the *Legends of Charlemagne*. In secret, long before the baron had agreed to let him be the librarian of the Apocalypticon, he had read, analyzed and divined great truth from the ancient fragment. It had opened his mind to the idea of a creature of singular destiny, a creature who could unite all his people in a war of liberation. It showed him the possibilities for a return of honor, for final justice against cruel despots, for an empire that would span the width and breadth of Deathlands, an empire cleansed of norms.

It had also taught him the concept of romantic love, which dovetailed nicely with his lifelong celibacy. Because there was only one mutie female meant for him—his true love—he was right to wait to mate. He named this unknown female Angelica, after a brave and beautiful princess in the fable of Rinaldo. It was for Angelica that he saved his seed. All that he had built so far, all that he would build in the future, he would share with her. And the two of them would found a dynasty that would rule for a thousand years.

He had carefully planned his escape from Willie ville. He had left only when he was ready, after a full year of winnowing through the stacks of predark material. When he went over the wall, Kaa carried one treasure under his arm. Stamped in red ink across the front of the slim, paper-bound document was the warning, Top Secret. For Your Eyes Only. Below the security clearance was the title: "Operation Cerberus: Sys Design and Config." The document wasn't all he took with him. Inside his mind he carried a framework of ancient stories memorized, of lessons learned, the bare scaffolding for his military campaign against the slave masters.

A high-pitched mewling at his feet brought Lord Kaa back to the here and now. At his feet a stickie was making the birthing sound, its stomach muscles corded and rippling with contractions, flaccid face flushed with strain. It was Rogero, one of Kaa's paladins. The piebald lord knelt down and thrust his hand into the stickie's gaping womb. With his fingertips he found the top of the unborn infant's head. Careful to avoid the teeth, he took a firm hold under the jaw and pulled the creature out into the world. For a moment he dangled the blood-bathed infant stickie by its umbilical cord. As it slowly spun, it snapped its jaws.

Kaa pressed the baby to one of the sucker-ringed purple teats on Rogero's hairless chest. It began to nurse at once. After a few hours of steady feeding, the baby stickie would be too big to carry; its own weight would uncouple it from the nipple. The little mutant would be able to run and hunt as soon as its feet touched earth, and at that moment it would be as dangerous as a full-grown adult—the only difference being, it took smaller bites.

By the time they reached Willie ville, many hundreds more would have been birthed and nursed, fattened and readied for war. Kaa's stickie army would number closer to six thousand than five. Under his command they would sweep over the baron's defenses as if they were nothing, lay waste to the great ville, to its norms, scourge the earth and leave only cinders in their wake. The baron's liberated mutie slaves would rise up and join the battle.

It was only the beginning.

Lord Kaa planned to march over the eastern baronies, one after another, burning the estates to the ground, at each stop adding many thousands of mutie fighters to his ranks. By the time he was done, he would head an army the likes of which the world hadn't seen in many generations, an army that could conquer all of Deathlands and unite it under a single banner.

Chapter Six

Johnson Lester squinted through the telescopic sight of the toll booth's 90 mm recoilless rifle and considered touching off a round or two, just to break the eerie silence.

It had been a particularly boring day for the baron's sec man. Although it was nearly sunset, Lester and his crew had collected no tolls.

For the twelve hours of their watch, the road had been free of traffic moving toward Willie ville from the south. The booth in which they sat was a partially buried, wheelless, axleless, windowless, doorless semi truck and trailer. Like a rusty red pimple, the cab of the junked truck stuck out of the base of the twenty-five-foot-high berm wall, facing the highway south. The berm formed a defensive perimeter around the Willie ville complex. Under the dirt barrier, fortifying it, were piles of trashed motor vehicles.

The berm had been constructed by hand by mutie slaves, at blasterpoint. Slaves had likewise hacksawed off the back of the semitractor's cab and cut an opening in the front of the trailer, turning the buried rig into a tunnel, a pedestrian passage through the earthen wall. Wheeled carts using the baron's highway were directed to a different entrance, a narrow break in the berm that was blocked by the side of a semitrailer which, because it still had wheels, could be rolled back and forth. The trailer gate opened onto a tight sec area—a killzone, really—where the human- and animal-drawn vehicles could be searched while under heavy guard.

As much as Lester wanted to, he didn't shoot the 90 mm weapon. Ammo for it was not to be wasted on sport—baron's orders. He set the bipod-mounted weapon back on the truck cab's roof and stretched his shoulders. He was standing halfway out of the top of the cab, in a crude hole hacked in the sheet steel. The day had been a hot one, and he was looking forward to the end of his shift, to a hard-earned tankard of tipple. Brewed in the kitchen of the Liberty Bell restaurant to Willie Elijah's own specifications, the harsh, powerfully alcoholic barley wine was part of every sec man's daily wage. The brew's cloying kick disappeared after the first few sips, followed in short order by the onset of a most satisfying, warm and fuzzy stupefaction.

If Lester stopped to think about it, most days in the booth were pretty dull. The sec men weren't allowed to shake down travelers for more than the baron's toll, which was ten percent of whatever they were carrying. Unofficial, additional extortion by sec men tended to divert wayfarers from the toll route, which reduced the baron's profits. Elijah, suspicious bastard that he was, kept watch on his toll-takers with a pair of binocs from his penthouse suite in the Freedom City Motor Hotel and Casino.

The only time Lester and his crew had any real fun was when travelers couldn't pay. Then the sec men could get a bit creative. They indentured the men as unpaid, unfed field slaves for up to a week, in exchange for the toll. They put the women, if they weren't too old, and the girls to work on their knees right there in the toll booth. The sec men always let on, after they had finished and buttoned up their flies, that the females were done paying for passage, that their trials were over. It was a kind of a private joke between toll-takers. They never mentioned that the travelers had to clear another barricade on the other side of Willie ville, and that once again the women would have to open wide if they wanted to pass on.

If the sec men came across a real interesting mutie among the migrants, say a baby with leathery vestigial wings and a spiky tail, they'd clobber the mother over the head and take it from her. The baron had a long-standing bounty on unique specimens of the mutie races, which was how he populated his private zoo these days. Old Elijah could be generous, too. A sec man could spend a week drunk in the Willie ville gaudy on the reward. If the mutie parents put up too much of a fuss over losing their deformed brat, or if Lester's boys had had an otherwise slow day at the booth, they would chill both father and mother on the spot. The sec men would then drag the carcasses over to the Liberty Bell, where the cooks would chop them up, boil them down with spent grain from the brewery and feed the stinking mess to the mutie field hands in slop buckets. The slaves, who were kept in hovels outside the berm, were always glad to get their grub. They never asked where—or whom—it came from.

The baron's slaves provided much-needed diversions for the one hundred sec men who guarded Willie ville. And not just in the gaudy. Sometimes the sec men staged mutie fights to the death over in the Independence Park Amusement Zone. They'd throw a couple of big mean ones into the mesh hopper of the Spin 'n' Whip ride and let them tear each other's guts out, with high-stakes wagers on the outcome. Elijah also allowed them to bait the inmates of the mutie zoo, during certain hours and within certain limits. They weren't permitted to hurt the specimens physically. Yelling and spitting, and occasionally pissing on them, were okay, although the latter had to be done with speed and care since the muties tended to piss back.

Baron Elijah was real touchy about keeping muties and norms separated. Before he had hired Lester as a mercie in the Mutie War, he had made him prove that he didn't have any bad blood in him. Lester was required to drag in his mother, father, sisters and brothers—and their kids—for a complete exam. The baron was big on physical exams. He would sit there in his predark lounger with a huge magnifying glass and a lit candle and look over the outside and as much of the inside of a prospect as he could get at without using a knife. He was an expert at finding a mutie sign.

As far as Johnson Lester was concerned, it had been well worth his trouble to get on the baron's payroll. After his service in the brief, one-sided war against the mutant rebels, he had become a sec man for Willie Elijah. It was a plum occupation in a world where most people scratched their living from the dirt and for all their pain and sweat ended up half-starved. The baron did require that his sec men remain single—this because he didn't want them "softened" by married life. Which wasn't a hardship because, what with the gaudy and the steady flow of destitute travelers wandering by, there were plenty of females to go around.

"Lester, we got company," said a gruff voice from the cab below. "Stragglers at ten o'clock."

When Lester scanned the road south, he saw a line of people jogging toward them. He counted six. "They're trying to beat sundown," he said as he lowered himself through the hole. Reaching the protection of the ville's walls before dark was something every traveler with a grain of sense tried to do. There was no guarantee of safety outside.

"They're all carrying heavy packs and long blasters," Pedro Hylander said, lowering his binocs. Under the thick brush of his auburn mustache, the tall sec man's mouth twisted into a grin. "Plenty of pickings there. This day might turn a profit for old Elijah, after all."

"Gill," Lester said to the third man in the booth, "when they're in range, give the signal cords a tug." Their toll booth was connected by lengths of rope to the others spaced along the outside of the berm. The ropes were tied to aluminum cans with pebbles in them. A soft rattle would alert every sec position that someone approached the barrier.

Lester picked up his battle-scarred KG-99 assault pistol. As he stepped from the cab, he thumbed the fire-selector switch to full-auto. Behind him Hylander and Gill spilled out of either side of the truck, spreading out to get the best firing angle and to offer the most difficult targets for return fire, if there was any.

"Hey!" Lester shouted at the line of travelers, who were veering to the left. "Over here, you triple stupes!"

When the six people headed toward him, Lester confirmed that they were heavily armed. He decided not to take any chances. "Stop there!" he hollered. "Stand in the circle painted on the road."

The travelers obeyed, stepping into a crude ring that was the aim point for the three other gun positions along the south side of the berm.

"Keep your hands away from your blasters," Lester warned as he moved closer, sighting on them down the barrel of the KG-99.

The male traveler in front shifted as Lester approached, putting his body between the compact 9 mm's muzzle and his companions. He had a black patch over his left eye.

"Well, nuke my nuts!" Lester exclaimed. "If it ain't an ol' war buddy come back to pay us a visit."

"Which one of them do you know?" Hylander

asked, keeping back from the edge of the circle, well out of the line of fire of the other berm emplacements.

"I know old One-eye there," Lester said, scratching his stubby chin. "Know him real good."

"Not *the* One-eye?" Hylander said. "Cawdor?"

"Same."

"My, my," Hylander said, beaming at Ryan. "You're gonna keep us knee deep in gaudy sluts for a week."

"To hell with them scabbies," Gill said as he stepped up to the ring of death. He eyed Krysty's long legs appreciatively. "I'd rather get to know the curvy redhead. Inside and out, if you know what I mean."

Krysty looked at him as if he were a bug, fit only for stomping.

"Hey, Firetop," Gill said, aiming his M-16 at her head, "you ready to pay Willie Elijah's toll?"

As he watched, her mane of red hair separated into tightly packed tendrils, which coiled and writhed like individual serpents.

Gill jumped back a yard. "Damn, she's a rad-blasted mutie!" he said, taking a two-handed grip on the assault rifle. Recovering from the shock, he said, "She'd make a hell of a brood mare for the baron's zoo."

"Wrong, Rabbit-face," Ryan said to him.

Gill switched his aim to the one-eyed man. "What you call me?" he snarled.

"Lester," Ryan said to the sec leader, "we don't have time for this droolie shit. We've got important business with the baron."

"You damn right you got business," Lester agreed. "The way I hear it, you forgot to tell Elijah goodbye when you went over the wall all those years ago. And he was set to give you a parade and medals for the rebel muties you chilled. Willie Elijah don't ever forgive a scornful hurt like that." Holding his weapon steady, Lester approached the one-eyed man. "Dump your blasters and knives down on the road," he ordered.

"We keep our weapons," Ryan told him. "There's an army of stickies coming up the road behind us. Don't know how far back they are."

The three sec men looked down the highway south.

There was nothing to see, except the sunset burnishing the long, straight stretch of concrete in shades of purple and orange.

"We got to tell the baron," Hylander said.

"Willie Elijah will be eatin' about now," Lester replied. "You know he doesn't like to be bothered at his meal."

"If you don't get us up to see him pretty damn quick," Ryan said, "more stickies than you ever saw are going to be joining him for dessert."

"One-eye is chock full of shit," Gill scoffed. "Stickies don't have no army."

"They do now, my arrogant young friend," Doc assured him.

"How about I kick your scrawny ass up and down the road?" Gill asked, crossing into the painted ring. "I could use the exercise."

There was something about the old man that Lester didn't like. Sure, he looked crusty and slow, but for an instant his eyes seemed to be measuring the distance between himself and Gill. It occurred to Lester that the crusty bit might be an act, that he might be playing possum in order to sucker the sec man in close. "Step back, Gill!" he snapped. "Step back now!"

Lester's combat instinct was correct, even if it was a bit hazy as to the details. Gill was within seconds of having his heart parted by the swordstick's double-edged blade. Through long practice Doc had refined his subtle kill-stroke. With a blindingly quick downward flick of the wrist, Doc could drop the ebony scabbard; a precise upward flick would sink the steel in to the hilt.

The sec leader waved his men back. "Dump the blasters now," he told Ryan, "or get blown to hell."

The one-eyed warrior glanced over Lester's shoulder, searching the front of the berm. Lester could see him take in the permanent gun emplacements, one by one. No way could he miss the sec men standing with blasters braced and ready to send a withering rain of fire into the painted circle.

Ryan Cawdor was never a stupe when it came to fighting, Lester thought. One-eye could see that even if he and his friends darted off in different directions all at once, no one would make it more than a dozen feet outside the ring before being chopped down.

With a pained expression that pleased Johnson Lester no end, Ryan faced his companions and nodded. On his silent order they carefully lowered their packs and collection of weapons to the ground.

HANDS IN THE AIR, Ryan let himself be shoved through the trailer tunnel in the berm. He felt naked and vulnerable without his blasters. As much as he hated being disarmed, he hated putting his friends in that position even more. Yet giving up their guns was a necessary evil, a calculated risk they had to take. It was the only way for them to get through the gates of Willie ville quickly and alive. Their sole task was to convince Willie Elijah that the stickies were coming. If they succeeded in making the baron believe he was in jeopardy, they would get their weapons back and have their chance to fight and perhaps to survive. If they didn't manage to convince him, whether they got their blasters back or not, it wouldn't make any difference in the long run.

A stickie army of the size they had seen on the road was unstoppable, unless all of the East Coast barons joined forces against it. If that didn't happen, if the baronies were defeated one by one, sooner or later Ryan and company would have to face the stickie legion and certain destruction.

As would the rest of humanity.

The situation was made more complicated—and dangerous—by Ryan's personal history with Willie Elijah. He was counting on the pressing nature of the stickie threat to outweigh, at least for the time being, whatever resentment the baron still held for the way he had bowed out of the genocidal campaign known as the Mutie War. Elijah had always been a greedy, possessive bastard. Ryan knew if there was one thing that would get his miserly back up, it was the possibility of losing everything he had accumulated.

As Ryan and his friends stepped out the rear doors of the trailer, six more armed sec men swung in behind them. After a rough pat-down for hidden weapons, they were escorted across an open field of yellow dirt and dried-up grass. Ryan was amused to see that the sec men had left Doc his "walking stick."

About a half mile away, above a high hurricane fence, loomed the post-Apocalypse metropolis of Willie ville. It was pretty much as Ryan remembered it.

Dominating the skyline was the tall predark building that served as the baron's headquarters and barracks for his sec men. Even in the soft and somewhat flattering rays of sunset, it looked like the last rotten tooth in a dead man's jaw. The side that faced them was checked from top to bottom with windows, many of them black and broken. Orange lights flickered in the rooms with intact glass.

As they passed through the rolling gate in the hurricane fence, Ryan could see the rest of the complex. The landscaping of the grounds, which had never been looked after, had deteriorated to bare dirt and mummified plant beds. The curving concrete or asphalt driveways, paths and parking areas were split and broken by bristling tufts of spike grass. Clustered around the base of the baron's HQ were a few low buildings.

With their peeling paint and crumbling masonry, all of the structures looked scabrous. On the other side of the broad scar of rilled dirt that in happier times had been an eighteen-hole golf course, Ryan could make out the top of a motionless Ferris wheel and the stark white skeleton that supported the roller coaster's tracks. The baron's infamous mutie zoo was back there, too, out of sight.

A slight shift in the wind brought the sickly sweet smell of Willie Elijah's brewery rushing over them. Ryan recalled that the beer was made in the one-story building off to the right of the golf course. He also remembered the way the malty, scorched stink permeated the entire ville in the dog days of summer. Farther to the right was the gaudy, which had once been a fuel-and-repair station for gas- and diesel-powered motor vehicles.

Beyond the decrepit amusement park, on the other side of the berm, were the ville's slave quarters. The baron liked to keep his muties outside the walls at night. The small number of muties who handled menial tasks inside the berm were hobbled by chains and shackles on their ankles. On the other side of the slave hovels, which the muties shared with the baron's livestock, were cultivated fields. Elijah maintained a kind of pecking order of deformity among his field workers. The least obviously mutated served as overseers to the more grossly rad-altered ones.

Because Ryan hadn't witnessed the full glory of late-twentieth-century humankind, he had no yardstick by which to judge the merit of this place. Willie ville and other decayed settlements like it were all that remained of human civilization. And the baron, grievously flawed leader though he was, had created a secure border for his subjects. Willie ville's defenses were so imposing that the town had never been successfully stormed and sacked, either by mutie bandits or by other barons' mercies. If there was to be a rebirth of human culture in Deathlands, it would have to begin someplace like this, where there was relative safety, agriculture and primitive industry.

Their armed escort steered them toward the massive steel-and-concrete-slab awning that protected the main building's front entrance and U-shaped driveway. Across the face of the structure were huge, faded, red, white and blue script letters that read Freedom City Motor Hotel And Casino.

They passed under the awning and through cracked plate-glass doors that were defended by a half-dozen armed guards. The lobby of the hotel was a bleak expanse of glue-stained concrete subfloor, which had been stripped of all furniture, rugs and other decoration. The lobby was barren except for off-duty sec men who eyed them contemptuously as they were herded past. There were no civilian residents of Willie ville in evidence.

Johnson Lester led the way to the ground floor's twin elevators and pointed at the elevator car visible between parted doors on the left. The doors on the right were open, as well, but there was no car to be seen, and there were no cables visible, either. "All of you get down on your knees," Lester said as he waved them into the car ahead of him. "Face the rear wall with your hands behind your backs. Don't move until I tell you to."

After Ryan and the others obeyed, a dozen sec men pushed in behind them. When all were aboard, Lester shouted into a funnel connected to a hollow tube set in the lobby wall. "Twenty-four!" he bellowed. "Twenty-four!"

There was a long pause, then, with a creak and groan, the car started to creep upward.

"How in the name of hell are they running this thing?" J.B. muttered.

"A few dozen slaves in the basement," Ryan answered. "Elijah keeps them chained to this gear contraption that winds up the cables as they push it around and around a big post. They push it the other way to let the car down."

"Dark night, there's a lot of weight in this thing to be lifting that way."

"It's safe enough going up," Ryan said. "Going down is the problem. Did you see the other shaft in the lobby, the empty one? That car got away from the slave crew years ago. They tried to stop it from crashing in the bottom of the shaft, but it was impossible. For their trouble they all got battered to death by the machinery."

It took ten minutes for them to get from the lobby to the twenty-fourth floor.

As soon as they stepped out of the car, it was clear where all the lobby furnishings had gone. The hallway was jammed with couches and armchairs. They sat along the opposing walls in unbroken lines, arm crushed against arm, like the showroom of a shabby discount-furniture warehouse. And above them the walls were covered with large, uninspired oil paintings of crashing surf on a rocky shore, quaint farms with red barns and snowdrifts, and storm-besieged sailing ships. The couches and chairs were filled to overflowing with the wives and children of the important men of the town: the baron's accountants, his sec chiefs, his skilled craftsmen, emissaries to other barons, licensed exporters of agricultural products and tipple. Well-dressed and clean, the children sat quietly beside their mothers or in their laps. Each child held a small bag of confetti on his or her knees. When the baron and his wives made their regal exit from the dining room along this corridor, they would be showered with bright bits of paper and excited cries of "Live forever!"

From a doorway at the end of the hall came the sounds of hoarse, braying laughter and clattering cutlery. Four sec men stood guard over the entrance, and as Lester approached, they blocked it with their bodies and rifles.

"I need to see the baron," Lester said.

"He's already started eating," the sec man in charge told him. "He doesn't want to see you while he's stuffing himself. You might break his rhythm or even put him off his feed. Come back later, after he's had his snooze and hump."

"This is important. It can't wait that long."

"Oh, yes, it can," the sec man said, leaning his face close to the toll-taker's. "It can wait as long as I say."

Lester knew he had the trump card. He seized Ryan by the arm and, holding the muzzle of the KG-99 hard against his temple, pulled him close. "This here's a deserter from the Mutie War the baron's been after for years. Go on in there and tell him I brought him a special dish. Tell him it's called One-eye Cawdor on a plate."

Chapter Seven

With blasters pointed at their heads, Ryan and the others were pushed into the suite the baron had converted into a cavernous dining hall. The place was lit by banks of candles set on stanchions. Though there were many people in the smoky room, Elijah and his family were the only ones eating. The rest were either servants, who scuttled back and forth with food trays and beverage tankards, or the baron's male toadies, who filled rows of straight-backed chairs like an audience gathered for an evening of chamber music.

Chewing pensively, Baron Willie Elijah sat in a black lounger behind a heavily laden table on a raised dais. The platform was so high, he risked bumping his head on the ceiling when he stood. Sitting at tables below him on the floor level, and also chewing, were his three wives and their three baby daughters. There was a strong resemblance between all the mothers, which came as no surprise to Ryan, since it was common knowledge that they had all been sired by the same man.

Johnson Lester bent in a low, scraping bow to his master, then half straightened and said, "Baron, I've captured the deserter, Ryan Cawdor."

The room went silent.

"So I see," Elijah said, looking up from his dinner to survey first Ryan, then his friends. On the dais beside Elijah's feet was a great, brimming jar of tipple. He drew the long-handled dipper from the beer bucket and sluiced a half pint through his cheeks to clear his palate. The meal set out before him was plain fare, and plenty of it: huge clods of pan-roasted flesh; a steaming pile of potatoes cooked in their jackets; a predark, one-gallon plastic bucket full of brown gravy; stacked loaves of crusty flat bread. The baron ate it all with his bare hands.

While they awaited his further word, Elijah picked up a hot potato and squeezed it until the skin split, then sucked the white starch out through the crack. He followed it with a swallow of gravy right from the bucket, then a gulp of beer and quickly back to the roasted clods and bread.

Lester cleared his throat to regain the baron's attention, then continued. "I caught him trying to sneak through the toll booth with these other stupes. I can't tell about the others, but for sure, two of his runnin' buddies got bad blood—the red-eyed boy and the red-haired bitch. Looks like the butcher of Coupe ville's gone mutie lover on us, Baron."

Lester's master failed to rise to the bait. Instead of exploding with rage, Elijah stared almost amiably at Ryan. He crunched into a fresh loaf of flat bread, sending a rain of crumbs and crust shards spraying over the table. After washing down the mouthful with more tipple, the baron leaned forward and said, "Well, Cawdor, it's been a good long while since you and me last faced off. What do you think of the way my little gals filled out?"

The baron's wives blinked their pale, straight, corn-silk eyelashes at Ryan. They looked so much alike they could have been born triplets. Their round faces bore the same blank expression, and their straight, fine, blond hair was parted in the middle and fell to the middle of their backs. They appeared to be in their early to middle teens and were clad in long dresses with extremely low, tight necklines that with every breath threatened to send plump breasts popping out of their tense confinement.

Though he wanted to skip the small talk and rush into the important subject at hand, Ryan couldn't risk offending Elijah with the very first words out of his mouth. "They look even younger than the last time I saw them," he said with a straight face. "Which one's Poonie? Which one's Toonie?"

The wives bounced the baby girls on their laps and said nothing.

"You're a whole generation off, Cawdor," the baron said. "You're looking at Poonie-Two, Toonie-Two and Roonie-Two."

"Your granddaughters," Ryan said, smiling at the three girls. "How're your mothers doing?" He guessed that Elijah's daughters were already long dead, killed by the baron just as their mother, his first wife, had been as soon as the new crop of females came ripe for harvest.

Again there was no response from the royal harem.

Time hadn't been so kind to Willie Elijah, Ryan thought. The baron's hair, his pride and joy, which had once been corn-silk blond like his granddaughters', was now stiff and white and unmanageable. He tied it in a loose bun at the back of his head. He had on a quilted, plum velvet smoking jacket, which leaked stuffing from holes in the shoulders and elbows. He wore no shirt under the smoking jacket; the coarse white bristle of his chest hair spilled over his food-stained lapels. Loosely draped around his neck was a blue silk scarf with black tassels on the ends. His trousers were baggy, wine-colored corduroy, and his shoes were a pair of predark sandals known as Birkenstocks. Because he wore no socks, Ryan could see his great, horny, yellow toenails. Even from across the room, the baron smelled like an unhosed bear pit.

Ryan remembered him as being a taller, more imposing figure. Certainly the flesh of his face didn't used to hang down below the line of his jaw. And his cheeks had never been scruffy with white stubble like that. Even his eyes looked ancient. They were bloodshot, and the whites had a yellowish tinge to them. From too much of his own brew, Ryan thought. But he knew it would be a mistake to underestimate Elijah, even in his present condition. Though the man had been scourged by time, he was still dangerous, cruelly perverse and unpredictable. And they had placed their fates in his hands.

"So, Cawdor," Elijah said, "did you come back to try and make amends after all these years? Mebbe beg me for forgiveness?"

The audience of toadies murmured its unanimous approval. They liked a good and proper show of begging, especially when it was doomed to be fruitless.

"We came to warn you," Ryan told him. "There's five thousand stickies on your toll road. They're coming north to level this place. They already wiped out your little way stop twenty miles south. Burned it to the ground."

The baron laughed, and the crowd of sycophants joined in with gusto.

"That's a good one, Cawdor," Elijah said. He picked up a potato and threw it at Ryan's head, but missed when his intended target easily ducked the warm missile, which brought more laughter from the audience.

"Baron," Lester spoke up over the tumult, "I think One-eye was sure he could sneak past Willie ville without anybody recognizing him."

Ryan didn't look at his friends, but he could feel their eyes on him. Everything depended on what he said next, and how he said it. "Baron, that is the dumbest thing I've ever heard," he argued. "I wasn't trying to sneak by your ville—fireblast it, I wasn't even wearing a disguise! With a face like mine, I'd have to wear a hood and mask to keep from being noticed. I came here for one purpose, and that was to warn you, and I did it knowing there was still a price on my head. Ask yourself why would I risk my life to sell you some nuke-shit, made-up story about stickies when I could've easily taken a ten-mile detour and avoided Willie ville altogether? You know I'm no stupe. What possibly could be in this for me, except mebbe an early death?"

The baron sipped from his tankard as he considered the question.

Ryan didn't wait for a response, but forged ahead while he still had the chance. "We talked to the only survivors from the burned ville of yours," he said. "They told us a mutie was leading the stickies up the toll road. We outflanked them on the highway and got close enough to see the bastard for ourselves. The survivors said you know him. Said that you used to keep him in your zoo. His name's Kaa."

Elijah shook his head. "I don't ever give my mutie pets formal names, Cawdor. They aren't worth the trouble. You should remember that from the old days." As if losing interest in the conversation, the baron started picking through the mound of meat in front of him.

At the table below, Roonie-Two reached up with a thumb and spilled her right breast out of the top of her dress. She deftly stuffed its pale nipple into her two-year-old daughter's face. As Roonie-Three began to nurse noisily the teat, Roonie-Two dipped a potato halfway into her one-gallon gravy boat. She plunged the dripping end of the baker into her mouth and, with hollowed cheeks, proceeded to suck off the coating of sauce. Her performance caught, but failed to hold, Ryan's attention. Krysty, on the other hand, glared daggers at her.

"We saw this mutie leader with our own eyes about six hours ago," Ryan said. "He's close to seven feet tall and powerfully built. He had unusual coloring on his skin. Brown-and-white patches all over."

Elijah squashed the chunk of cooked flesh in his fist, squirting warm grease on his jacket. Ryan had touched a raw nerve. "You lie!" the baron snarled at him. "You lie trying to save your cowardly deserting hide! And it isn't going to work. Nobody I hired walks out on me and lives. Nobody!"

It was time to play the hole card, shaky though it was.

"If I'm lying to you, Baron," Ryan said, "you'll know it soon enough. The stickie army couldn't be more than a few hours behind us. They'll sure be here before daybreak. Until then, what's it going to hurt to get your sec men ready for the attack? What's it going to hurt to send out a warning to the other barons around here? Mebbe they'll even give you some reinforcements, which you'll need. But whatever you do, you've got to start now, before the stickies lay siege to Willie ville."

The room again went silent.

"Me and my friends will fight alongside you," Ryan said.

"He could be a spy, Poppadaddy," Toonie-Two piped up.

"Yeah, a spy from Byrum ville, working for Black-heart Hutton," Roonie-Two added.

"I don't grow no stupe girls, One-eye," Elijah told him with pride. "They can smell a dead mutie a mile off. What do you say? Did you sell me out to that thieving, rad-tainted bastard who runs Byrum ville? Is it a trick to get Blackheart's sec men inside my walls so he can take my treasure and diddle my pure-norm gals?"

"I'm no spy," Ryan said. "Just think about what I'm saying for a minute. Protecting yourself from the other barons isn't a problem. If you're worried about some-body pulling a trick on you, don't let any of their sec men inside the walls. But put every one of your men on triple red tonight. You've got nothing to lose."

Elijah pondered the matter in silence for a moment or two, then rose to his feet. "I don't see no downside to me here," he announced to the crowd. "Anybody see a downside?"

If they did, they kept real quiet about it.

"I'm going to do what you say, Cawdor, but don't think it's going to buy you any mercy from me, even if ten thousand stickies show up at my gates." He pointed a thick finger at Ryan's face. "You're mine, and you're going to die the way I see fit. I got to think a while on how I want to do it, though. I've been wait-ing so long for this, it's got to be something extraspe-cial. Something extrapainful."

"Do whatever you want with me," Ryan said, "but

let my friends go. They don't owe you anything. They came here to help save your skin."

The baron looked over his companions, then said, "Take One-eye, the old bastard and the one with glasses and stick them in the cooler overnight. For now the red-eye boy goes to the zoo."

"He's not a mutie," Ryan protested.

"Shut it, Cawdor."

"And the women?" Lester asked.

Before Elijah answered, one of the toadies stood and raised his hand for permission to speak. Even though he'd lost ninety percent of his hair and put on seventy pounds around his middle, Ryan recognized Lee Strootz from the old days.

"Baron," Elijah's whoremaster said, "if you haven't already made up your mind about the black one, I'd like to stake a claim on her. She's got a sturdy look I like. With a little training from me and my boys, she'd take it any way you'd want to put it to her, as long as you want. Make a nice addition to the gaudy stable."

Mildred went rigid beside Ryan, the expression on her face mingled fury and horror. The physician had been willing to give up her life if necessary to save these norms from the stickie hordes; she certainly hadn't figured on being turned out as a gaudy slut. Ryan had to physically restrain J.B. from starting forward.

"No, Strootz," Elijah said, "you've got enough warm bodies down there. She goes to the cooler with the men. And when they die, she dies, too."

Ryan watched Mildred relax. Death was something she knew she could face—after all, she had already done it once.

"Get them out of my sight," Elijah said to Lester. "All but the red-hair. She stays here with me."

To one of the servants, he said, "Bring me my magnifier glass!"

Applause and scattered cheers burst from the crowd.

"Would you boys like to see how a real expert mutie exam is done?" the baron asked his toadies. "Mebbe get your faces right up against the lens so you could learn something interesting?"

The men jumped to their feet, cheering and catcalling.

Ryan leaned close to Krysty. "I'm sorry," he said. "We'll get out of this mess somehow. Hang on."

"You, too," she said. Under the bravery and defiance that flashed in her green eyes, there was fear.

Before Ryan could say more, the sec men separated him from Krysty with the muzzles of their blasters, then roughly shoved him, Mildred, Jak, J.B. and Doc toward the exit.

"Wait a minute!" the baron bellowed down from his dais. When they stopped and turned to look back, he said, "What's that stick the old one's carrying?"

"Nothing, Baron," Lester said. "He's a crippie. Needs it to walk. Otherwise, he'd have to be carried."

"Let me see it."

Lester snatched the ebony cane away from Doc and passed it up to Elijah.

The baron examined the silver handle, found the release catch and unsheathed the rapier. "What's this? You let a weapon get past your search? You let him bring a sword in here?"

A groan went up among the toadies.

"Baron, uh, I, uh…"

Elijah resheathed the blade and threw the stick back at the sec man. "Put it in my quarters with the rest of their gear. You're going to pay for that mistake, Lester. Tomorrow you're going to take a turn on the wheel."

The audience whistled and clapped.

The sec man's jaw went slack, his face suddenly pale. He didn't protest the sentence. Those who protested did two turns.

At this point Elijah's servant rushed up with the magnifier. Set in a brass frame and handle, it had a convex lens six inches across. With a sweep of his arm, the baron sent the food platters on the table before him crashing to the floor. Having cleared his exam table, he said, "Bring her up here to me."

As Ryan and the others were pushed from the dining room, they heard Elijah say, "Strip her down and move the candles closer. I need plenty of light for this kind of work."

The wives and children waiting in the hallway didn't laugh and throw confetti when the five companions were paraded past them at blasterpoint. Instead, they yelled insults, kicked and slapped. It was all part of the evening's entertainment.

With the sec men's blasters pressed hard into their

flesh, Ryan and his friends rode the elevator down in silence. Finally J.B. said, "We all knew this could happen, Ryan. We all knew the risk."

"Yes, we did," Doc said. "Be assured of that."

"You're not to blame, Ryan," Mildred told him.

Ryan could think of nothing to say to Jak, no way to make things right. Words could only do so much. And they were cheap. Young Jak was headed for the mutie zoo, where death came slowly, sometimes over the course of decades, and only after unspeakable suffering and degradation. He had every right to be angry. With any luck he wouldn't be there long.

When they reached the lobby, the car stopped and six of the sec men separated Jak from the others. The white-haired teen stepped out of the elevator surrounded by his armed escort.

"Your friend seemed awfully quiet," Lester said to Ryan as he ignited a hand torch from the one already burning in the elevator. "Guess you must've told him what goes on in the zoo. Actually it's a lot worse than when you saw it last. Baron's got the whole place full now. He's collected some of the damnedest-looking muties you ever seen. Kind of hard for any of them to get to sleep, I imagine. Bunches of them are always screaming, screwing and carrying on."

The car started down again. It didn't make a stop in the basement, but kept on going. The deeper they went, the darker it got. The two torches in the elevator barely cut the gloom. As they descended, they could hear the sound of gears clacking, chains creaking and men groaning. The sounds of labor and pain grew louder, the farther down they went.

"By the Three Kennedys," Doc said, "what's that hellish commotion?"

"Tell him, Lester," Ryan said.

"Shut up."

"It's the wheel," Ryan answered for him.

"I said shut up," Lester growled.

When they stopped at the bottom of the shaft, the mechanical sounds ceased. The groaning continued, but softly.

Lester and the sec men pushed Ryan and company out into the dim corridor. Its dripping concrete walls were unpainted; it was bathed in flickering half-light from the torches stuck in stanchions along the walls. Water in the corridor was ankle deep in places, and it reeked of decay and mildew.

"Dark night, it's colder than a dead stickie's butt down here," J.B. stated.

"Now you know why they call it the cooler," Ryan said.

As they were quick-marched along the corridor, they could see steel doors open on both sides, but the light was too poor to make out anything inside the rooms. They followed the corridor around a dogleg to the right and came upon four rooms in a row with closed doors and no doorknobs. Wired to screws bored into the steel at eye level were bunches of sorry-looking plastic flowers.

White lilies.

"What's in there?" Mildred asked. "Looks like a tomb."

"Good guess," Ryan said. "Baron Willie Elijah locked his first wife down here years ago. Left her to starve to death. Probably did the same to his three daughters when they got too long in the tooth for him."

"All right, hold it there," Lester ordered. He stepped around the others and over to a door locked with two big bolts. Then he opened the door and showed them the cooler's prison cells in the ten-by-ten room. The two iron-barred cages had been constructed on-site. Each stood about four feet high, and one was stacked on top of the other. Three inches of water covered the barred floor of the bottom cage. Even in the weak torchlight they could see the bloated corpse facedown in the far corner.

Lester opened the door to the top cage and started shoving his prisoners in. Once inside, they had to crawl or crabwalk forward as there wasn't enough room to stand.

"Faith, it stinks to high heavens in here!" Doc said, fumbling in his frock coat for a hankie to cover his nose.

"That's because your toilet is underneath you," Lester said. "Be glad you don't have to sit in it."

He saved Ryan for last. He actually let him get his head in the top cage before jerking him back out. "No, I'd better not put you up there," Lester told him. "Might overcrowd the other prisoners. Might cause them unnecessary distress. Can't have that."

The sec man shut the top cage and opened the bottom one. At blasterpoint he forced Ryan to crawl inside on his hands and knees. There was no way to stay out of the vile water or avoid the rank, soft stalactites hung from the bars of the cage floor above his head. Ryan hunkered down, making himself as small as he possibly could.

Lester clanged the door shut. "Like it, Cawdor?"

Ryan stared up at him. "Look on the bright side, Lester," he said, "mebbe the stickies will overrun Willie ville tonight. Mebbe you won't live long enough to do your time on the wheel."

Lester slammed the hallway door, plunging them in total darkness.

For a long time no one said anything. Talking meant drawing extra breath, and no one wanted to breathe more than necessary.

"Ryan," J.B. asked from somewhere above him, "what's the wheel, anyway?"

"It's what the baron calls his elevator motor."

"Is it as bad as this?"

"No. It's worse."

"Good."

Chapter Eight

Jak had two alternatives in mind as he walked out the front of the Freedom City Motor Hotel and Casino: to escape or die trying. Daylight was completely gone; the color had all but drained out of the world. Jak's ruby red eyes worked better at night than most other people's. If he could put some distance between himself and the sec men, he knew he could evade them and reach the wall. True, he was unarmed and without food or water, facing an army of stickies in the dark. But any death he could think of was better than a life sentence in the baron's zoo. He couldn't count on Ryan for a rescue. The one-eyed man had his own troubles.

The sec men didn't make it easy for him. Figuring that their captive would try to make a break for it, they stopped long enough to bind his wrists together with a thong. They lit their hand torches from a stanchion, then led him across the fractured parking lot toward the entrance to the Independence Park Amusement Zone. As Jak glanced back, he saw the baron's men running out of the hotel with torches in their hands. On orders of their feudal lord, they were setting alight every lamppost that they passed. If the stickies broke through the berm and entered the grounds tonight, Elijah wanted his defenders to be able to see them.

The amusement zone's entrance was framed by a tall arch made of bands of wrought iron. Human-sized statuettes capered across it. Because Jak had never seen a cartoon, he didn't recognize them as fictional characters. With their distorted heads and bodies, spindly legs and oversize hands, he thought Mumbly Mouse, Wazoo Wildcat, and Peewee Poodle were muties. He thought the arch had been specially constructed to mark the way to the baron's zoo.

At that moment Jak felt more kinship to the cartoon characters than to his trusted companions of so many years. Since the jump dream his attitude toward his friends had changed.

The stickie nightmare had done something to him that he couldn't explain to the others. New and powerful ideas swirled through his head in a torrent. After all, he had sat at the feet of Lord Kaa and listened to his teachings not with ears, because he had none in the dream, but with the core of his mind. He was an albino, not a mutie, but the seed had been planted that told him who his true enemies were.

The norms. He was one, but not.

According to Kaa, norms had only one purpose in the great scheme of things, and that was to bring Deathlands and its people into being. Having done that, the norms were worse than useless; they were an obstacle to further progress because they refused to relinquish the power they had held for so long.

Throughout their history the norms had proved they had no lasting allegiance to their own kind. And yet they continually fooled themselves into believing such bonds existed. Ryan Cawdor was no exception. Hardened fighter though he was, he still thought that Baron Elijah would see the light and act according to reason, in the best interests of all. Ryan believed that Willie ville and everything it stood for was worth not only his blood, but the blood of his comrades. How long he would hold this opinion, it was impossible to say. In the jump dream Kaa had shown Jak that norms couldn't be trusted to see past their own short-term self-interest. Their federations and alliances were doomed to split apart. They would die as they had been born, as individuals, in isolation—and in isolation they would become extinct.

Kaa had explained that at the root of much of the endless dissension and bloodshed among the norms were arguments over which of their many races had come first—and which, therefore, were the most favored children of their creator. Kaa taught that the new people had no such internal divisions. Muties of every stripe, no matter when they were born, shared a common date of origin: January 20, 2001. Nuke day. They suffered a common oppression. They had a common destiny, which was to unite and remake, to unite and rule Deathlands forever.

There was glory here on a scale that Jak had never imagined.

And in that glory was a place for him.

As they penetrated the amusement zone, the sec men set fire to the torches atop the lampposts. Ahead of them the wide, curving asphalt lane was dark. The place practically cried out for an ambush. Jak could sense the guards' growing nervousness. Even if they didn't completely believe the stickies were drawing near, the idea made them jumpy all the same.

On either side of the path loomed the strange, mechanical-looking structures of the fun rides: cylinders of wire mesh, hoops of steel I-beams, cages attached to long metal arms. All were frozen, dead. At the entrances to each ride were low chain-link fences and steel turnstiles, for crowd and ticket control, which hadn't been a concern for more than a century.

Then they approached a two-story building with more of the mutielike figures decorating its side and roof. Jak could hear moans and sobs coming from inside and thought they'd already arrived at the zoo. For a moment he was sure that he'd blown it, that he'd waited too long to make his break. But the building turned out to be just another deserted ride: the Ghost Castle Spook Train. Like the other amusement rides, it was no longer powered by fossil fuel or electricity; it was powered by live beings. Mutie slaves dragged the miniature railroad cars through the darkened spook house; muties in chains leaped out of hiding places in the blackness to try to scare the norm passengers.

Jak decided he was as close to the rear of the park— and freedom—as he was going to get. He had to act now or never.

"Stickies!" he cried, pointing at the shadows beside the building.

"Where?" one of the sec men yelped.

"What?" shouted another as he brought up his blaster.

The white-haired teen snapped a spin kick into the closest sec man's face and felt the satisfying crunch of a nose breaking under his heel. A hand grabbed his neck from behind, fingers sinking into his flesh. He twisted away, slamming his doubled fists into the man's side. As he started to run, he saw the path he'd chosen was blocked by a huge guard with arms outstretched.

"Get the little shit!"

"Don't let him get away!"

The sec men dropped their torches and closed in on him.

"Hey, snow-hair," one of them said, "where do you think you're going?"

Jak didn't answer. He feinted right, then spun left, shooting a snap kick hard into the center of the speaker's throat. The sec man dropped to his knees, clawing at his neck and gasping for air. Before Jak could make his dash, the other sec men jumped him, and by the sheer weight of their bodies, drove him to his back on the ground.

"We'll fix you, you bastard runt!" the sec man on his chest said as he cocked back a fist. He laughed and smashed the youth full in the face.

Jak saw stars as he was hit repeatedly, then kicked and stomped up and down the length of his torso. And when the first sec man got tired of the game, the others spelled him. As consciousness began to slip away, Jak prayed the bastards would lose control and beat him to death.

But they were pros; they knew just when to stop.

Grabbing him by the armpits, they hauled his battered and bloody body to the gates of the mutie zoo. Jak was dimly aware of their being met at the door by a stout man with greasy, gray hair and knee-high rubber boots—the baron's zoomaster.

"Got a fresh one for you, Knackerman," a sec man said.

The zoo master leaned down and lifted Jak's head by the hair. "Pure albino variant, mebbe," he said, squinting at the boy's pale, scarred features. "Kind of hard to tell the way you messed him up."

"Tried to get away," a sec man said.

"He'll live, don't worry," another added. "He's a tough little bugger. Where do you want him?"

"I don't want him," Knackerman said. "Baron's got too damn many packed in here as it is. Pretty soon they're going to start dying from the scour sickness. They're already killing each other every chance they get. I keep telling him it's a mistake to overcrowd his zoo. Baron doesn't care. He likes variety. Always more muties, he says. This way."

Jak started to come around as he was dragged into the building. The concrete corridor was dark and dank, and it reeked of the unwashed creatures imprisoned behind its floor-to-ceiling cages. The hallway rang with their earsplitting shrieks, tortured sobs and inarticulate screams.

"They seem wilder than usual tonight," one of the sec men shouted over the din.

"Mebbe they smell this one's blood."

"Something's got into them, all right," Knackerman agreed.

A cage door opened with a creak, and Jak was hurled inside. He landed facedown on the foul, matted straw. He didn't move until the voices of the guards trailed off and the lights they carried disappeared. As he pushed himself up onto his elbows, he felt sharp pain as his facial wounds reopened. He tasted fresh blood inside his mouth. Rising to his knees, he scanned his surroundings. He couldn't see much, even with his mutated eyes, but he could see enough to know he wasn't alone in the cage.

At the back of the enclosure, where it was darker than dark, a huge pair of yellow cat eyes glittered at him.

WITH THE SOUNDS of the mutie zoo raging at their backs, Lester, Hylander and Gill lay belly down in a shallow pit they had scraped in the dirt.

"Listen to them rad-blasted buggers howl!" Gill said.

"Chillin' each other...like always," Hylander stated.

"Naw, it's different," Lester told them. "I don't know how, but it is. It's like they know something's about to happen."

"Mebbe it's all the lights," Gill suggested. "Some muties get strange around fire. Makes them go animal."

The baron had ordered every torch in Willie ville lit. The ruined highway rest stop glowed orange and golden from thousands upon thousands of points of firelight.

Lester and his men were stationed at the edge of the open ground between the zoo and the berm wall. On the other side of the berm were the slave quarters. Their mission was to observe, then pull back and report if the stickies broke through.

As precarious as their position was, Lester found it hard to keep his attention focused on the top of the berm. Ryan Cawdor's words kept running through his head. They raised questions he didn't want to face but couldn't stop thinking about. How many norms actually survived a turn at the wheel, especially sec men? Offhand he couldn't remember any. After all, unless there was an accident, it wasn't the wheel that killed you; it was your fellow workers. The muties slaving in the subbasement were condemned to death, sentenced by the baron to labor until they dropped in their chains. They had nothing to lose by chilling a sec man; they looked at the opportunity as a kind of bonus. Even though the muties were manacled to their posts as they pushed the wheel around, Lester knew they had their own ways of doing the deed, none of them pleasant. If he wanted to live through the baron's punishment, he had to bribe the overseers into keeping the mutie slaves off his back.

His good buddies, Gill and Hylander, hadn't once mentioned his impending ordeal. Maybe they figured they already had enough to worry about tonight. Maybe they didn't want to have to lend him any jack in case he came up short with the overseers. In either case, Lester was too bone tired to take offense.

None of it probably mattered, anyway.

If there really were five thousand stickies coming, the odds of a hundred or so sec men holding them off until dawn were slim. There was just too much ville to defend. Realizing this, the baron had ordered explosive charges planted along the most likely attack routes. The battle plan was to retreat, then detonate the explosives under the stickies, retreat and detonate, all the way back to the hotel, and in the process, reduce the enemy numbers as much as possible. Once the sec men had pulled back to the hotel, they'd defend it from the ground up, room by room.

If the stickie force turned out to be smaller than what Ryan Cawdor had described—and this was what every sec man in Willie ville was fervently praying for—the initial retreat of the baron's defenders would mask a massing of their forces. It would let groups of stickies break through the berm barrier in specific places, funneling them into prearranged killzones.

Lester, Hylander and Gill had drawn the unenviable task of leading the stickies to slaughter.

In the grand scheme of things, they were live bait.

Chapter Nine

It could be worse, Krysty kept telling herself.

But that was hard to believe.

Stripped naked, she was stretched out on her belly across the baron's dining table. At Elijah's command, his sec men held her wrists and ankles, and pinned her hipbones against the edge of the tabletop. She couldn't see what was going on behind her, but she could feel it. Fingers lightly brushed the red shock of her pubic hair, then cold glass pressed against her upturned buttocks.

"Hmm," the baron said, with his free hand tipping the bank of candles closer.

Molten wax dripped and splattered onto the sensitive skin at the base of Krysty's spine, making her flinch and jerk against the grip of the sec men.

"Got to check them for pustules right off," the baron said as he raised his face from between her splayed thighs. "Can't be putting the new ones in the zoo and doing it later. Never know what kind of sickness these muties might be carrying. Before you know it, whatever they've got, it spreads through the rest of them like wildfire. Learned that the hard way, years ago. This little scalie bitch I bought off a trader from the

Darks came in infected with some kind of rad-mutated STD. It nearly wiped out my zoo, killed half my adult specimens before I got control of things. No, you can't be too careful with the pustules. I always check the new females for rad cancer, too. They can look okay on the outside, but then they ooze and drip like a dead dog's belly once you try to breed them."

Krysty craned her head around as far as she was able. She could see the white frizz of hair on top of Elijah's head. He was writing with a pencil stub in a thick, cloth-bound book. Was he making some kind of measurements of her private parts? Taking notes on her general physical appearance? Was it sheer nonsense and bluster meant to impress ignorant sec men with his command of pre-Apocalyptic scientific procedure? She had no way of telling, but her instinct told her he was a fraud.

"Turn her over," the baron said, "and hold her head real still."

When the sec men twisted her onto her back, Krysty saw that Elijah had picked up a short, sharp knife. From the look on his face, she thought he was going to gut-slit her for sure. The situation seemed so desperate that she was on the verge of summoning her Gaia power—something she was very reluctant to do except as a last resort. She had no doubt that her unique connection to the feminine forces of the earth could give her enough strength to break free of the guards who held her spread-eagled. But then what? There were other blaster-armed sec men in the room; even with

Gaia's help, it would take several strokes of luck for her to chill them all. And if she managed it, using the power left her weak and trembly, and she still had nowhere to go. Krysty forced herself to relax. The time wasn't right. The power had to be saved and used only when it could be most effective.

As it turned out, she made the right choice.

"I want to take a sample of hair," Elijah told his men.

At least, Krysty thought, there were only a handful of sec men to see the show. At least the baron had cleared the room of his wives and assorted toadies. Like most malevolent despots, Willie Elijah found he enjoyed depriving his subjects of pleasure more than he liked granting it to them.

The baron rounded the side of the table, then grabbed a thick lock of her prehensile red hair. Stretching it out, he lopped it off near the root with a quick slash of the blade.

Krysty screamed in pain, and the sinuous mass of her hair retracted at the insult, coiling tightly against her skull. Krysty felt as if she had lost a finger or a toe, and the pain rushed across her scalp in burning waves.

Elijah dropped the severed strand onto a plate and watched it writhe. It didn't bleed from the cut end. Other than the violent motion, it appeared to be normal hair. The thrashing continued for a few seconds, then it slowed and the hair gradually became still.

"Unusual," the baron said. He reached across her

breasts for his notebook, which lay open on the table. Pulling the ledger onto her belly, he hastily scribbled something with his pencil stub.

"Which mutie are you going to mate her with first?" asked the sec man who was holding her head.

All the sec men wanted to know the answer to that; in fact they were practically drooling to find out. They considered the baron's practice of mutie husbandry a spectator sport, a recreational activity that ranked right up there with the baiting of zoo inmates.

"Too soon to decide," Elijah replied. "I'll isolate her for a few months. Have Knackerman time her periods. When I figure out when she's due to be fertile, I'll chain her down on her back and let one of my best mutie studs have a go at her for a few days."

"Lucky rad-ass bastard," muttered the sec man at her head.

The prospect of being mated against her will momentarily plunged Krysty back into the primal terror of her jump dream. It wasn't just the threat of sexual violence and victimization that scared her; it was the idea of being forced to bear live young when there was no way of telling what kind of baby would emerge at the end of term. Once again Krysty experienced the helplessness of the nightmare. Once again her enormously swollen belly contained a staggering weight and dozens of tiny legs kicking, hands scratching, needle teeth piercing, ripping. With an effort of will, she fought off the sensations.

The fear of giving birth to monsters was something

she shared with practically all of Deathlands' sentient females. What with lingering radiation hot spots, polluted aquifers and chem-saturated rain, post-Armageddon genetics was an ongoing game of Russian roulette. Everyone realized that most of the fresh mutations induced by the environment were lethal—and if not that, then debilitating or disfiguring in some way. Though outwardly she didn't seem to have been impacted negatively by the changes in her mother's genetic structure, Krysty couldn't know whether the genes she now carried had been damaged in the course of her life, and if so, all her future offspring. Deep down she understood that it was possible her DNA had already been compromised so badly that the Gaia line would end with her.

The concern had to have shown on her face.

The baron smiled at her almost paternally. "I'm done for now," he said. "Let her put her clothes back on."

Under the prying gaze of all those male eyes, Krysty dressed herself with all the dignity she could muster. She had won a pair of small victories. She had gotten through the exam alive, and she had kept her Gaia power a secret. When she had finished zipping up her coveralls, the baron addressed her directly for the first time.

"Is there anything else I should know about you?" he asked. "Any other interesting mutie peculiarities?"

She looked at him for a moment, as if trying to decide whether she should speak at all. Then she shrugged. "I do have a power that can't be seen," she told him.

"And that is...?"

"I'm a doomie," Krysty said. This was an exaggeration, if not an outright lie. She did have some ability to visualize the future, and in particular, impending danger, but her gift was very limited and imprecise.

"Really?" the baron said. "What do you see in store for me?"

Krysty closed her eyes. "A bright future for you and yours. A long and healthy life. I see many girl great-great-grandbabies. Much power. You will gain a broader reach throughout the east. Before you draw your last breath, fear of your name will have spread across all of Deathlands."

"So you don't see any stickies in my future?" Elijah said, grinning. "Don't you believe what your friend One-eye says about a conquering army coming this way?"

"Oh, I believe," she told him. "I believe because I saw the stickies on the toll road with my own eyes."

"You saw this mutie leader, too?"

"Yes, I did. He was big, with brown-and-white patches on his skin."

One of the sec men leaned close to the baron and said, "Could it be him coming back after all this while? Could it be Zit?"

Elijah silenced the man with a wave of his hand.

Krysty looked the baron in the eye and said, "For some reason the stickies don't seem to influence any part of your future. Either they don't attack or you repel them when they do. It isn't clear to me."

"I like this doomie bitch," Elijah said.

Which was exactly what Krysty had intended. She smiled fetchingly at him. She was bartering now for any small advantage she could get. Though her situation looked fairly hopeless, the game wasn't over until the last shot was fired. Krysty knew there was any number of ways that things could still work out for her and friends. She had to keep focused, ready to seize the chance when it came.

"How long you been running with Cawdor?" Elijah asked.

"Not long. A few months."

More lies.

"You must be screwing him, then."

Krysty didn't answer.

"Funny that One-eye should take up with a mutie slut like you," the baron said. "Or that you'd take up with him after what he done. Although, mebbe he didn't tell you...."

"Tell me what?"

"That he hired out to me as a mercie during the Mutie War. He was part of a special chill crew I sent into rebel-held territory. A bunch of escaped mutie slaves had built up this scratch-ass little ville in the middle of nowhere and named it Coupe, after one of their dead. They were nothing but a bunch of dirt farmers armed with blasters they stole from me. My orders were to make an example out of them, to chill the ones that put up a fight and drag the others back here, where I could work them to death, good and proper. Your pal Cawdor and the other mercies and sec men surrounded Coupe ville. The muties saw them coming, though, and barricaded themselves in their huts. My men blasted the place up a little to show that they meant business.

"The way the other mercies tell the story, after the rebels knew they were licked, they threw out their weapons. They wanted to surrender and go home in chains. One-eye wouldn't hear of it. Kind of went crazy. He was a coldheart bastard back then. He set fire to the place and burned them up in their huts, women and mutie brats, too. My crew didn't bring back a single prisoner from Coupe ville. Word about the massacre spread real quick through the rebel territory. Lots of them gave up without a fight after that. Cawdor did me a big favor by going wild. Too bad he lost his taste for mass chilling. He lit out on me not long after."

"No, he never said anything about that to me," Krysty said. She figured it was what the baron wanted to hear. That it was close to the truth was just a coincidence. Ryan had told her and the others that he and the baron had had a disagreement over prisoner policy. He hadn't given them any of the details. Krysty had no way of knowing whether the baron had made up the massacre story. She knew Elijah could be trying to turn her against Ryan in order to make her a more pliant zoo specimen, or to get information from her about him and about whoever supposedly was backing him.

"Take her down to the zoo," the baron told his sec men. "Tell Knackerman I want her kept isolated. Have him put females in the cages on either side of her. I don't want any males getting at her until I say so."

For Krysty it was a brief stay of execution, a small consolation, but better than none.

As the sec men grabbed her arms and started dragging her off, she resisted. Determined to make a last attempt to convince Elijah whose side she was on, she stomped the toes of the nearest guard with the stacked heel of her cowboy boot. When he released her with a curse, she twisted back to face the baron.

"If it comes down to a fight tonight between you and the stickies," Krysty said, "my skin is going to be on the line just like everybody else's. I can handle a blaster pretty good. I'd like the chance to die with one in my hand. If the stickies come, you're going to need every blaster you can get."

"I don't need no mutie slut with a blaster aimed at the back of my head, though," the baron said. "Get her out of here."

Chapter Ten

The creature crouched so low in the straw that even as Jak rose to his feet, he couldn't make out the shape of its body. He had no way of telling what kind of mutated being he was sharing the cell with, no clue whether it was friend or foe. The teenager retreated as far as he could go, pressing his back against the bars at the front of the cage.

"Hey, you, over there!" he said to the pair of huge yellow eyes. He practically had to shout to hear himself over the yelling and screaming in the zoo corridor.

At the sound of his voice, the creature started to advance. It moved toward him very slowly, with utmost caution and stealth. And as it closed the distance, Jak noticed that the position of its eyes had dropped nearer to the ground. It was coiling, preparing to spring on him.

Jak wiped his battered mouth with the back of his hand. Was the smell of his blood attracting it? There was nothing he could do about that. He couldn't stop the flow. The eyes speared into him, shifting as the creature moved to his left. It was trying to back him into a corner. Jak knew better than to let that happen. He countered by shifting to the left, as well.

The creature froze.

It began to growl. Jak didn't hear it as much as he felt it, through the concrete floor, right up through the soles of his feet. The growl climaxed in a roar so loud it rattled Jak's heart in his chest. He knew those enormous cat eyes didn't augur well. In the world of adaptation, they indicated hunter, carnivore, killer by instinct.

Which meant death was just a matter of time.

Jak accepted his fate with a broad, defiant grin. He saw it as a blessing, not a curse. It was his chance to escape the baron's animal farm with his head held high, a chance to go out quick, and to go out fighting.

"Come on," he said, kicking straw at the yellow eyes. "Let's go."

Jak had no plan, as such. In order to plan, one had to know what one was up against. He blanked his mind and steeled his body to counter whatever was thrown at it.

He didn't see the beast make its jump.

When the eyes blinked, he ducked to the right. Soft fur brushed his shoulder, and with it came raging body heat and the scent of musk and urine. Claws clattered against the iron bars, and a shriek of feline frustration ripped the air.

Without thinking, Jak whirled and leaped onto the creature's back. There really was no place else to go.

The cat was big. Its body was over six feet long, not counting the tail. The great knobs of bone along its spine gouged Jak's chest and crotch. His hands found and gripped the pointed horns curving out from the sides of its neck, a permanent defense against throat attacks by larger predators. Jak locked his legs around the beast's narrow waist and held on for dear life.

Bellowing its fury, the mutie mountain lion tried to dislodge the boy by crashing its sides against the bars. Jak wouldn't be scraped off. The cat twisted its head around as far as the horns would permit and tried to snap a bite out of him. Jak choked on its fetid breath and kept out of range. He couldn't control the animal's head; it was too strong. The cat lunged forward, bending almost double as it ducked its head under its chest. It struck upward along its sides with its front claws, missing him by inches. When this failed, it threw itself on the straw and tried to roll him off. Though the full weight of the beast crashed down on top of him, Jak wouldn't let go of the horns.

The mutie cat wallowed on him for several long moments, then rolled back onto its belly. Jak punched it in the rib cage with everything he had, the jolt of the impact registering all the way to his shoulder joint. It was like hitting a side of beef. He hit it again and again. The cat's massive ribs absorbed the rain of blows, which had no effect, other than to tire Jak out. There was no way to get at the creature's vitals, its soft underbelly, without exposing himself to the tearing fangs and claws. His only hope was to wear out the great beast.

Leaping to its feet, the cat crashed around the cell again, scraping its rider against the walls. It was trying to grind him down, if it couldn't knock him off.

The standoff continued for what seemed like hours. Both combatants had the same idea: to exhaust the opponent and then take advantage. The contest of wills dragged on and on. Neither fighter would yield. Though both gradually weakened, neither gained the upper hand.

Finally the mutie cat began to slow down, which was lucky for Jak because his arms were exhausted. Still, the creature wouldn't quit. It moved in tighter and tighter circles, until it collapsed to its stomach on the straw, wheezing for breath.

Jak sensed the beast's huge tongue lolling out of its mouth. He could hardly hear its panting over the rasp of his own gasping. Against Jak's chest the cat's fur was warm and soft. Under him the lion started to purr, a deep, baritone rumbling, a very relaxing sound, hypnotic, even.

After a few minutes the lion put its chin on its front paws. A little later it began to sputter and snort. Its breathing slowed; the purring continued. Jak let go of a horn and reached out to touch its ear. It was pointed, fat and furry. The teenager suddenly found it difficult to keep his eyes open. His every muscle felt drained and limp. He knew he had to get up and find a way to kill the cat before it recovered. But he needed to rest for just a minute.

Soon they were both snoring in the dark.

"STUFF AND DAMN taradiddle!" Doc's angry voice drifted, disembodied and ghostly, through the blackness of the Willie ville cooler.

"This is by far the vilest jail in which I've ever passed a night," he announced in a half-strangled croak. "Fouler by far than the infamous torture dungeon of the late and unlamented Baron Jordan Teague, of Mocsin ville. More loathsome than the human terrarium of Baron Sean Sharpe. And having had the benefit of an abundance of personal experience with the inventors and operators of similar establishments between here and proverbial Piss Town, U.S.A., I can tell you this—only a pox-riddled brain could have devised such a hellhole. Only a soulless beast could confine a fellow being to such a filthy pit."

"From what I've seen, you've described Baron Willie Elijah to a tee, Doc," Mildred said. "Not only demented by his own self-indulgent addictions, but savagely cruel to boot."

"I knew what a psycho he used to be in the old days," Ryan said, "but I still didn't think we'd end up here."

"'Tis water over the dam, my dear Ryan," Doc told him, "water over the dam. There's no going back now.

Our fates are well and truly cast. And though grim they are, it behooves us to try to make the best of them."

"How long has it been?" Mildred asked J.B.

It was so dark in the cooler that the radium dial of J.B.'s wrist chron gave off an eerie green glow, partially illuminating his face.

"We've been down here for close to five hours," he said. "I make daylight another four hours off."

"So what happened to the army of stickies?" Mildred asked.

"If they had shown up," Ryan said, "we'd have known about it. Even down here we should have been able to hear the sec men's blasterfire. You can bet they aren't going to hold anything back."

"But where the blazes are they?" Mildred went on. "Why haven't they attacked? We all know they couldn't have been more than three hours behind us on the toll road. They should've been here by now, if they're coming."

"Dark night, Mildred," J.B. groaned, "don't say that."

"Why not?" she countered. "It's a possibility we've got to face at some point. The stickies might just be headed someplace else. Maybe our guy with the brown-and-white patches has other plans we don't know about. Hey, for all we know, they all turned around and headed south after we left them. It's possible we could have screwed up."

Ryan shifted in his narrow, waterlogged, lower cell,

moving from agonizing pain to somewhat lesser discomfort. His back, neck and legs were cramping from so many hours of a permanently hunched-over position and near-constant shivering. The stench of death and excrement remained as thick as fog in the airless, sealed room, but it now only occasionally made him dry-heave; his senses of smell and taste had been overloaded and largely negated by prolonged, concentrated exposure to the stink.

A product of a diseased brain or not, Ryan had to admit that the cooler was a most efficient torture chamber. It required no personnel and no maintenance; in fact the nastier it got inside, the better it worked. He knew the baron's cooler could break even a strong prisoner's spirit, often with a speed that was amazing. He had seen it done himself.

"We assumed Elijah would free us to help him fight stickies," J.B. said. "If there's no battle, he could just leave us in here to die."

"Think about this," Mildred said. "If the stickies get the upper hand early on, the baron might lose the contest before he can let us out to fight. Nobody would ever look for us in here."

"My friends," Doc interrupted, "you are not making the best of what is an admittedly bad situation. You are, in fact, further confounding matters by dwelling on the morbid and defeatist."

"Doc's right," Ryan said. "If we let ourselves think we're done for, we are. I know Elijah, and he's not going to leave us to die here in the dark. He's going to want to watch. More than that, he's the kind of cheap bastard that likes to milk some benefit out of a chilling, as a spectacle for his followers. Or a few days of slave labor he didn't have to pay for. At least the sec men didn't manacle us. They figured we'd be so weak after an overnight session in here that we couldn't put up a fight. We've still got our hands and feet free. Save your strength as best you can."

After a moment the sounds of splashing water filled the closed chamber.

"Ryan, what are you doing down there?" J.B. asked.

The one-eyed man had dropped to his hands and knees and was crawling toward the corner of his cell. "I'm looking over our dead friend," he said. "Thought I'd better get on with it. He isn't getting any sweeter."

Ryan fumbled in the darkness in front of him until he touched the back of the corpse. Then he ran his hands over the distended body. Its flesh was as hard as concrete and just as cold.

"How long's he been dead?" Mildred asked.

"Who knows?" Ryan replied. "All I can say is, his hair sloughs off in big clumps whenever I touch it."

"What about weapons?" J.B. said. "Has he got anything on him that we can use?"

"Haven't found anything yet," Ryan replied. He braced his foot against the cell wall and, grabbing the corpse's shoulder, tried to lever it onto its side toward him. "Fireblast!" he swore. "I can't turn the damn thing over. Its underside is stuck to the bars, and it's swelled up. If I pull any harder, it's going to split open."

Ryan fumbled under the water for a second, then said, "It's got ankle shackles. They're made of some kind of metal, hinged in the back. No chain between them—the sec men must've taken it off before they dumped the poor bastard in here. The shackles've got possibilities, but, damn, I can't slide them off! The ankles are too swollen."

"Are the shackles welded shut?" J.B. asked.

"No," Ryan answered at once, "they've got a lock. I can feel the hole for the key."

"If I was down there with you, I could pick the locks easy. I got a piece of wire in my pocket that the sec men missed."

"Can you lift the corpse's legs?" Mildred asked. "If you can raise the feet up close to the ceiling, J.B. can reach through the bars and work."

Ryan tried. He discovered that the dead man's legs didn't bend at the knees anymore. They were locked out straight. Not to be denied, Ryan sat on the corpse's back, grabbed an ankle and pulled back with all his strength. After a moment of teeth-grinding impasse, something snapped underwater and the leg swung up at the knee joint.

"Oh, sweet sufferance!" Doc gasped. "What a smell!"

"I think his guts broke loose," Ryan said.

J.B. reached down through the bars and, finding the dead man's foot, set to picking the crude lock that held the shackle shut. As he'd said, it was quick and simple work. It took Ryan twice as long to break the other leg, but after he'd done so, J.B. had the remaining shackle off in no time.

"Feels like they're made of soft iron," the Armorer said, testing the tab end of a shackle against the bars of the cage. The hinged bands were two and a half inches wide and an eighth of an inch thick. "They should take an edge okay, but they won't hold one for long."

"Don't need it for long," Ryan said.

"That's right," Mildred added. "Just a couple of well-timed slashes."

They started taking turns scraping the iron against the concrete floor and walls. It was slow work, and noisy. Every so often, the results would be passed over to J.B. who checked the angle they were putting on the edges.

Nobody mentioned the pathetic nature of this effort.

Whether the makeshift weapons would ultimately help to advance their cause or not, at least they were doing something.

Chapter Eleven

Flanked by a small group of stickies, Lord Kaa and Rogero had crawled to a hilltop vantage point within a half mile of the Willie ville defensive berm. Nestled in the black hollow of the valley below, Baron Elijah's township twinkled in outline. Yellow points of light defined its perimeter, its height, its breadth. There were so many torches burning, it looked as if the whole ville had been set on fire.

"The norms are expecting us to pay them a visit tonight," Lord Kaa said. He spoke with his lips almost touching the side of Rogero's head, to make sure that his officer would hear his words and understand them. "Baron Elijah only lights his ville like that when he suspects an attack. Word of our victory in the south must've spread up the toll road ahead of us. It's a safe guess that every one of Elijah's sec men is standing watch at the barricades, with blaster in hand. Won't they all be disappointed when dawn comes and we still haven't shown ourselves?"

Rogero made a soft, whimpering sound. As the stickie watched the distant flames, its fingers clawed furrows in the dirt.

Kaa understood his paladin's need, and the needs of

the other members of the recce party. The sight of fires in the valley excited them and kindled an urge to wreak mindless havoc. Kaa knew that if he hadn't been there to help them contain their enthusiasm, the stickies' primal blood lust would have taken over. Rogero and the others would have rushed down into the light and hurled themselves upon the ville's walls, dying pointlessly there under the baron's concentrated blasterfire, dying in an attempt to satisfy what could never be satisfied: their species' thirst for violence and slaughter.

The piebald lord reached up and carefully peeled back the lids of his third eye. All the stickies on the hilltop jerked as one, called to attention by some invisible puppet master. They saw not through their own eyes, but through the dead white, glistening orb in their leader's forehead.

With infinite patience, in a series of carefully constructed mental images, Kaa showed them the tactical situation. He showed them groups of their fellow stickies already in position, concealed at various points around Willie ville's perimeter. He explained that no matter what the baron did, they were in complete control of the battlefield; there was no escape from their wrath, no survival for the norms inside the ville. This night the baron would stew in his own fatty juices, pacing the halls of his palace like a prisoner, waiting for an assault that wouldn't come. His sec men would go without sleep. By daybreak they would have lost confidence that a real enemy even existed. By noon of the following day, after eighteen hours of full combat alert and no hint of a foe, they would be mentally and physically drained, and even easier to defeat.

Kaa expected the baron to send morning patrols outside the berm, patrols that, when the time came, would be quickly and quietly taken care of. They would simply vanish. The baron never committed his sec men to outside night sweeps. He and his colony of norms had always counted on the barrier to secure them against the forces of darkness, and relied on the perimeter's stationary blasterposts to concentrate and control any would-be attackers.

Night had always belonged to the muties.

They were about to expand their sphere of influence.

Having made his point, Lord Kaa placed a calming hand on top of his paladin's head. Rogero's hairless scalp was clammy with sweat, its eyes as dead and emotionless as polished black stones. Kaa pulled the side of the stickie's flabby face close to his mouth. "There will be victims yet tonight," he assured Rogero. And with detailed mind pictures he gave the recce squad a foretaste of the banquet of pain that was to come.

The stickies pressed their faces into the dirt, demonstrating their gratitude and subservience.

The lord of the mutants pinched his third eyelid shut and picked up his treasured M-60 machine gun. He had named it "Joyeuse" after the fabled enchanted sword of Charlemagne. A blind scalie witch had decorated the blaster for him, painting it with neon spells against harm. "He who wields this weapon," the witch had promised, "shall not fall in battle."

Kaa scooted back behind the crest of the hill, then started along the track that led to his main encampment. He was the only member of the recce party carrying a blaster or a stabber. Stickies as a rule weren't fond of weapons, predark or otherwise. They found that tools interfered with their pleasure during slaughter. They preferred to use their sucker hands and needle teeth for chilling. Rogero refused to carry even so much as a club. Their other mutie kin, the scalies and scabbies, the swampies and cannies, had no such qualms about using blasters or blades or blunts in battle. If they weren't as physically powerful as the stickies, the other muties' blood lust was at least tempered by a healthy desire for self-preservation.

The stickies' propensity to violence was such that nothing pleased them more than tearing apart a victim while they themselves were being ripped asunder. This perverted, Bushido-gone-amok was an integral, defining part of their nature as were their instinctive urges to hunt living prey, to nest in great masses and in great masses to breed in profusion. As with other hunter species, most of the space in their brains was devoted to fine control of their primary sensory apparatus. All their pink matter went to smell, taste and sight; there was no room for higher thought. The stickies' mental shortcomings notwithstanding, Kaa had the greatest respect for their physical abilities. And their loyalty.

They killed for him, bred for him, died for him.

What more could any general ask of a foot soldier?

It took almost an hour for Kaa and his party to circle around to the back side of the hills and reach the base camp. He had located it well beyond the range of the baron's daylight foot patrols, in a shallow bowl between a pair of rounded peaks. There were no structures of any kind in the camp. Stickies slept and ate rough. There were fires, though, and his army danced and cavorted around the scattered blazes.

Kaa was pleased to see how rapidly the young ones were maturing. It was already hard to tell the generations apart. That was the other positive side to delaying the attack on Baron Elijah by twenty-four hours. Instead of fielding an extra thousand ankle-biters, Kaa would have that many three-quarters adults fighting at his side.

A cheer went up as his army sensed his presence. They shouted his name and jerked their arms overhead as they spun wildly through the clouds of wood smoke.

It was time to spill some blood, Kaa thought.

The throng parted before his advance, and stickies by the hundreds prostrated themselves, falling to earth in waves of supplicating flesh. Kaa walked upon their backs to the center of the camp, where a small knot of figures knelt on the ground. The baron's couriers, sent to bring reinforcements from the bordering feudal lords, were bound hand and foot.

They knew what was coming; he could see it in their eyes.

Only one of them, a norm Kaa had known from the

old days in Willie ville, mustered the courage to speak. "Zit," he said in a shaking, tearful voice, "whatever I did to you way back when, I'm sorry for. Honest, I am. I was only following orders. Same as you. If I hadn't done what the baron told me to, he'd have put me on the wheel, you know that. It was nothing personal. It was never personal."

"That's funny," Kaa said, "with me it's *always* personal."

He pointed his M-60 at the stars and cut loose a long burst of 7.62 mm tracer fire. When the arcs of light vanished from the sky, when the gunshot echoes faded, he peeled open his pineal eye.

"Don't do this," the sec man moaned.

It was too late.

It was already done.

Orders had been given, and orders had been accepted.

Movement stirred through the crowd. The young ones hurried forward, some carrying metal cans high over their heads. A dozen of them immediately jumped on one of the defenseless sec men and with suckered fingers pried open his jaws. They held his mouth wide while others ripped off the top of an olive green can.

"You dirty, rad-tainted fuckers!" one of the other sec men cried. "You lousy, stinking mutie bastards!"

The immature stickies dumped a good pound of black powder into their prisoner's mouth and down his throat before releasing him. While he sputtered and choked on the load of explosive, a young mutie capered up and touched a firebrand to his black-dusted chin. A fountain of sparks and flame erupted from the sec man's face. With a whoosh his features melted like wax, and his eyes dripped off his chin.

The army of stickies screamed in jubilation and triumph as the ruined but still-living norm toppled to his side in the dirt and fell into a shuddering, shivering fit.

The young muties repeated the procedure with two of the three remaining sec men. They saved the norm who had used Kaa's slave name for last. They had something special in mind for him. After filling his mouth with gunpowder, they used strips of his clothing to bind his jaws shut. The sec man's eyes bulged enormously as one of the little stickies wedged a crude twist of fuse deep into his right nostril.

As one, the army moved back, making room for the big finale. Another young stickie hopped up and set the fuse alight. With fire sputtering, creeping up the front of his face, the norm captive shook his head violently, trying to dislodge the fuse. Flame entered his nostril, making it glow red. He clamped his eyes shut, then his head exploded with a solid whack, leaving nothing between his shoulders but a smoking stump of neck.

The little stickies rushed forward en masse, picked up the corpse and threw it into the bonfire. While their fathers-mothers cheered, they stomped the mortally wounded sec men to death. And when they had reduced the luckless norms to ragged heaps of bone and muscle, they tossed the remains into the fire, too.

The earth trembled from the impacts of thousands of dancing feet.

Kaa raised his arms to the sky, tipped back his head and roared his approval.

His baby soldiers had been well and truly blooded.

Chapter Twelve

Baron Willie Elijah gave up trying to sleep. Scowling, he opened his eyes and took in the glitter-flecked, rough-textured, white plaster ceiling of the penthouse master bedroom. On his left on the king-size bed, in a tangled mass of untucked covers, lay Poonie-Two and Toonie-Two. The sisters were snoozing in each other's arms. On his right, stretched out on top of the rumpled sheets, was Roonie-Two. His pure-norm gals were producing a rhythmic chorus of snorts, pops and nasal whistlings. Poonie-Two's legs kept twitching, kicking him in the shin.

This, the baron decided, was what it must be like to try to doze off in an overcrowded pigsty, like one of his mutie slaves.

In the normal course of events, Elijah was the first one asleep and missed the snore chorus of his three wives. The night past had been different, however. Not only hadn't he gotten to sleep first, but he hadn't dozed off at all. He had left orders with his sec men to be roused at the first sign of an attack. Then he had lain wide-awake, waiting for the crackle of blasterfire.

Elijah gazed across the snowy expanse of Roonie-Two's bare behind, to the sunrise spilling through the curtainless floor-to-ceiling windows of the baronial penthouse.

Evidently there had been no attack.

No one had tried to wake him.

So much for One-eye Cawdor's stickie army.

What had the traitorous coward been thinking? He had to have known that his pack of lies would be uncovered and his fate sealed by dawn. Maybe he was hoping that the chaos of a full nighttime mobilization would allow him and his friends to escape. Now there was a dumbfuck move.

Feeling the pressure of a full bladder, the baron climbed over his granddaughter-wives and padded naked and barefoot across the bedroom suite. He threw back the sliding glass door to the patio. The day looked promising, not too hot, not too wet. A good day for business. Stepping up onto the seat of a metal chair, he sent a yellow stream arching over the balcony's rail and down twenty-five stories onto the unprotected heads of his subjects.

Willie the Sun King.

When Elijah turned back to the room, some of the things he had passed the long night thinking about— things he hadn't bothered to consider for years—resurfaced in his head. He relived the single most formative incident of his childhood. When the baron was a boy, his old man, who had always appeared to be a perfect norm, had gone cannie after skinning and eating a three-foot-tall mutie bear he'd found stiff-dead in a clearing. Willie's mother had tried to talk him out of keeping the foul-smelling meat, but the old man had insisted on making a meal of it.

The following day, while Willie was away from their camp, his father had attacked his mother, sisters and brothers. When Willie returned, he found his entire family gutted, skinned and staked out to dry in the sun. His father was just sitting there with his belly all pooched out and a stupid grin on his face. He was so stuffed with hearts, lungs and livers he could hardly move. Which made it a whole lot easier for young Willie to crack his skull open with a sharp bit of rock. The baron-to-be beat his old man's mutie-contaminated brains into pink mist. Willie figured it was do-or-die time, that as soon as the jerky ran out, his dad would go after him. He dumped all the bodies down a fissure in the earth. All he kept back were a few locks of his mother's and sisters' hair, which he still had, tied up in ribbons somewhere.

Shortly after the patricide, Elijah had begun his career as a coldheart robber along a desolate reach of the six-lane highway that ran past Freedom City, U.S.A. His modus operandi was simple. He crept up on travelers while they were sleeping and clubbed them to death for their worldly goods. His first real break came when he took a blaster and some bullets off one of his victims. After that he moved up in the world rapidly. He headed a gang of other coldhearts that specialized in trading mutie slaves and pushing a cheap and inferior grade of jolt. Eventually he got hired on by Baron George Frederic Sokolow, the previous lord of Freedom City. Elijah's job was to supply fresh slaves to work the baron's plowed fields. With the help of the baron's wife, he had murdered old Sokolow and taken his place, in both the feudal and matrimonial arenas. He had done away with his princess-wife after she had borne and raised him three healthy and ripe norm daughters.

Elijah's longevity at the helm was due to a combination of factors. Certainly his ruthlessness played a large part in his success. He also had an ability to manipulate people and keep them at a disadvantage. He stirred up constant intrigues among sec men and toadies, then conducted bloody purges of those he considered the most dangerous. No one had dared to raise a hand to him in more than twenty years.

The baron had spent a good deal of the night thinking about Zit, and wondering what, if anything, the mutie had taken with him when he'd run off some years ago. At the time Elijah had vowed that Zit would be the last mutie he'd ever trust. He'd raised up a lot of others from pups. He could always look in their eyes and read their intentions as plain as day. He'd thought he could read Zit, too, but he couldn't. Maybe it had something to do with the slave's screwed-up genes. He'd never seen a mutie go through a change the way Zit had. According to the mercies who'd brought him in, he'd been born with that patchy-colored skin and weepy sore in his forehead. About the time the boy started to show signs of manhood, the sore crusted over, and when the scab dropped off, it had turned into a full-fledged eyeball, albeit as white as an egg, with loose, lashless eyelids.

Zit had grown up to be a big bastard, but the way he always walked around, with his head hanging down so meek, none of the Willie ville norms were afraid of him. He never gave any of them a harsh look. Muties were another story. Zit put the fear of God into his own kind. Once he had his growth, Elijah worked Zit as an overseer, first in the fields, then in the elevator "motor." He did such a good job bullying and beating that the baron let him handle the duties of executioner whenever the job came up. Sometimes Elijah would get a mutie slave who wouldn't be tamed and had to be destroyed. Death sentences were also imposed if a mutie stole something or looked at a norm funny.

Elijah had been stunned to learn that his archivist had gone over the wall. It was like a slap in the face to him. He'd been sure if any damn mutie was ready to lick his baronial ass and beg for more, it was Zit. He blamed book learning for a lot of the trouble, which was why he never let his girls get any education. He didn't want them getting any ideas he hadn't planted. Zit had somehow managed to sneak off and teach himself to read better than almost anybody in Willie ville. The baron really had no way of telling whether Zit had got his dangerous notions about freedom from the Apocalypticon or whether he already had them when he started to work on the collection. The rare books and secret papers had strange powers; after all, they had run the whole predark world.

Elijah had always been a hoarder, a pack rat. As a boy, he was always picking up bright, shiny objects he found during the family's food-gathering expeditions. Now that he was rich, he freely indulged his compulsion. He had spent much time and treasure accumulating the trove of material. He had put out the word on the trader network that he would pay top jack for anything predark and in good shape. Of course, there were practical reasons for the expenditure, too. The mystery of the Apocalypticon added to his wealth and power because it furthered his legend as a master of the arcane and dark. It didn't matter that the legend was a bald-faced lie. Elijah could read, but haltingly. And he certainly couldn't make heads or tails of the acronym-littered technobabble that much of the documentation was written in.

"Where you goin', Poppadaddy?" Roonie-Two asked, squinting over at him.

Elijah picked up his corduroy pants from the floor and started to pull them on.

"Come back to bed, now," she moaned. "It's too early."

"Got important work to do, gal," he told her. He stepped into his shoes and left the bedroom.

At the far end of the penthouse suite, with a commanding view of the highway and valley to the north, was his operations room. The sec men and high-level toadies sitting around the long table jumped to their feet when he entered. All their eyes were red rimmed and dark circled; the toadies' faces looked even sallower than usual.

"I take it we had a quiet night," he said as he rounded the head of the table.

Murchisson, his longtime sec chief, spoke up first. "So quiet you might even call it dull, Baron. Except for a report of some possible blasterfire around 2:00 a.m."

Elijah tipped the lid off a bucket of tipple on the floor and used a dipper to ladle himself a breakfast pint. "No one saw anything?" he asked, taking a deep draft of the high-octane ale.

"No, sir," Murchisson answered. "Could've just been a string of thunderclaps. We had some chain lightning off to the east around that time."

"I don't suppose any of the runners are back yet," Elijah said.

"No, sir. Don't expect to see them until midday, if then."

Elijah caught the wry look in the head sec man's eye. "You don't think Old Blackheart Hutton and the other barons are going to send any men our way, do you?" he asked. "You think they're more likely to sit back and hope we get eaten alive. Let the rad-blasted stickies do their dirty work for them. Then come by after the smoke clears and fight over the pickings."

"My thoughts exactly, sir."

"Well, you're probably right. They know I'd do the same thing to them, if the opportunity ever came up." Elijah refilled his dipper and sipped from it.

One of the assembled toadies cleared his throat. "Baron Elijah," said Skeen, a short, wide man with heavy jowls, "I'd just like to say that in my opinion last night was a great victory for your leadership." Skeen showed his lord the balding top of his head.

"Victory? How so?" Elijah said.

"Baron, if there were any stickies out there threatening us, you scared them off. They didn't dare attack Willie ville. They knew they'd get ripped to pieces. The way you handled the situation demonstrated once again the depth of your wisdom and insight. I want you to know how grateful I am."

Elijah stared at him over the rim of the dipper. "And how grateful is that, Skeen?"

"I'm sorry, Baron, I don't understand."

"Grateful enough to double your tithe to me?" Elijah asked.

The toadie nearly swallowed his tongue.

"I...I..." he sputtered.

"Come on, Skeen," the baron goaded, "you know you owe me your worthless life. If it wasn't for my patronage, you wouldn't have a scrap of bread to your name. You and that brainless wife of yours, and all your brats, would starve to death without me. You know, looking at your pinhead missus and cross-eyed offspring, it makes me wonder if there ain't a bit of rad taint coming out in blood there somewhere."

The sec men smirked as they watched the toadie squirm.

"Of course I'll pay."

"Not only that," Elijah said, "you'll get down on your knees and beg me to take your jack." He scanned the faces of the other coattail riders, the middlemen who fed off his bounty. "And what about the rest of you?" he said. "Don't you have anything to say? Aren't you grateful that I saved your miserable skins with my 'wisdom and insight'?"

The toadies bowed and fawned and assured him that they were just as grateful as anyone. Shooting hateful glances at Skeen, they agreed to double their taxes to their lord.

"An excellent morning so far," Elijah said to his sec chief as they swept out of the ops room.

"Yes, sir," Murchisson agreed. "Real profitable."

A phalanx of armed sec men fell into step behind them as they headed for the elevator. They were about halfway there when Murchisson spoke up again. "Baron," he said, "the boys all been pestering me, wanting to know what you've got in mind for the yellow-belly Cawdor."

"I haven't decided yet," Elijah told him. "I need to spend some time with the Apocalypticon. Got to review my options."

The baron, Murchisson and a dozen sec men bunched into the elevator car. As it started to inch its way down to the lobby, Elijah turned to his sec chief and said, "Murch, I want you to send some patrols outside the wall. Look for any sign that stickies passed through during the night. Start the patrols in close and have them gradually fan out, but keep them in sight of the berm at all times."

"Better to be safe than sorry, sir."

"If they find anything, I want to know about it at once."

Then Elijah noticed one of the sec men standing off to the side. The guard was staring at his own boot tops, trying to become invisible. "Rad-blast it!" the baron shouted at his sec chief. "What the hell's Lester doing up here? He's supposed to be serving time on the wheel today."

"I'm on my way to report for punishment now, sir," Lester said.

Elijah stared at the two men standing beside Lester. They, too, were trying their best to vanish. And they had reason. The baron recognized them as Gill and Hylander, Lester's bunker mates, the other dilwads responsible for allowing a prisoner to bring a weapon into his royal presence. "Murch," Elijah said, "I want you to send these two south. Have them run down and check on the damage to my way stop, if any."

Gill and Hylander looked at each other, then at Lester, who wouldn't meet their gaze. None of them said a word. Because of Lester's screwup, it was death sentences all around if there were stickies about.

The crew split up when the car reached the lobby. Gil and Hylander got out first, stepping to one side to let Elijah and a half dozen sec men pass by. Murchisson and three other sec men remained in the elevator, which was carrying Lester to the subbasement.

As the baron exited the lobby, his sec team stepped forward, creating a living shield on all sides of him. They escorted him in formation to the bank entrance. He left them there with orders to guard his back. Once inside the one-story building's foyer, the baron lit a torch. He walked past the tellers' counter and proceeded through the barred, stainless-steel gate to the vault door. Only he had the combination to the lock.

At least he'd had the sense to keep that from Zit.

Inside the vault the mutie librarian's handiwork was evident. Zit had gone through the diverse and voluminous material and organized it under various appropriate subject headings. He'd had no file cabinets to work with, so he just stacked the stuff in neat mounds along the walls. Elijah went straight for the section marked Chilling. Even though he couldn't read very well, many of the books and magazines had pictures, and the baron satisfied himself with reviewing those.

He set the torch in a stanchion and took his time, rejecting the quick and easy deaths out of hand. What he was looking for was something slow and spectacular. Something that his subjects would tell their grandchildren about. He scanned through the piles of documents until he found a photograph that intrigued him. It combined great height with dizzying speed and helplessness.

He'd never chilled anyone like that, but it sure looked like a crowd pleaser.

Chapter Thirteen

Krysty had never spent a night in a nineteenth-century lunatic asylum, so she had no yardstick to measure the first few hours of her zoo experience. She didn't even know what a loonie bin was because the practice of locking up the insane hadn't survived the nukecaust; it had been vaporized along with the whitecoat shrinks and their leather-upholstered Porsches, the canvas straitjackets and the humming machines that administered "therapeutic" doses of electroconvulsive shock.

In the days preholocaust, the days before the first successful flight of an airplane, before the development of pharmacological restraints and adult disposable diapers, madmen and -women were kept in cages like animals. They slept on beds of straw and padded barefoot through their own filth. Like animals, they were left to scream, pull out their hair and beat their heads against the bars of their cells. Only the lucky—the catatonic and comatose—slept. Everyone else raged or cowered.

If Krysty had ever seen a bedlam depicted in a film, or read about one in a book, she would've been able to say, "Aha! So *that's* where I am!" As it was, all she could do was shut her eyes tight and try to stop up her ears with her fingers.

Her cage was long and narrow and divided from those on either side by floor-to-ceiling iron bars. At the corridor end of her enclosure were more bars with a small entry gate and feeding slot. A steel-clad drop-door was set in a concrete wall at the other end. The door was down. There was concrete under the matted, rotting straw of the cage.

In the first moments after she'd been forced into the cell, Krysty had learned that the only safe place was in the exact center of its space. If she sat right in the middle, the prisoners caged on either side of her couldn't quite reach her when they stretched their arms through gaps between the bars. After a few hours of trying to claw out her green eyes, her fellow inmates had almost given up the game. They took only occasional swipes at her face with their nails. Krysty could have broken either of their arms quite easily any time they made a grab for her, but there didn't seem to be much point in hurting them if she wasn't in any real danger.

Now that it was light enough to see her nearest neighbors, Krysty decided she liked the look of the scabbie the least. As the mutant's name suggested, its skin was covered with ulcers and lesions, these in varying shades of yellow, black, brown, purple and pus green. This particular example of the scabbie subspecies still had a few irregularly shaped patches of pink, normal-looking skin, which were bordered by thin bands of fiery red flesh. But for the random patterning of its clots, the scabbie was naked. It was about eight months pregnant. Its bloated belly's crust was seamed with deep fissures and weeping cracks. There was no face to speak of, just two eyes peering out of a mound of scabs. Its hair, which was pale orange in color and quite long, sprouted out of a scalp crust in widely spaced tufts. Inside the mouth the skin looked soft and normal, as did what Krysty could see of the tongue.

The scabbie helped to support its vast stomach by cupping it with its hands.

"What're you lookin' at, bitch?" it snarled at Krysty.

"Mebbe countin' your sores," suggested the prisoner in the cage to Krysty's back.

Krysty turned to face her other neighbor, a scalie. Its rad mutation was a bit more subtle that the scabbie's. The striations of its fine scales were visible only when the light hit it a certain way. To the casual observer, it could look like a severe case of dry skin. There was a vague reptilian cast to the slant of its eyes and the turned-up corners of its lipless mouth. The scalie was also pregnant. It wore a short skirt of pieced rags that looked like a ratty pom-pom, but nothing on top. The scalie's breasts were pendulous and doughy, and the large nipples were an angry, infected maroon.

"When's your baby due?" Krysty asked the scabbie. To be heard over the din, she practically had to shout.

"Another few weeks," the inmate replied.

"Question is," the scalie said, "what's it gonna look

like? Elijah bred her with about twenty males, one after another. She didn't mind, though." The scalie looked over at the pregnant mutant and said, "Did ya?"

The scabbie screamed something at the scalie through Krysty's cell. The words were unintelligible.

"The baron did that to you?" Krysty asked the scabbie mother-to-be. "He set that many men on you?"

"Yeah," the scabbie said, then pointed through the bars, past Krysty, to the scalie. "And her, too. She's got a bun in the oven. She's just not showing yet."

"The baron keeps track of who he's mated with who. And who he's gonna mate with who next. Kind of like breeding hogs. Only his idea is to switch around the fathers and mothers to git the most unusual-looking specimens for his zoo."

"Why so many fathers?" Krysty said.

The scalie answered. "Elijah doesn't like to waste any of his females' breeding cycles, so he always makes sure we git well seeded."

"It'll happen to you, too, soon enough," the scabbie assured Krysty. "None of us ever escapes...."

Krysty choked back the fear and revulsion that threatened to overwhelm her. She refused to give in to the urge to go ballistic, to throw herself at the bars of her cell and scream her outrage. She knew she had to stay calm if she was going to have a prayer of getting free of the zoo, calm and clearheaded as she'd need to be to help Ryan and the others.

An eerie quiet settled over the zoo enclosure. The

lull in the uproar was broken by a few scattered cries, but they, too, quickly faded out.

Like Ryan, Krysty was puzzled and worried by the stickie army's failure to show up during the night. Without a battle, or the threat of an assault, they were dead. In the hope that her neighbors might be able to shed some light on the situation, she decided to pump them for information. "I saw someone on the road yesterday," she said softly. "Mebbe you know him?"

When she described the piebald man for them, the scalie let out a squeal, slumped onto its butt on the floor of the cage and started drumming its heels in the straw.

"Shut up!" the scabbie shrieked. "Don't say a word! You don't know who she is."

"Do you think she's spy for Elijah?" the scalie countered. "Since when does he give a damn about what his animals are thinkin'?"

"Red-hair looks like she could pass for norm. Mebbe she's not a mutie at all."

Krysty made her prehensile hair stand up in full-length spikes, then coil back against her head in tight curls.

"Oh, yeah, she's one of us."

"Mebbe so," the scabbie said. "Still could be workin' for the baron."

"This piebald man," Krysty said, "he had an army with him. Biggest I ever saw. An army of stickies. They were comin' this way."

"It's him!" cried the scalie, unable to contain itself.

"He's come back! I told you something strange was in the air. He's come back to us. Just like he promised!"

The scalie started to turn away to spread the word to the adjoining cage. The scabbie barked a warning. "You wait! Wait!" When the scalie looked back, the scabbie said, "We got to make sure of this before we pass it on." Then it faced Krysty and demanded, "What else did you see?"

"The stickies on the highway called their leader Kaa," Krysty explained. "I heard a rumor that he used to be a pet here in the baron's zoo."

This last bit of news seemed to excite the scabbie. "Don't know him by that name," it said, "but I might know who you're talkin' about. Never saw him myself, and neither has she, no matter what she lets on. We heard about him from the others who been here longer than us. The way the story goes, the baron used to have a patchy-colored mutie he called Three Eyes or Zit. He called him that on account of he had an extra eye in the middle of his forehead. Zit's eye opened up for the first time right here in the zoo—I heard a cannie spouting off about it once. Said he was in the next cage and the eye was as clear as glass and it cried blood. And when Zit looked through it, just trying it out, he killed four stickies on the other side of the zoo. They started shaking, their eyes bugged out and then they shit themselves and died."

"From what I hear, nobody said nothing to Knackerman about what that eye could do," the scalie said.

"Everybody hates Knackerman, the zoo master. And I guess nobody much cared for those stickies, either."

"Story goes that Zit had himself an inside track with the baron," the scabbie went on. "He'd act real mean to muties whenever there were norms around, but when he was alone with his own kind he'd be different. He knew lots of things because he could read. He'd tell them all about the rebellion and the Mutie War and the slave heroes. He even made them remember the heroes' names. We all still say the names. Coupe. Marrowbone. Peltier. Balwan."

"Zit did some bad things for the baron," the scalie said, "chillin' muties and all. Some say he had to do it, to stay on the baron's good side. Others say he was a murdering, blowhard liar, that he was just using everybody to get a better deal for himself. They said he'd never come back if he left."

"You figure he's going to sack Willie ville with that army?" Krysty asked. "Or is he headed somewhere else?"

The scalie beamed at her. "Oh, he's comin' here, all right. And he's gonna do more than sack the place. He's gonna set all his people free. No more torture. No more starvin'. No more gettin' worked to death. Our babies are gonna be born free!"

"He's gonna get blasters to those that can handle them," the scabbie said. "Then we're gonna take Deathlands from the norms. Nobody in this damn zoo and nobody in the fields has a drip of sympathy for them. If Zit or Kaa, or whatever he calls himself now, gives us the chance, we'll show them norms what the other end of the whip feels like."

With that, the mutants moved to the opposite sides of their cells and spread the word through the bars. In a matter of minutes, the zoo was rocking with cheers and shouts.

THE SUDDEN SURGE of noise roused Jak from a deep sleep. Eyes still shut, he drowsily stretched his arms. Something wet, hot and scratchy slapped the side of his face.

Meat breath gusted over him.

Jak looked into the face of his cell mate. The mutie mountain lion's eyes were slitted with pleasure as it washed his cheek with its bristling tongue.

"Stop," the teenager cried, trying to hold the beast at arm's length.

"First it cleans you, then it eats you," a swampie shouted gleefully from the next cell.

The mutie lion whirled away from Jak, throwing itself at the bars. The startled swampie jumped back so hard that it crashed into the opposite wall. The swampie was a little gnomelike creature, dressed in a ragged scrap of an overcoat and gum boots. It had the typical feral teeth and wide nose of its subspecies. Swampies weren't big, but they were a sneaky bunch and mean.

Jak steeled himself for another attack from the lion.

When the beast looked back at him, it got that happy expression on its face again. Its tongue lolled out, and its eyes narrowed to slits. Jak noticed that it had some wicked fangs on it, long and sharp, and claws to match. It padded up to him and rested its chin on his shoulder.

"Thinking about some other lion," Jak told the swampie. "This is pussycat."

"And you are a triple stupe," the swampie said, keeping well back from the bars. "That thing ain't no lion, ain't no kitty cat, neither. Baron's been workin' on that one's line for eight, mebbe ten years. It can talk almost as good you or me, when it wants to. And as for chewing you up, it just ain't hungry right now."

"Mebbe," Jak said, roughing up the big cat's ears, "but think he'd rather eat you. Stick little head through the bars and find out."

"Nope," the swampie said, "don't care to do that."

Actually Jak had no idea why the cat's attitude about him had changed. He gazed into the huge yellow eyes. The rad-blasted thing was purring again and huffing its rotten-meat breath in his face.

At the other end of the zoo, a new ruckus started up, spreading like wildfire from cage to cage. Everyone was yelling and screaming, but it was different than the racket they made the previous night or earlier that morning. This wasn't just a way to blow off steam.

This seemed to have a point.

Jak and lion moved to the side of their cell that faced the uproar.

"He's here!" the swampie chirped as it spun away from the bars opposite. It kicked up a wild jig in the straw.

"Who's here?" Jak asked. "What's happening?"

The big cat turned nose to nose with him, opened its mouth and bellowed, "Kaa!"

The blast of sound and hot air knocked Jak flat on his rear. All around him the muties' inarticulate cries were changing, crystallizing. They became a chant, which was repeated over and over.

Kaa!

The noise was so loud that it shook the building to the foundation. The baron's zoo master came running down the corridor to see what was happening. Knackerman didn't stay for long. The muties pelted him with their droppings. Cursing, he covered his head with his arms and dashed back the way he had come.

Chapter Fourteen

When the door to the cooler creaked open, a shaft of torchlight cut through the gloom. Ryan shielded his face from the blinding glare. Even after his eye adjusted to the light, he couldn't see who was in the doorway. He was too close to the floor, and there were too many iron bars in the way. He could see boots, though. Lots of boots.

A key rattled in the lock of the top cage.

"How'd you like the accommodations?" someone asked from the corridor.

None of Ryan's companions said a word. They didn't want to do anything that might interfere with their getting out of the cooler. When the door was flung back, they crawled through it. Ryan moved closer to the bars. All of his friends were stiff and bent over, Doc the most of all. They groaned and moaned as they straightened for the first time in many hours.

When the sec man in charge stepped back, Ryan recognized him from the old days. Murchisson was no stupe, but he didn't notice the single shackle on J.B.'s right ankle. He stood the other prisoners against the corridor wall, had his men hold them at blasterpoint, then unlocked Ryan's cell.

The one-eyed man crawled out of the filth and rose slowly to his feet.

"Man," Murchisson said, stepping back and covering his nose with a hand, "you need a hose-down. You all need a hose-down."

Because the iron cuff around Ryan's ankle was covered with reeking muck, the sec chief failed to see it.

"Your stickies didn't show last night, One-eye," Murchisson told him. "Old Elijah was real disappointed. He was lookin' forward to puttin' a bunch of mutie scum on the last train West. He was going to watch the whole deal from his penthouse while drinking beer."

"The baron send out patrols yet?" Ryan asked.

"Sure. So?"

"Hope you kissed them goodbye."

"Somehow, after last night, that doesn't scare me much," Murchisson said. "What's got into you, Cawdor? I never figured you for pulling a dumb shot like this. You sick and tired of living?"

When Ryan didn't answer, the sec chief used the muzzle of his Uzi carbine like a cattle prod to urge them in the direction of the elevator. They rounded the dogleg in the hall and came face-to-face with the open elevator car.

To their left, Johnson Lester was standing in front of a closed door labeled Power Plant. Not only had he been stripped of his rank, but everything else he owned. Lester was bare-assed naked. While he tried to cover himself with his hands, three mutie overseers squabbled over the division of his clothes and personal effects. The squat, hairy-backed bastards weren't satisfied with the pickings.

"This all you got?" one of them shouted into Lester's face. He shook the sec man's worn jungle boots in his face. "It ain't enough!"

"Not near enough," said another.

The third overseer opened the power-plant door, and for an instant Ryan and the others could see inside. The wide room was lit by torches in the walls. Its central feature was an enormous steel turnstile with spokes that nearly touched the sides of the room. Each spoke had four or five naked men chained to its rings. In the middle of the turnstile was a large gear, which was connected by a pinion the size of a man to other massive gears just overhead. The floor under the turnstile had ribs on it, to give the slaves better traction as they pushed the wheel around. They needed all the help they could get. Grease from the gears was smeared over the slaves, over the floor, over everything.

As Ryan and the others neared the elevator, the overseers shoved Lester toward the open doorway. He twisted to glare over his shoulder at them.

J.B. couldn't help himself. He shot the sec man a huge grin.

"What're you smiling at, stupe?" Lester hissed. "You think you're not as dead as me?"

The overseers slammed the door behind him.

Murchisson used the sole of his boot to push Ryan

into the elevator. "Don't touch anything," he warned all of them, "till we get you washed down."

It took a few extra minutes for the elevator to start up. Probably, Ryan thought, because the slave drivers first had to chain Lester to the spoke. When they reached the lobby level, Murchisson and the other sec men marched them outside, under the building's awning, then across the parking lot to where a makeshift water tower had been erected.

"Cawdor, step over here," Murchisson said, pointing at a mound of dirt that had once been a decorative plant bed. He picked up the end of a hose that hung down the side of the rusting metal tank. "The rest of you stay back."

When Murchisson opened the hose's nozzle, a powerful stream of coffee-colored water rushed out and onto Ryan's chest. At Murchisson's direction, Ryan turned around and around so he could wash the muck off his clothes. This done, the sec man said, "Now, get those duds off. You don't just have stink on the outside. You got it everywhere."

Ryan peeled off his shirt and set it aside. When he started to untie his boots, Murchisson stopped him. "Just drop your pants and roll them down over your boot tops. That'll do just fine."

As Ryan unbuckled his belt and unbuttoned his fly, Mildred looked the other way.

"Yoo-hoo!" called a high-pitched voice from above and behind them. "Yoo-hoo!"

Ryan looked back at the hotel while Murchisson sprayed his bare backside with the hose.

"Yoo-hoo!"

A pair of pale white asses had been stuck over the rail to the penthouse patio. While her sisters exposed themselves, Willie Elijah's other granddaughter-wife was checking out Ryan through the telescope.

"Yoo-hoo," she called, waving.

Her sisters waggled their asses at him.

"If they don't watch it, they're going to fall off there," Mildred observed.

"Aw, hell, they do that all the time," Murchisson said. "Ain't nobody for twenty miles around who hasn't seen everything they've got."

"Not bright," Ryan said. "Considering what Elijah did to their mothers."

"Oh, he don't ever get mad," the sec chief said. "He likes for everybody to see what he's getting—and what they can't have none of. Mebbe he even put the gals up to it the first time. They sure took a liking to it, though. Hang their asses out like that every day, weather permitting."

"Two moons over Willie ville," Doc muttered, squinting against the sun's glare.

"Get your drawers up quick, Cawdor, or I'm going to put a brand-new hole in your behind," Murchisson said.

Ryan turned as he lifted his sopping-wet pants, keeping the shackled leg out of the sec man's view.

"All right," Murchisson said to the others, "get over here where I can get some water on you."

J.B. started to take his shirt off as soon as he was hit by the spray, but Murchisson stopped him. "Naw, you three don't need no deep cleaning. You're not going nowhere near any norm folk. You're going to be chained up with the slaves in the fields. The muties don't care how bad you smell."

Murchisson hosed J.B. down from head to foot, splashing the water right on the shackle.

Ryan could almost see the light bulb go on over his head.

"Wait a minute!" Murchisson said. "Keep the blasters on them boys. Something isn't right."

The head sec man ducked down and looked at the shackle. "What's this here? An ankle cuff with no chain? Who put that on you?"

J.B. didn't answer.

Murchisson took it off his ankle and held the tab end up to the light. "Man, you could almost shave with that edge," he said.

"One-eye's got one, too, Murch," another sec man said. "Good thing you caught them, boss, or we'd be cranking up the elevator, too."

"What were you going to do with these?" the sec chief asked after Ryan, too, had been disarmed. "Cut somebody's throat?"

"Mebbe."

"Should of cut your own last night, Cawdor," Murchisson told him. "You made a big mistake there. Elijah's got special plans for you. Says he's going to make history with your chilling."

GILL AND HYLANDER STARED through the glassless front window of the semitractor cab. The view from the berm blasterport was due south, down the empty six-lane highway. Nothing moved on the valley floor or on the hillsides. The sky was clear and blue, the sun hot. There was no wind to speak of.

"What're you two so worried about?" asked the sec man standing behind them. "Aren't no stickies out there." He paused for effect, then added, "Of course, they could be just over that far rise."

"Why don't you stuff a rag in it?" Hylander said, getting up in the guy's face.

"Come on, Pedro," Gill said, taking hold of his shoulder. "Let's get going. It stinks in here."

He and Hylander hopped down from the cab to the tarmac and checked their weapons. They each carried a Beretta Model 12-S 9 mm machine pistol. The 12-S looked like a five-dollar caulking gun with a pistol foregrip and a 32-round stick mag jammed underneath. The classiest parts of the blasters were the black web nylon shoulder slings, and they had seen better days.

"At least we got a fighting chance," Gill said to Hylander as they shouldered their packs and walked away from the berm. "That's a hell of a lot more than poor old Lester."

"Did you see the look on his face?" Hylander said. "Man! He was sorely tore up."

"Not half so bad as he's going to be by tomorrow. And that's okay with me. It's that stupe's fault that all our butts are on the line."

"Yeah, he should've caught that old-timer's rad-blasted swordstick."

They started moving at a leisurely pace, testing the waters, so to speak. If there were stickies around, it figured that they'd be lying in close to Willie ville. Gill and Hylander could see a long way off, better than two miles, and that was how they liked it. After they'd traveled a mile or so, they stopped to recce the terrain. Standing on the concrete center divider, they scanned all around, and saw no sign of one stickie, let alone five thousand.

"Looks good to me," Hylander said, wiping the sweat from under his mustache with the side of his finger.

"One thing's worrying me, though," Gill stated.

"What's that?"

"Wasn't any traffic on the road yesterday, except for One-eye. And there hasn't been any this morning, either."

"It happens like that sometimes. Doesn't necessarily mean anything."

"Mebbe not. But I'd feel a lot better if we saw a caravan of travelers humping up from the south."

"How long you think it'll take us to make the way stop?"

"Never make it there and back before dark."

"I wouldn't mind spending the night, even though

it's a pesthole. It'd give old Elijah a chance to forget about us."

"Hadn't thought of that. Good idea. We'd better get rolling, though, or we won't even get there by dark. We don't want to get caught out on the road after sundown."

The sec men fell into an easy, loping gait. At about two miles out of Willie ville, they paused to look back. They could see the hotel and part of the amusement zone sticking up above the berm line. As they watched, a three-man patrol crossed the highway a half mile behind them. They waved. Gill and Hylander waved back.

Fifteen minutes farther down the road, the two sec men came upon their first obstacle—a downed overpass that blocked the entire highway, one of many between Willie ville and the way stop. They approached the mound of rubble slowly and carefully, watching for any sign of movement on the ends or along the top. When they got closer, they could see coils of wire fencing—part of a ruined antisuicide barrier—blocked the path across the top. They were going to have to go around.

"Looks clear up to the overpass," Hylander said.

A hot wind, the first of the day, swept down the valley, rattling the wire.

"Could be a thousand of them hiding on the other side," Gill said, "ready to jump us."

"That isn't going to happen. Cover my ass."

Hylander lowered his head and charged up the rubble. Leaping from chunk to chunk, he didn't stop until he reached the crest. With his Beretta out front, he peered through the wire.

Gill knelt in the roadway, braced for full-auto fire, his finger on the machine pistol's trigger.

"Nothing," Hylander said to him as he started back down. "Just empty road. I told you it was okay."

"Yeah, yeah," Gill said. "Let's go."

At the end of the rubble to the right, where the edge of the road ended, a makeshift path began. It had been tramped into the dirt. Everything looked clean. There was no cover for stickies to hide behind. They had gone less than a dozen steps when something cracked and the earth opened up under them.

Gill cried out in alarm, clutching at the collapsing sides of the hole. He couldn't stop himself from falling and dropped fifteen feet down into the mantrap. Hylander landed beside him in a blinding cloud of dust and leaves.

The hole was ten feet across and full of waiting stickies.

Hylander and Gill didn't get off a shot before their blasters were ripped from their hands. They yelled then, yelled as they'd never yelled before.

But no one heard.

Chapter Fifteen

The mutie overseer stood waiting for Mildred, J.B., and Doc at the open rear doors of a four-ton panel van buried in the berm. His muscular torso was bare from the waist up. From the front he looked like a norm; from the back it was a different story. The length of his spine, from his tailbone up to the back of his head, was covered with masses of tiny, worm-shaped tumors. The tendrils were long and densely packed over his spinal column, thinning out toward the sides of his rib cage. The mohawk of soft growth was caked with dirt and body oils. There was no way he could clean in and around the fringe—unless he mowed it off first.

Inside the sheet-steel tunnel of the van's cargo compartment, while their sec-man escort held the companions covered, the mutie overseer clapped ankle shackles on them. "This old one won't last the day," he said to the sec men as he sized up Doc. "The other two I might get some work out of before they drop dead."

Mildred shrugged off his hand as it squeezed her bicep.

"Don't get too many norms out in the fields," the overseer said as he led the way out of the cab of the van. He had a bullwhip coiled on his hip. "Only when the baron wants to make a special example of somebody. That's something I know how to do."

The sec men walked J.B., Doc and Mildred just as far as the van's cab. They let them head into the squalor of the slave quarters in the custody of the overseer. The Willie ville slave quarters were built right up against the berm wall. They spilled down from the high dirt barrier in an avalanche of wood, metal and plastic scraps. Some of the structures weren't much more than lean-tos, and barely tall enough for one person to crawl under to get out of the acid rain. Other hovels were more elaborate, connected by shared walls, doors and roofs. The whole shantytown looked as if it would collapse on itself in the next chem storm. The air was thick with the caustic odor of burned garbage and the buzz of carrion insects.

There were no slaves in any of the huts, but there were quite a few animals. Pigs, goats and the odd cow were tethered inside the rickety doorways. The slave population was in the fields, working. Mildred could see them in the distance. She assumed that the bundles strapped to the adults' backs were babies.

The dirt path that wound between the huts was deeply rilled and fairly steep. It sloped down to the green fields in the river valley. Mildred found it hard to keep up with the others because the length of chain between her ankles was so short. It forced her to take little, mincing steps. The sun blazed on her head and back. Her clothes were already drying from its heat.

The overseer steered them along a path that bordered the cultivated fields. Stooped-over field hands tended the rows of green, leafy plants. Only the slaves a good distance away stopped working to look at them. The ones closest to the path, and the overseer, kept their backs bent and their arms moving. Mildred grimaced as she was hit by a familiar smell. In a shallow, water-filled ditch alongside the field was a pair of swollen corpses. They were still in their shackles, but all their clothes had been either stripped or cut off.

The overseer took a path to the left, away from the crop rows and the fouled ditch, and toward Willie ville. Mildred could see a group of people ahead. They were digging in a wide, shallow pit. Over the clank of her ankle chain she could hear the scrape of shovels.

"Looks like a quarry," J.B. said softly.

"Looks like where we're headed," Mildred stated.

"What, pray tell, are they digging, sir?" Doc asked the overseer.

The mutie answered with a cut of his whip. The lash sizzled and cracked, and Doc cried out and spun away.

"Digging your rad-blasted graves," the overseer told him. "No more talk."

Mildred saw the tear in the thigh of Doc's breeches, and blood trickled through it. Though Doc's face was pale, he got up and got moving. He was a game old bird.

The slaves working in the pit paused as the overseer approached. They were mostly young, and all males. Their ankles were chained, and they were sweaty and covered with grime. They stood in a depression four feet deep and roughly fifty feet in diameter. What exactly they were "quarrying" wasn't immediately apparent. Nothing was piled up, except the dirt that had already been excavated.

"Pick up the shovels," the overseer ordered, "and get to work."

J.B., Doc and Mildred got their tools from a stack on the ground.

"Start over there," he told them.

Then he turned to Mildred. "And you, bitch, keep your pants on. I won't have my slavies wasting the whole day screwing in the dirt."

Mildred didn't bother to tell him that she had no intention of doing anything of the kind, not as long as she could swing a shovel. As the overseer walked away, she, Doc and J.B. started to work. If walking in chains was hard, digging in chains was triple-tough. The earth was baked clay, and it had to be chipped away, like marble.

The other pit workers kept their distance and said nothing. Occasionally one of them shot the companions a hateful look.

When the overseer was a good way off, J.B. spoke up. "What are we supposed to be doing here?" he asked the slaves.

They didn't reply right away. They just looked at one another. After a bit the mutie who was their leader stepped forward and answered. It was tall and thin, and its head was wrapped in a long strip of dirty rag. Except for a slit for the eyes, its whole head was hidden by the cloth.

"Ain't no 'we' here," it said. "There's us, and there's you."

"But we're all in the same boat," J.B. replied. "Baron's going to work us to death."

The raghead leaned on the shovel handle. "You're wrong both times," it said. "You norms got your boat, which is sinking. We got our boat, which is gonna sail away."

"Huzzah," one of the slaves said.

"You're going to escape? How?"

The slave leader laughed. "Oh, yeah, just ask me and I'll tell you everything. I'm nothing but a dumb mutie, after all."

"Listen," Mildred said, "we're not from around here. We don't even know the baron. We never did you people any harm."

"You're norms, aren't you?"

"What difference does that make?"

"Try living with the face I got hidden under these wraps, and you'll see." The mutie pointed a finger at her nose. "You norms are outnumbered, and your days are just about over."

The other slaves quickly moved in, encircling J.B., Doc and Mildred. The companions shifted into back-to-back defensive positions as the muties raised their shovels to strike.

"No," the leader said, "it ain't time for that yet. We don't want to tip our hand to the boss man." The mutie looked at each of the newcomers in turn. "None of us ever chilled any norms before," it said. "We're gonna enjoy chillin' you."

When the slaves moved back to their side of the pit, J.B. said, "Why do I get the feeling that these guys are expecting some help to come along soon?"

"Our friend Kaa?" Doc said.

"Looks like," J.B. agreed.

"Sounds like, too," Mildred added. "For a second, bandage boy was talking Kaa's kind of talk. Can't really blame the slaves for wanting to get even with the baron."

"Kaa seems to have rather more extravagant aspirations than that," Doc said.

"Point is," Mildred went on, "what are we going to do?"

"Pretend to dig, for a start," J.B. said.

The overseer had turned and was looking their way. As they hacked at the earth at the edge of the pit, J.B. said, "We can't stay out here. If the stickies come, we're dead meat. We've got to get back inside the berm. If we get our blasters, mebbe we can free Ryan, Krysty and Jak."

"How about these?" Mildred asked, holding up her ankle chain.

"That's the easy part." J.B. fished around in his pants pocket and produced the short piece of steel wire. "We're going to lose these cuffs right now."

J.B. worked quickly, unlocking the shackles.

"Where do you think you're going?" the raghead

asked as J.B., Doc and Mildred hopped up out of the pit. "Overseer's gonna run you down and beat the skin off you!"

When the slaves started yelling for the boss man, the trio took off across the flat, heading for a big, smooth rock in the distance.

"What now?" Mildred asked as they huddled momentarily behind the stone.

"Look for a way in," J.B. replied.

They moved low and fast, keeping parallel to the berm and about a quarter mile out. Every once in a while they looked back to see if the overseer was in pursuit. If he was, he was too far behind to make out. North of the cultivated area was riverbed scrubland. There were no dwellings and no people. The terrain sloped gently away from the Willie ville boundary, then dropped off in a low, eroded ridge. Over the top of the berm wall, they could see the roller coaster's framework and the rim of the Ferris wheel. At the foot of the berm, the sun flared off the chrome bumper of a buried truck.

"There's nothing but open ground between us and the bunker," Doc said. "We'll never make it that way."

"Let's try it farther up," J.B. suggested.

They put the bunker well behind them before they turned, following an erosion scar that led toward Willie ville. They crept to within 150 feet of the berm. As they advanced the last thirty feet, they saw something strange, right under their noses.

The dirt was suddenly a different color and texture.

J.B. brushed the surface earth aside. It was damp underneath. "Somebody's been burrowing," he said.

Ahead of them, at the head of the scar where it intersected the ridge, was a hole. It was less than three feet across and angled slightly down.

J.B. approached the entrance and peered in.

Mildred crawled up beside him and stared into the blackness. "What do you think?" she said.

"It's recent work," he told her. "From the look of it, it could be our stickies trying to sneak in under the berm."

"They dug all this out overnight?" Mildred said. "They must be digging fools."

"The inside of the tunnel has got some kind of adhesive smeared all over it," J.B. said. "It's set up like concrete. Man, that's a neat trick. It means they don't need to shore up the hole with wood or anything as they go. Speeds things, big time."

"They might not be done with their digging," Doc cautioned. "They could still be working somewhere inside."

"There's only one way to find out," J.B. said.

WITH MURCHISSON behind him and sec men on either side, Ryan was marched out of the elevator and onto the twenty-fifth floor of the hotel. He didn't kid himself. His chances for survival were looking grim. He'd been cut off from his friends and his weapons, and he was sorely outnumbered by guards with blasters. In the back of his mind, he held out the hope that maybe he'd still get one chance to chill the baron.

A single full-force kick to the heart would do it.

As if reading his mind, Murchisson stopped him before he was taken into Elijah's presence. He bent and clamped a pair of leg restraints on Ryan's ankles. "Behave yourself now," the sec man warned.

Elijah's penthouse was furnished in the same grotesque style as the dining-hall floor below. He had looted the other hotel suites for their "art" and decorator touches. Everything that the baron could get his hands on, he had crammed into the rooms, the halls, the corners. For him quantity was the hallmark of taste.

The sec men ushered Ryan through a wide but densely cluttered living room. The one-eyed warrior saw the G-12 caseless rifles and other gear piled in a corner—J.B.'s beloved fedora was on top of the heap. The sliding doors to the balcony were open.

"Outside," Murchisson ordered.

Ryan hobbled out onto the patio. The whole Elijah clan was there. The baron, his granddaughters/wives and his great-granddaughters/daughters sat on lawn chairs, enjoying the sun in matching straw hats. Some sec men and toadies were crouched at one end of the patio, doing something along the steel-pipe railing. Heavy sandbags and a huge coil of nylon rope sat at their feet.

"Great day for a public chilling, huh?" Elijah said, standing and opening his arms to the blue sky. "Guess there aren't going to be any stickies in the audience, though. You sure struck out there, Cawdor. Mebbe you just dreamed you saw them?"

Ryan stared out over the broad vista. He knew he hadn't dreamed them. He knew they could be hidden out there, easy; hell, they could even be looking up at him right now.

Elijah's wives were whispering to one another, looking at Ryan and giggling into their hands.

"Sure seems a shame to waste a good-looking man like that, Poppadaddy," Roonie-Two said. "Specially when he could die giving pleasure to some deserving girl."

"Girls," Poonie-Two corrected her.

"And I suppose you've got some particular girls in mind?" Elijah said.

All three blond heads nodded.

"Well, Cawdor, what do you say? Want to croak in the saddle?"

Ryan looked at the girls. They were showing off for him, sticking their tongues out, swishing their hips back and forth. It made him want to laugh. According to Baron Elijah, Roonie-Two, Poonie-Two and Toonie-Two were supposed to be the pinnacle of Deathlands' pure-norm genetics. But they were so inbred that they couldn't function, except as sex beasts and brood mares. Ryan decided that was just the kind of chain-jerking that the baron got off on nowadays.

"Are you going to hurry up and hang me," he said to Elijah, "or am I going to have to jump off of here on my own?"

The girls' faces drooped in disappointment.

"Are you turning down my pure-norm gals?" Elijah asked.

"You were never offering them."

"You always were a tough, smart sucker, One-eye. I got to ask you one thing, though. Why did you run out on me after Coupe ville? You done me a real favor there. Practically broke the back of the rebellion on your own. It was just sweep-up op after that. You know I was ready to make you an important man around here. What scared you off?"

"Me," Ryan said.

"What?"

"I scared myself off. I knew I could get hooked on chilling, just like jolt. Then I wouldn't be my own man. I could see myself turning into just another bought-and-paid-for sec man shit-heap like Murch here. I'd rather be dead."

"Going to get your wish," Murchisson said, grabbing him by the shirtfront.

"Easy, now," the baron said. "He's just messing with your mind. Mebbe hoping he'll get an easy way out of here. Isn't going to happen." As Elijah walked over to the rail, the workers stepped aside for him.

"What do you figure he weighs, Murch?" the baron asked.

"Two hundred, mebbe a little less."

"Let's test it."

The sec men tied four of the sandbags to the end of the rope, then tipped the weights off the patio. Everyone moved to peer over the rail as the line snaked over the balcony. The quartet of bags hurtled down, then smashed open against the sidewalk, spraying sand in a wide circle.

"Too much rope," the baron said. "Shorten it up."

After adjusting the length, the workmen tied on four more bags and chucked them over the balcony. This time the line came up tight before the bags hit. The rope squeaked as it stretched under the weight, but the sandbags missed the ground by at least ten feet. Coming to the end of the rope, they bounced high in the air, then fell back.

"Better," the baron said. "Much better."

"So, you're going to hang me?" Ryan said, watching the sec men pull the two hundred pounds of deadweight back up to the penthouse. It was the kind of grueling job normally reserved for mutie slaves. Ryan figured the sec men had to have volunteered for the duty.

"Not exactly," the baron said. "Hanging you can only do the once."

When the sandbags had been hauled over the rail and untied, Murchisson shoved Ryan closer to the sec men. "Tie it good and tight," the sec chief instructed. "We wouldn't want it to come loose the very first time."

Instead of tying up a noose and dropping it over Ryan's head, the sec men lashed the free end of the rope to his right ankle. They tied it so tight his foot went numb almost immediately. Then they hoisted him up onto the balcony's rail.

The hot wind whipped his black hair as he looked down. A crowd had already gathered in the parking lot below.

"Dump him," Elijah ordered.

The sec men pushed, but not hard enough. Elijah's girls tittered as Ryan fought to keep his balance on the rail. When the cause was lost, when he knew he was going over, Ryan committed himself to the farthest dive he could muster. He knew if he didn't get well clear of the side of the building, the row of patios would beat him to death on the way down.

The wind howled in his face as he dropped. The outward thrust of the dive quickly faded, and he plummeted headfirst at the onrushing ground. He couldn't feel the tension of the rope on his ankle. He thought maybe the sec men had cut it loose.

Just when he was sure he was going to hit, everything stopped short. His leg was nearly wrenched from its hip socket, and his guts lurched up into his mouth. He stretched to the max, the rope stretched to the max, then both sprang back up into air. Ryan sprawled in space like a rag doll, then dropped to the end of the rope.

The second time he didn't bounce.

The audience of norms applauded and whooped. Someone started shouting, "Do it again! Do it again!"

The sec men on the penthouse started hoisting him up, feet first.

By the time they pulled Ryan's legs back over the railing, his face had turned beet red.

"It's called bungee-jumping, Cawdor," Elijah said. "The predarks used to do it for sport. They used a different kind of rope, of course. Springier. They didn't want to rip their legs off." The baron laughed.

His sec men laughed, too.

"Ready for another go?" Elijah asked.

Before Ryan could answer, the sec men grabbed him by the legs and threw him bodily over the railing. There was no opportunity for a swan dive this time, no putting some distance between himself and the building. He dropped straight as a rock, skimming past the hotel's jutting patios.

The falling was the easy part.

Stopping was what hurt.

Again his entire weight crashed onto his right hip and ankle. He groaned as he was ripped back up in the air by the rope's stretch. Something inside his nose burst, and blood gushed out of his nostrils.

The crowd squealed as they moved out of the way of the spray.

This was what they'd come to see.

Chapter Sixteen

For the first time in his life, Lord Kaa was one color, and that color was mocha brown.

He lay on his back with his powerful arms and legs spread wide. He was well within sight of the berm. If anyone had known where to look, and if they had looked hard and long enough, they might have caught the outline of his upper torso shadowed against the base of the earthen bank. As Kaa lay there, baking in a shell of mud, tears of pink raced down his clay-daubed temples and curled behind his ears. In the middle of his forehead and sticking up out of the uniform brown of the landscape like a piece of river-rounded, white quartzite, his mutant pineal eye was open. Its protective lids had no muscles, no nerves. They couldn't blink. To protect itself from drying out as it stared up into the cloudless sky, the eye leaked a steady stream of watery gore.

Kaa couldn't see the blue vastness above him. Because his norm eyes were closed, he saw nothing directly. Nothing outwardly. Everything he viewed was indirect, channeled through the psychic network that he enabled and controlled. While his third eye peeked through twelve thousand keyholes, the dead eyes of an army of stickies scattered around and under Baron Elijah's fortress, his mutant brain collated and integrated the flood of images. His brain acted as a central processor for all the stickies' input.

Holding his soldiers still for so many hours was the hardest thing Kaa had ever done. They didn't want to lie there; they wanted to kill. The feat of mental dominance required unwavering focus on his part. Over and over he showed them the plan, the order, the outcome. Like a chess match he had already played and won, he knew how it would unfold. The murderous stickies lay where he had positioned them the previous night, hardly breathing while the sun cooked cracks in their mud coats. They awaited the completion of the last and longest tunnel. It ran under the berm at the north end of the ville, near the rear of the hotel.

A dagger was poised over the heart of Willie ville, and the time had nearly come to drive in the blade, to watch the blood well up around the hilt.

Lord Kaa knew that the only way to defeat the baron's perimeter defenses was to get a small force behind them. The system of bunker blasterports fielded overlapping zones of fire that could control 360 degrees of access, for as long as the ammo held out. But if three of the bunkers in a row were knocked out, a clear path opened up down the middle. Once the berm was breached and his army was pouring through the gap, it would be no contest.

In fact it would be a slaughter party, a butcher game.

It pleased Kaa to think that if anyone was to blame

for the destruction of the norm mecca of Willie ville, it was the baron's own zoo master. Years ago Knackerman had been so bored that he had amused himself by sitting the future mutant lord on his lap and teaching him to read. He'd chosen Kaa because, unlike the other young muties in the zoo, he wasn't physically repulsive—the scalies and scabbies had their skin problems, the constant oozing and the feral stink. Stickies were too dangerous to make pets of, as were cannies. Doomies made poor companions, as they were off in their own worlds most of the time or telling you things you didn't want to hear.

Knackerman had let him follow along like a dog as he did his brutal chores: the forced matings, the cullings of live young that looked too normal to suit the baron's breeding plan. In retrospect it seemed to Kaa that the zoo master had wanted him to be a naive witness, someone he knew he could impress with his power as a norm, with his supposed moral authority. The zoo master had made a big mistake by showing the boy so much. Without meaning to, Knackerman had taught Kaa that the baron's zoo was an evil that had to be erased at any cost.

As the north tunnel broke through into the light of day, the piebald lord's mind filled with bouncing images of earth and sky and the chem-scorched motor hotel. His stickies were pouring up through the narrow opening in the ground, racing for the cover of the side of the building and then moving quickly along it.

From a trio of simultaneous viewpoints, he saw his

strategy unfold. The rear doors of each of the three semitrailers were open and unguarded. The sec men never expected an attack from the rear; all their weapons were aimed the other way. The squads of stickies dashed unchallenged across the open ground, then burst into the backs of the trailers, arms waving.

Kaa's brain staggered under a jumble of superimposed images, different but similar. He saw a blur of norm faces full of shock, eyes wide with terror. The sec men tried to turn and get their weapons up, but there wasn't time. The world rocked as heaps of wildly scuffling bodies crashed to the trailers' steel floors.

Their cries muffled by stickie palms, their shoulders and heels pinned by stickie arms, the sec men came undone in long, raggedy strips.

A tremor rippled through the army that lay hidden in plain sight, a yearning that rattled their very bones.

They smelled blood.

Kaa strained to hold them back a few seconds more. If they waited, they would lose no soldiers to the berm's blasterposts. They would enter Willie ville at full strength. He held them back because he didn't want their beautiful lives wasted. He held them back because he loved them.

Like his hero Charlemagne, he was a king after God's own heart.

J.B. CRAWLED FORWARD into the cramped darkness. By the time he'd advanced thirty feet, the light from the hole behind him had vanished. It was so black that he couldn't tell whether his eyes were open or shut. He had to feel his way along, fumbling for the walls of the tunnel in front of him. When he stopped to make sure the others were close, the top of Mildred's head rammed into his behind.

"Sorry, John," she said, sounding nervous.

"Is Doc back there?" J.B. asked.

"I'm here, John Barrymore."

"Keep tight to me," the Armorer said, then started forward again. At least, he told himself, there wasn't enough room in the tunnel to turn around, which meant that if he stumbled onto a stickie digging in the dark, he would most likely come on it from behind. Perhaps the kill-crazy mutant wouldn't be able to get its sucker fingers on his face.

J.B. counted his crawling steps as he proceeded, trying to keep track of where he was in relation to the berm. After a few minutes of travel, he figured he had to be beyond it. But the tunnel showed no signs of ending. It seemed to be angling to the left, though he couldn't be sure. Ahead was only more blackness. He decided to give up counting and concentrated instead on speed.

It was hot work in the confined space. The sweat poured off him as he scrambled along on hands and knees. Behind him he could hear the steady rasp of Mildred's breath.

When a light appeared in front of him, J.B. wasn't sure what it was. It looked like an orange blob hanging in space. At first he thought it might be a stickie, so he stopped short—and immediately took another direct hit from behind.

"What is it?" Mildred asked.

"End of the tunnel. Let me go up and take a look."

J.B. crawled ahead, into the circle of unfiltered sunlight. He let his eyes adjust, then slowly raised himself up and poked his head out of the hole. The tunnel surfaced near the amusement zone's back fence in the middle of a strip of parched dirt that had once been a lawn. As J.B. turned his head, he saw ten stickies creeping along the fence line, away from him. They had dried mud plastered over their backs and legs.

The Armorer dropped back into the hole. "Come on!" he urged his companions. "Hurry!" Then he crawled out and lay belly down on the dirt. When Doc and Mildred joined him, he pointed out the pack of stickies. They were running across the parking lot.

"Somebody's in for it," he said.

"Shouldn't we raise an alarm?" Mildred said. "Warn everybody?"

"Too late for that. All hell's going to break loose here in a minute or two."

"I concur with J.B.," Doc told her. "To thank us for our previous attempts to help them, the residents of Willie ville have jailed us, chained us and abused us. We have done more than enough for them. We have to find our friends and make our escape if we can."

Mildred nodded. "Okay," she said, "you guys have convinced me. Which way do we go?"

J.B. led them over the hurricane fence and into the

shadows behind the building that housed the Ghost Castle Spook Train. The sounds of cheers coming from the other side of the Freedom City compound made them crane their necks around the corner for a look-see.

"That's Ryan!" Mildred said, pointing at the dark figure falling from the top of the hotel.

"Dark night!" J.B. exclaimed as Ryan jounced up in the air at the end of the rope.

"We have to do something quick," Doc said.

No sooner had he spoken than someone shouted at them. "Hey, you! Hey! Hold it!"

A pair of sec men was running toward them, up the path from the Ferris wheel. The baron's men suddenly stopped and raised their blasters.

As J.B., Doc and Mildred dived for cover, a flurry of autofire rang out. The burst of slugs clipped the corner of the building, spraying splinters across the dirt. J.B. grabbed Doc's shoulder and pulled him to his feet.

"Move!" he said to Mildred. He rounded the back of the building and sprinted up the short flight of stairs to the heavily curtained doorway of the Ghost Castle Spook Train ride. An empty, two-person tram sat on the tracks in front of the portal. It was shaped like a miniature railroad flatcar. In the predark days the ride's little tram was powered by electricity. Now an empty slave harness dangled from its bow.

J.B. led them around the tram and through the curtain. Inside, it was dark, cool and very quiet. They followed the pair of tracks as they curved deeper into the building. There was bare metal scaffolding on the ceiling and, on either side of the tracks, a clutter of deceased mechanical and electrical devices, power cables, a conduit. In the weak light everything looked dim, gray and dusty. J.B. scanned the layout, searching for some kind of weapon and a likely spot to stage an ambush if they were pursued.

They hadn't gone very far when they heard footsteps hurrying in the darkness behind them. J.B. pulled the others behind a plastic boulder covered with a century-thick carpet of dust. While they listened, the footfalls slowed. They were getting closer. Then torchlight leaped across the girdered ceiling.

"We know you're in here," a male voice said.

"We got your asses cold," another added.

The light blazed brighter, sending a distorted shadow of the plastic boulder across the floor.

J.B. was hoping the sec men would pass by without seeing them, that they'd get a chance to jump on their backs and overpower them.

He hadn't counted on the spooks.

With a roar and a clanking of heavy chains, something huge and angry lunged at them from the dimness. Powerful fingers brushed J.B.'s face, nearly knocking loose his glasses. Mildred was so startled by the attack that she yelped and jumped out from behind the rock.

"Hold it right there," the sec man with the torch said. He held her covered with the rifle in his other hand. "The rest of you come on out."

His partner stepped to one side, aiming at the rock with a battered, wood-stocked AK-47. "Yeah, come on out."

As J.B. and Doc rose from cover, there was another roar and clank. This time it came from behind the second sec man. As they watched, a loop of heavy chain flopped over his head and down around his neck. With a crunch the loop cinched tight. The sec man dropped his blaster and clawed at the links that were crushing his throat. He was hauled, kicking, back into the darkness.

It all happened in a heartbeat.

The man with the torch swung around and, with his autorifle aimed at belly level, rushed to help his buddy. Mildred timed her kick perfectly. She caught the sec man moving forward, with one foot on the ground. She booted him sideways, in the direction of the plastic rock. The rifle and torch went flying as he crashed on top of the boulder. He disappeared behind it.

Darkness closed in as the torch sputtered out.

A second passed, then a blood-curdling scream ripped the air. It was followed by the loud *whap* of heavy steel chain slamming into meat and concrete, and the guttural grunt of an all-out effort.

Slap. Grunt. Over and over.

By the time J.B. found the rifle and the AK-47, the screams had become a bubbling moan. When the three of them reached the Ghost Castle Spook Train's entrance, it was dead quiet behind them. Doc held back a corner of the curtain so the Armorer could check the actions and mags of their newly acquired blasters.

Mildred drew back the curtain on the other side of the doorway, stuck her face outside and sucked in some fresh air.

"Scary ride, huh?" J.B. stated, slapping the 30-round box back into the Armalite rifle.

Chapter Seventeen

When his psychic network told him the three berm bunkers were out of commission, Lord Kaa pushed himself up from the mud and grabbed his M-60. He was already running for the middle bunker when he visualized the rising of his troops. As he pinched closed his middle eyelid, the scrubland dirt plain behind him jumped to life. Thousands of stickies joined him in the charge.

His creatures had their marching orders. Once the wave of shrieking stickies reached the wall, it split into three parts. The middle section funneled straight on through the center bunker. The other two turned in opposite directions and sprinted along the barrier to the unmanned blasterports, where they, too, broke into the Willie ville compound.

Kaa led the middle force through the tractor-cab gateway. Inside the trailer blood was splattered everywhere. His stickies had to pass through the puddles of gore, to walk in them barefoot, to smell them. And as they did, their excitement reached a fever pitch.

Lord Kaa, too, was excited. On the inside of the berm, his split forces rejoined. He ran at the head of a mass of bodies. They moved quickly toward the paved lane between the end of the Independence Park Amusement Zone and the baron's brewery.

Though there was no real resistance yet, he could hear distant screams of panic and sustained bursts of blasterfire. His prelim entry teams were already at the hotel, where the sec men were the most concentrated.

The baron's sec men didn't open fire until the main force was almost to the brewery. A blaster position on the roof of the building sprayed their right side with autofire and scored scattered hits. Stickies along the flank leaped and spun in the air as they were drilled. The mist of blood raised by the blasterfire only made the survivors more frantic to kill.

Kaa stepped to the edge of the throng and returned fire from the hip. Bullets from the rooftop whined off the asphalt on either side of him. He paid them no more mind than drops of chem rain. Joyeuse, his neon autoblaster, bucked in his fists, spitting smoking casings in a yellow stream. The tracers spanged off the edge of the roof, and the sec men disappeared in a flurry of impact smoke puffs. Kaa swept the M-60's muzzle back and forth, hosing the sec men off their perch.

While he was so occupied, Kaa's troops advanced without him, starting up the wide strip of parking lot that passed by the front of the amusement zone and led to the entrance of the hotel. He shouldered Joyeuse and melded with the advancing pack. All he could see ahead of him was the bobbing mass of bald heads, gleaming in the sun.

More blasterfire erupted from the direction of the

hotel. The stickies in the lead were absorbing it, the first ripple of a living wave sweeping over the baron's blaster emplacements. Those that were shot and fell became the carpet for their comrades. Kaa felt sadness and joy, and above all, pride. This was the true measure of the hardness of the hearts of his soldiers. That they would all gleefully die in the hope of getting their sucker hands on a live norm.

The massed blasterfire from the entrance to the hotel was suddenly joined by an attack on their right flank. Sec men along the fence line of the amusement zone and high in the scaffolding of the roller coaster peppered the mob with salvos of lead. It took many hits to chill a stickie. Kaa saw them dropped by bullet impacts, only to rise up and run. The combined assault did have an effect, though. It compressed Kaa's army, forcing it to run along a narrow strip of golf course.

The piebald man saw the danger, but before he could reroute his troops, the earth rocked violently and Kaa was thrown to the ground. As he was trying to get up, another explosion ripped the air.

Then it was raining body parts.

The baron had mined his own compound.

His ears ringing from the pressure of the blasts, Kaa sprang to his feet. Clouds of smoke billowed across the parking lot. Dozens of his soldiers were down, and many more had simply been vaporized. His stunned army paused, struggling to regain its momentum.

He had to do something.

The mutant lord could see the little figures hanging

over the balcony of the penthouse. He knew that the baron and his head toadies were up there watching the show, confident in their own safety. Bracing Joyeuse against his hip, he opened fire. He stitched a line of slugs across the front of the patio. The tiny figures scattered. Maybe some fell; he couldn't tell. Or they ducked below the balcony wall.

It was a foretaste of hell.

Another explosion sent Kaa staggering to his knees.

Chaos and panic swept through the ranks of the stickies, who hadn't yet recovered from the effects of the first two blasts. If his army stayed out in the open, tightly packed together, it would be annihilated, either by blasterfire or an explosion. He was too far back in the pack to lead them away from danger with a shout or a raised arm.

He unpeeled his eye and showed them how to escape.

ELIJAH WAS BUSY browbeating his sec men when the stickies jumped up from the river plain. The volunteers were getting tired of raising the prisoner twenty-five stories and were working more and more slowly.

If Elijah didn't see the stickies pop up, the toadie Skeen sure did. He screamed and pointed to the far side of the amusement zone.

"Look! Look!" he cried.

Everyone looked. Because of their angle of view and the intervening structures, they could only see the rear-most portion of the force.

"My blasterports can handle them," the baron said. "This should be very interesting. Come on over, gals, and watch this." Elijah got a fresh tankard of beer and joined them at the rail. They watched the mass of stickies disappear behind the lee of the berm wall.

There was no blasterfire.

"Why aren't they shooting?" Skeen said.

Elijah didn't know. He whirled on Murchisson. "Are your men asleep? The stickies are going to breach the wall!"

The head sec man looked dumbfounded. His mouth opened and closed, but no sounds came out.

"Fix it, damn you!" Elijah snarled.

"I'm on it, sir."

"Take the stairs," the baron shouted at his back. "We'll all be dead before you get down to the lobby in the elevator."

"Right, sir."

As the sec man vanished through the open slider, blasterfire crackled close to the base of the hotel tower. The crowd of norms in the parking lot started screaming and running in a panic for the lobby doors.

"This is fun," Roonie-Two said. She held Roonie-Three up over the railing so she could see the silly people fleeing for their lives and crushing one another in the process.

Only when the army of mutants rounded the end of the amusement zone and came charging up the golf course did Willie Elijah realize what he was up against.

A sea of dead-eye faces boiled up his avenue.

The sec men holding Ryan at the eighteenth floor let go of the rope, and once more he dropped to the end.

Autofire raged from the brewery's roof. He could see the smoke and the flash.

"At least somebody's shooting at them!" Elijah said, reaching for his telescope. He was watching his sec men spray the stickies when the machine gun opened up on them from the ground. He saw his soldiers shot to pieces. Lowering the telescope, the baron scanned the throng and located the mutie shooter. "Zit!" he cried. "It's that goddamn Zit!"

Meeting no serious opposition, the first wave of stickies closed the distance to the hotel.

"Come on, Murch!" Elijah shouted. "Do it! Do it!"

As if on cue, the ville's defensive plan kicked in. Autofire rattled from the front of the lobby and chattered from the amusement zone across the way. The stickie force was channeled between walls of lead, forced to close ranks in a long, narrow line.

Elijah could see the mutants dropping on the edges of the mass. They soaked up full-metal-jacketed slugs like frogs absorbing BBs. They were damn hard to chill.

A flash of light, followed by a thunderclap, bloomed in the middle of the former golf course, right at the head of the stickie army. A huge ball of smoke and dirt rolled away from the heart of the explosion.

It was spectacle.

It was mass slaughter.

It was glorious.

Elijah whooped so wildly that he spilled tipple all over his pants.

"Yay!" the norm girls cheered.

The toadies cheered, too, and pounded their fists on the railing.

The celebration quickly died when stickies kept on coming, tramping over the broken bodies of their comrades.

Another explosion, this one under the parking lot, closer to the hotel, sent mutants and mutant parts flying across the compound. The pall of smoke drifted away, and the penthouse spectators saw stickies blown down in a circle like trees felled by a windstorm. There was movement at the outer edges of the destruction. Stickies were getting up and continuing the attack.

"Hit them again, Murch!" Elijah shouted over the rail.

Then the balcony started coming apart.

Heavy-caliber slugs sparked as they clipped the steel rail, cutting three of the sec men almost in two, splattering their guts in a wide swathe across the exterior wall. The spray of bullets went through babies and moms and shattered the patio's sliding doors behind them. The patio furniture was jumping and shuddering from impacts as the survivors dived for the doorway to the penthouse.

From the floor inside, Elijah could see Poonie-Two, Poonie-Three and Toonie-Two and Toonie-Three—dead in pools of red on the deck. The moms were still twitching, the infants weren't.

Two-thirds of his pure-norm gene bank was gone in the blink of an eye.

"Roonie-Two! Where are you?" Elijah cried. When she didn't answer at once, he thought he'd lost her, as well. "Roonie-Two!"

Then a faint voice said, "Over here, Poppadaddy."

It took a moment for him to locate her in the clutter of the overfurnished suite. She was belly down on the rug in front of a sofa, covering her baby with her body.

Skeen was trying to hide under the lamp table beside her. All he'd managed to conceal was his bald head and narrow shoulders.

As J.B. APPROACHED the roller coaster on a dead run, he saw movement in the scaffolding to his right. Several figures were struggling wildly. One fell, bouncing off the struts, and landed on the ground. The Armorer held up his hand, signaling his comrades for a quick stop. He, Doc and Mildred closed ranks behind the ticket kiosk.

At the bottom of the scaffolding, not sixty feet from where they knelt, ten stickies huddled in a tight circle over the fallen sec man, their arms flailing as they ripped and tore at him. The mutants in the scaffolding dropped beside them and joined in the fun.

Mildred raised her AK, but J.B. caught hold of the barrel before she could fire. He shook his head. They had only the two mags between them. If they used up all their ammo to kill these few stickies, they'd never make it to the hotel.

Not that their chances looked good, anyway.

It was clear that the first stickies into Willie ville, the ones who'd come in under the berm, were already ahead of them, thereby cutting off the most direct line of access. They watched the stickies pull the sec man apart and scatter the bits of flesh like confetti. As the mutants moved back toward the asphalt path, J.B., Doc and Mildred retreated out of sight around the kiosk.

The stickies didn't go far. They stopped at a manhole set in the middle of the path and lifted the cover. One by one the stickies disappeared down the hole. When they were gone, Mildred covered Doc and J.B. while they stepped up to have a look.

"It's a power-line conduit," the Armorer said. "It's heading in the direction of the hotel. It might be our only way in."

"What about the stickies?"

"At least we know how many are ahead of us, Doc," he said.

J.B. climbed down the metal ladder, and Mildred and Doc quickly followed. The conduit was six feet in diameter. Most of its width was packed with cables and plastic pipes, leaving a narrow slit down the middle for them to pass through. There was a channel cut in the floor for water runoff. The only light was coming down through the opening above them.

"Shh," J.B. said. "Listen."

They could hear scuffling sounds ahead. The stickies were moving away, and fast. With J.B. on point, the trio went after them. They had gone only a few hundred feet when the earth began to rumble behind them. Dust from the ceiling fluttered down like gray snow.

"It's the stickies," J.B. said. "The whole damn army's up there. We've got to beat them to the hotel. Run!"

Running wasn't easy inside the pipe because the space was so narrow and the water-filled channel in the floor tended to snag the sides of their boots. But they made good time, maintaining their distance from the hordes behind them and rapidly gaining on the stickies in front of them.

It came as a complete surprise when everything went white.

Hard light of impossible brilliance filled the inside of their skulls. The whiteness billowed out, and when it shrank back, it left in its wake only black. J.B., Doc and Mildred were unconscious before they hit the ground, stunned by the concussive pressure of the explosion above and behind them. Debris rained on them, but they didn't feel it.

RYAN HAD HIS HAND clamped over his face, trying to staunch his nosebleed when cries from the crowd of norms below caught his attention—not cries of pleasure at his pain and suffering, but cries of terror.

From a height of twelve stories, he looked down to see the mob rushing for the lobby. And he saw the reason why, too.

Stickies leaped and hurled themselves into the edge of the audience. There couldn't have been more than fifteen of the mutants, and the crowd numbered better than two hundred, but the norm spectators were toadies, women and children. Instead of cornering the few attackers and stomping them to death, the crowd turned its back on the threat, allowing the stickies to pluck people out of the mass at will and tear them to pieces.

Ryan had to squirm around to keep the scene in view. He was still being pulled up toward the penthouse, and the motion caused him to twist at the end of the rope.

The upward movement stopped at the eighteenth floor, at about the same instant that autofire broke out from the brewery.

Ryan arched his back to get a better look and saw the horde of stickies running toward the hotel. Then the rope slipped, his stomach lurched and he dropped almost two hundred feet to the end of his tether.

Close blasterfire roused him from momentary unconsciousness. Sec men had stepped around the civilians fighting to get into the lobby and formed a firing squad. Their barrage of autofire sailed downrange, driving the onrushing stickies closer together.

A powerful explosion scattered the mutants into the wind.

Ryan twisted around to get a better look.

There was another explosion, and a wall of autofire erupted from the lobby.

Ryan groaned and clapped his hand over his nose as blood started gushing again. As he struggled, the autofire behind him ceased. When the one-eyed man looked back, he saw the sec men retreating through the lobby doors, leaving him hanging there ten feet above the ground.

Like a party favor.

THE SOUNDS of sustained blasterfire and the tremors of the explosions reached even the dim recesses of the hotel's subbasement. In the elevator's power plant, the condemned slaves leaned on the great wheel, resting while they could. Faint screams filtered down through the layers of concrete and steel. The slaves looked at one another and at the overseers. They said nothing, but their eyes betrayed their anxiety.

Johnson Lester knew what it all meant.

"Stickies are inside the compound," Lester confided to the slave chained to the spoke beside him. "The sec men are blowing the mines to stop them."

The mutie slave was a dual breather, with sets of vestigial gills below and behind the ears, feathery pink frills that peeked out of crimson-lipped slits. Its neck and cheeks were smeared with the black grease that had dripped from the gears above. "Who cares?" the mutie said. "Don't change nothin' down here."

A shrill whistling sound sent one of the overseers hustling over to a plastic tube that hung from the ceiling. He unblocked the funnel at the end, removed the whistle and bellowed into it. "What floor?"

A voice shrilled back through the communication tube. "Up! Take us up, quick!"

The overseer glanced at the dial on the wall over his

head. The elevator's floor indicator said the car was at the lobby.

"You heard them," the overseer said, "crank it up." When the slaves didn't obey quickly enough to suit him, he unlimbered his bullwhip. The twelve-foot, braided leather lash sizzled across the radius of the wheel, the man's aim surgically precise. He flicked the lobe of the gill mutie's ear with the whip's leather tip, cutting the lobe in two.

"I said move!"

The other two overseers cracked their whips just over the heads of the frantically scrambling slaves. The condemned threw themselves at their spokes, trying to lift the car far enough for the overseer to unlock the gears. Groaning, their feet braced against the floor treads, they couldn't raise the car so much as an inch.

"Work!" the overseer shouted.

Whips cracked. Backs arched, and leg muscles began to quiver from the strain.

The overseer had both hands on the gear lever and was pulling with all his might. Still, he couldn't free the dog.

"Too many people in the car," one of the other slave drivers told him. "These stupes can't lift it. And if they do, they'll never hold it."

Letting go of the lever, the overseer picked up the end of the communication tube. "You're overloaded!" he shouted into the funnel. "Half the passengers have to get out!"

"Help us!" the disembodied voice called back. The

words were hard to make it out over the yelling in the background. "Help us! The stickies are almost at the door!"

"Lighten the load!" was the overseer's only advice.

Lester smirked. The panic-stricken toadies were going nowhere. They, their wives and brats would have to take the stairs. Before this, the former sec man had never considered the number of trips he made up and down the tower's elevator every day, never considered the pain and suffering each trip caused some invisible, doomed lackey.

Now he knew how much it hurt.

Bringing the car down was the worst. There were no brakes. The slaves had to back around the floor circle, holding the weight with their legs while the overseers feathered the clutch.

With a foot sweep that he only barely saw, the gill mutie knocked Lester on his face on the floor, which brought him into range of the feet of the mutie chained to the spoke ahead. Lester took a glancing blow to the side of the face, making him see stars. But he was already rolling back, out of reach.

As he straightened, the gill mutie was glaring at him. So was the would-be stomper, a hairy-backed troll of a mutie.

It had been a planned attack, somehow hatched between them when he wasn't looking.

There was no use complaining to the overseers. All that would get him was a cut from their whips. His meager possessions hadn't bought him much in the way of protection.

Fusillades of blasterfire echoed down the nearby elevator shaft. The racket was much louder, as the sec men were now shooting inside the lobby. The hotel was under all-out attack.

The overseers nodded to one another. They didn't say anything. They just left the power plant, heading for higher and presumably safer ground while they still could.

"Hey!" Lester shouted at the open doorway. "Hey, don't just leave us here!"

His words boomed down the corridor.

None of the other prisoners made a sound. Every mutie eye around the wheel was focused on the sec man.

THOUGH HE DIDN'T ALLOW IT to crack his battle face, Murchisson was stunned by the tenacity of the stickies. Two or three of the bastards were bad enough, but when there were more they seemed to spur one another on. Standing under the hotel marquee, he directed fire for the forty-odd sec men lined up in front of him.

The stickie that charged right into the line of muzzles had lost its right foot and ankle to an explosion. The assembled sec men had seen it get up from the ground and watched it hop toward them, undaunted while blood spurted from its wounds. Behind it, others, equally grievously wounded, were also resuming the assault.

Murchisson could tell his men were unnerved. Intact stickies were tough enough to face, let alone these mutilated banshees. "Wait!" he shouted at his men, walking up and down the firing line. "Hold your fire."

He was vaguely aware of the chaos inside the lobby, the crowds of toadies trying to jam into the elevator, rushing for the staircase. He shut out the sounds of their screams.

The head sec man let the first wave of muties get within thirty feet of the building, until he could see the black centers of their dead eyes, the glint of their needle teeth, until he could hear the tortured rasp of their wounded breathing.

Forty autorifles opened fire.

A meat grinder of lead drilled into stickie flesh, bone and blood, blowing the onrushing monsters off their feet. Gun smoke swirled across the field of view, then it was caught, lifted by the wind, and gone.

Murchisson squinted down the slight incline to the golf course and the tightly packed mass of stickie soldiers, on the verge of being hit by another explosion. What he saw in the next instant made his mouth fall open. All the stickies moved at once. As if choreographed, they split into two forces, which rushed apart, one to the left, the other to the right. It reminded him of a colony of foraging ants, suddenly diverting from a threat.

The sec men controlling the buried mines detonated them, but too late. They blew up stickies who were already dead.

The movement of troops was so massive and so quick that there was no way to counter it. The hotel was being flanked.

"Pull back!" he shouted to his men. "Inside!"

The real battle for Freedom City Motor Hotel and Casino had begun.

A STICKIE'S HAND SWEPT past Ryan's face. It came so close he could feel the breeze it made, so close he could smell the sharp chemical odor of its adhesive glands. There were five more below him, each trying to jump the ten feet or so and clamp their suckers onto his defenseless head.

If he hadn't held his arms folded tightly to his chest, they would have grabbed them for sure. In their eagerness to rip him, they fought and jostled one another for the best position. He could see they were getting more and more frantic with frustration. They hissed and spit as they leaped. Then they started to climb on top of one another, which made them instantly taller.

The sec men kneeling inside front doors of the lobby were still shooting, but not in his direction. He didn't expect covering fire from them anyway.

Ryan curled at the waist in a vertical sit-up. As a piggyback stickie clawed for him and missed, he caught hold of his own shins with both hands. Then he snatched hold of the rope on his ankle, first with one hand, then the other. He hauled himself up the line, until he was well out of reach of the hissing, screeching creatures below, then locked the loose rope around his legs.

Looking out over the golf course from his perch, Ryan saw the stickie formation split in two parts. He knew right away what it meant. He shinnied up the line until he was even with the hotel's fourth story. Then he started to swing back and forth on the rope.

Chapter Eighteen

Lord Kaa stood frozen in the middle of the battlefield, jostled this way and that by his own troops as they darted away from danger. Though only his white orb was open, all three of his eyes wept. There was no way he could have prepared himself for the profound emotion of this networking. Once he folded back the lids of his mutant eye, once he was connected to his legion, he saw what each of his soldiers saw, felt what they felt through their own nerve endings. Not just the exhilaration of battle, the fever joy of chilling, but the pleasure they took in dying in his service, the pleasure they took in their own excruciating pain.

It burned him to the ground. These were warriors the likes of which the world had never seen.

The humility he felt, the honor to be leading such troops in a just and noble war, reduced him to impotence, to catatonic immobility.

Explosions ripped the air again, but over empty ground.

This Kaa saw with borrowed eyes, the eyes of both the living and the dying. He saw the golf course littered with the bodies of those who could no longer see or fight. These glorious dead, these heroes, would never be mourned, he vowed. They would be celebrated always. As the smoke shifted, so did the thousands of troops that remained in the field. Soon the slaves would be free, and he would have even more. He formed a mental picture for his army of what was to come. It described the tightening of the noose, the strangulation of Willie ville.

Bullets screamed overhead as Kaa pinched closed his lids with his fingertips. He brushed away his tears with the back of his hand. Then with Rogero at his side, he followed the right half of the stickie formation. They left the golf course and ran through the arch of the amusement zone.

Blasterfire from the top of the Ferris wheel chopped down a half dozen of the mud-daubed soldiers at the front of the pack.

Kaa swung Joyeuse up and answered fire, raking the little swing-seats with 7.62 mm lead. The strings of slugs tore the chairs apart and dumped out limp, dark forms that dropped, pinwheeling, crashing limply into the Ferris wheel's hub. He pushed Rogero onward, and they turned down the path for the mutie zoo.

As they approached that shameful prison, they could see the stickies had already broken down the door. And even from a good way off, they could hear the tumult coming from inside. Kaa and Rogero reached the entrance just as a pair of the killer mutants came running out holding a length of fat, pinkish gray hose over their heads.

They were uncoiling someone's guts.

Kaa followed the grisly streamer into the corridor. A knot of stickies hid its source from view.

"Back!" he bellowed.

The mutants parted, hands dripping red to the wrists, to expose what was left of Kaa's old teacher, Knackerman. The norm no longer had a face or eyes, and his belly had been clawed open from sternum to groin. His dead heart floated in a cavity awash in blood; it had a chunk bitten out of it.

The mutie worm had turned, all right, turned most vicious.

The shrill noise that surrounded him made Kaa's head reel. "Enough!" he shouted. And when they wouldn't be quiet, he let Joyeuse gavel the inmates to silence. The M-60 roared in the concrete building, its ricochets singing merrily off the walls and bars.

The effect was instantaneous.

No one even breathed.

The piebald lord sent Rogero to Knackerman's office for the keys to the cages. When Rogero returned, Kaa sent the paladin on to the slave quarters to free the muties there.

Then Kaa moved to the center of the zoo, where all could hear him speak. His voice was loud and deep and it made the prison walls ring. "I am Kaa," he said, "once called Zit, once called Blotch. Once shamed like you, once defamed like you, once degraded like you, I have liberated myself from the tyranny of the norms. And I have come to liberate you."

He did a quick circuit of the zoo's cells. He did this

trotting with his arms raised over his head, turning to display his mutant skin and his mutant eye. He wanted each of them to know who was responsible for their release, that it was a brother freak they owed their lives to. When he was done with the victory lap, it took a second burst of 7.62 mm tracers to quiet the ecstatic prisoners.

"The baron's hotel is surrounded," he said. "His sec men are in full retreat. With your help we will soon chill them all. There will be blasters and beaters and stickers for you. There will be revenge for all your suffering. And there will be booty. As much as you can carry."

Kaa started to open the cells himself, and he laid hands on each of his new recruits as they were freed. The former zoo specimens didn't rush out of the building where they had been kept and abused for so long, but remained in the corridor to watch the liberation of the very last captive.

He had released about half the prisoners when he came to a cage with two beings in it. Unlike the others, they weren't frantic to be freed; by comparison, the red-eyed teenager with shoulder-length white hair and the enormous mutie mountain lion seemed almost tranquil. The youth had his hand resting on the big cat's back. Both were smiling fierce, proud smiles. The lion's grin exposed canines like yellow daggers.

Kaa put the key in the lock and turned it. "Come out," he said, swinging open the gate, "and help me fight for the freedom of our race."

The boy and the lion didn't move for the exit.

"Can you speak?" Kaa asked.

"I can speak," Jak replied.

"What are you waiting for?"

"Friend," the teenager said. "She put her same time I was. She's here somewhere. I not fight anyone or go anywhere without her."

"Come out and follow me. We'll find your friend."

Jak and the lion hopped down from the cage. The other muties gave them a wide berth, practically falling over themselves to clear a path. It wasn't because of the slim teenager with the ruby eyes; it was because of his new sidekick with the curving, yellow fangs.

Kaa continued through the cells, releasing all the prisoners. The first thing most of them did was to throw themselves at his feet and kiss or lick his muddy boots. Most were crying as they ran down the corridor. They had never expected to live to see this day.

"There. That's her," Jak said.

The lord of the mutants stopped short, stopped breathing when he saw the red-haired female with the luminous green eyes. Even through the bars of the cage, he sensed the immense gravity of the power at her center. And he knew at once that she was the one he sought.

"Angelica," he said softly.

The red-eyed boy stepped up to the bars. "Getting out of here, Krysty," he told her. "Going to be okay."

The red-haired female's eyes met Kaa's.

But instead of the warmth and affection that he felt

at first sight of her, upon seeing him, she radiated anxiety, even fear. Her reaction shocked him and was painful to his heart.

He unlocked her cage and let her out.

"You know me," he said to her.

"I know you."

"And you are Angelica," he said, "the one promised me by fate."

She didn't deny it. Her emerald eyes stared straight into his. Apparently she had overcome her fear.

Touching her chin lightly, he turned her face to the torchlight so he could see it better. Her red hair slithered around his wrist, seizing it with amazing power. It surprised him, but he didn't jerk back his hand.

"Come, Angelica," he said, "I will show you our brand-new world."

DOC WAS SURE that he was dead. He couldn't see anything, couldn't hear anything, couldn't feel anything.

Finally, he thought. The ordeal of his fragmented, torturous existence was finally over.

Then a hand shook him.

"Get up, Doc."

It wasn't God, calling him to the Throne of Judgment.

It was Mildred Wyeth.

He awoke with his cheek resting in the conduit's water channel. It was very dark. He tried to sit up and couldn't manage it in the narrow space. He pulled himself up to his feet using the cables mounted along the walls as handholds.

"What happened?" he asked.

"Explosion," J.B. said. "Must've gone off right over the tunnel. If you can move, let's go."

"I can move."

They soon discovered that the stickies who'd been in front of them hadn't been so lucky. The concussion of the explosion had torn them apart. The tunnel dripped with their fluids, and the channel was clogged with their limp bodies. The friends had to walk on the corpses to get by them.

"I didn't count them," J.B. said, "but I think all of the stickies ahead of us bought the farm."

More explosions rocked the conduit behind them. However, the detonations were farther away this time and didn't have the same stunning effect. They continued on at top speed until they could see golden light at the end of the conduit, then they proceeded with caution. The passage opened onto a low-ceilinged room crammed with electrical boards, fuse panels, pipes, air ducts and long-dead machinery. The cables in the conduit fanned out over a broad wall lit by torches. Along the floor were stacked sealed cans of paint, solvent and cleaners, reminders of a time when everything still ran and had to be maintained.

J.B. kicked one of the cans, and something sloshed inside.

"I think we're in the hotel," he said, taking a torch off the wall. "Let's find out where."

He opened the door at the end of the long room and faced a dripping concrete corridor, much like the one they had seen when they were taken to the cooler. As they headed down the hall, they quickly confirmed their location. They saw the plastic lilies wired to the doors of Baron Elijah's crypts.

"The elevator is that way," Mildred said.

As they neared it, they could hear the noise from the lobby rolling down the empty shaft: people screaming, gunfire. There was no sign of sec men. Apparently they were all upstairs, fighting for their lives.

J.B. rounded the last corner with the Armalite's butt against his shoulder. He swept the sights across the fronts of the elevators. The good news was there were no targets, norm or stickie. The bad news was that both sides of the shaft were empty. The elevator that still worked wasn't on this floor. Then he saw the door to the power plant standing ajar. He waved for Mildred and Doc to follow him, but cautiously.

When J.B. barged into the power room, the slaves jerked their heads up from the wheel's spokes.

"It's okay," he said. "Everybody relax."

Doc and Mildred took up positions just inside the doorway.

"Unlock us so we can fight," one of the slaves said.

"It's the sec man," Mildred said, "the one who turned us in. Hardly recognized him under all that grease."

"We aren't doing anybody any good chained down here," Lester said.

The other slaves shouted their agreement, but there was something in their eyes that J.B. didn't like. He wasn't sure which side they'd fight on if they were freed.

Through the end of the communication tube, they could hear the canvas-ripping sounds of sustained auto-fire, only distorted, tinny.

"There is something you can do," J.B. told them. "Does the elevator still work?"

The slaves nodded.

"We had to stop running it because there were too many people trying to pack into it," Lester said.

"But you can bring the elevator car down to this floor?"

"Sure," the sec man said.

"What are you thinking, John?" Mildred asked.

"I'm thinking I might have a way to get us out of here alive."

Chapter Nineteen

Murchisson rammed the steel-shod butt of his Uzi carbine into the face of the resisting toadie. Clutching his shattered nose, the man abruptly sat on the staircase. Blood squirted out between his fingers.

"Out of the way!" Murchisson shouted at the others. "Clear a path!"

Things weren't going well.

When the head sec man and the baron had laid out the plans for the defense of Willie ville, they hadn't thought an attack would happen in daylight, with most of the norm population outside the hotel's tower. The plan, should the berm walls fail, should the mines fail to stop an advance, was to make the stickies pursue the baron's sec men up the twisting stairwells, where they could unleash withering, concentrated firepower. The key to the strategy was an orderly and rapid retreat. They needed to be able to withdraw in order to keep the mutants at a safe and proper blasting distance.

In the real world of unforeseen events, that wasn't possible.

The line of retreat was blocked by the bodies of the toadies and their kin packing the stairs. The sec men at the bottom of the stairwell couldn't back up without falling over their own.

Over Murchisson's shoulder the din of autofire shook the stairs. Cordite smoke coiled up the well. When he turned and looked down, he could see the stickies hurling themselves onto the barrels of his men's weapons. The suicidal bastards absorbed dozens of high-power rounds so the monsters who followed could climb over them and onto the momentarily trapped sec men.

The baron's sec chief considered using fraggers to clear the bottom of the stairwell, but he knew the shrapnel spray would take out many of his men. He glared at the clot of norms on the stairs above him.

What was holding things up?

Using the butt of his Uzi, Murchisson battered his way through the crowd. "Move! You worthless sacks of shit," he told them.

When he reached the next landing, he found it blocked by a mass of people. They were pounding on the steel fire door, which was closed and evidently locked.

"Let us in!" the toadies cried.

"No. You've got to go higher. Keep moving up the stairs!"

He pushed back the blockage and looked around the corner of the landing. People packed the stairs all the way up as far as he could see.

"Damn!" the sec man said. Turning back, he shouted for a squad of the rearmost sec men. They came crashing, kicking up the steps. The toadies and their families crushed to the sides of the well to get out of their way.

"All right," Murchisson said, "I want a path opened all the way to the top. Get going."

The sec men were only too glad to oblige, because it put distance and bodies between them and the raging stickies. Tramping up the staircase, they used fists and feet to drive a wedge between the norms. The stubborn ones were knocked over the railing.

Murchisson stepped into the wake his troops made. "Up!" he said to the toadies. "Follow us up!"

Above the seventeenth floor the stairwell was clear. Murchisson and his men took the steps three at a time. When the head sec man reached the open fire door to the twenty-fourth floor, he immediately started herding the norms behind him inside.

"Move to the end, dammit!" he shouted, waving them past the elevators. "To the end!"

The cream of Willie ville funneled, dazed and shaking, down the hallway lined with looted couches and chairs.

RYAN SWUNG HIMSELF over the rail of the fourth-floor balcony. Hobbled by ankle chains, he made an ungainly landing on a patio table. He tied off the end of the rope on the rail. Finding the slider locked, he picked up a metal chair and smashed in the glass.

The dark hotel room consisted of a bathroom, bedroom, open closet and a built-in dresser. The wall mirror was long gone, as was every other bit of furnishing not nailed or screwed down. He checked the bath, which was empty. When he stepped out into the dim hall, he came face-to-face with the crowned muzzle of a hogleg, stainless-steel blaster—a Ruger Redhawk .44 Magnum with a seven-and-a-half-inch barrel.

The toadie norm on the other end of the Redhawk was shaking up a storm. He could hardly miss at this range, though.

"K-k-kill you," the man said.

Ryan swept the Ruger's long barrel aside and clamped his hand over the blaster's cylinder. The toadie tried to discharge the weapon into Ryan's leg, but with the cylinder trapped, the hammer wouldn't rise on double action.

Ryan hit him once in the stomach with his left hand. The blow doubled the man over and dropped him to his knees. He let go of the .44-caliber blaster.

The one-eyed warrior turned the handcannon around and cocked it.

"Don't shoot me," the toadie begged between gasps for air.

Ryan ignored him. He put the pistol's muzzle against the first link of the ankle chain and fired. Flame belched from the barrel, and the hallway rocked from the blast. His ankles were no longer connected. He swung out the cylinder and saw he had three live rounds left.

"You shouldn't be down here," Ryan told the man as he snapped the action closed. "Nobody should be this close to the ground. The stickies can climb up the outside of the building. Is anybody else on this floor?"

"Uh-huh."

"Well, get them the hell out. And quick. Before the stairwell is cut off."

When the toadie just stood there, Ryan realized he was going to have to do it himself. He shoved the man ahead of him as he stormed down the hall, kicking and pounding on the doors. "Everybody out!" he yelled. "Stickies are coming! You can't stay here. You're not safe!"

Behind him the doors opened a crack, and the hiding norms started filing out.

Ryan had just one immediate goal, which was to recover their weapons. The last time he'd seen them, they were twenty-one floors up. He headed for the stairwell door. He didn't have to put his ear to it to hear gunshots and screams.

It was already too late. The sec men had retreated to a higher floor. There was nothing but stickies in the stairwell.

Ryan didn't say anything to the norms. He couldn't help them. He abruptly turned and pushed past them, moving back the way he had come.

"What do we do?" one of the toadies cried. "What do we do?"

Die, Ryan thought. You die.

When the one-eyed warrior reentered the balcony room where he had tied off the rope, stickies were already scrambling over the rail onto the patio. Three of them rushed at him through the broken slider. He raised the Redhawk and fired once.

A foot of flame leaped from the muzzle as the weapon roared. The single 240-grain slug smashed through the first mutant's head, then the second and finally the third. They toppled like dominoes. He walked over their shuddering hulks and out onto the balcony. As he did, another stickie popped up over the railing. The massive handblaster bucked as Ryan shot it in the face, point-blank. The stickie's bald head blurred into a red mist. Its body dropped, then stopped. The sucker hands were still stuck to the steel railing. They held the headless corpse dangling there while blood bubbled from the stump of its neck.

Tucking the Ruger into his waistband, Ryan untied the rope, jumped up on the railing and launched himself into space. As he swung out, he could see stickies climbing from patio to patio on the outside of the hotel. In seconds they would be swarming over the fourth floor.

Ryan started to pull himself up the rope. It was much easier going with his ankles free, but still a long, dangerous climb to the penthouse. As he inched past the floors, he could see figures running about and he heard almost constant blasterfire.

As he reached the nineteenth floor, a sec man rushed out onto the balcony. The man paid him only a quick glance. He leaned over the rail and, seeing the tiny forms scaling the side of the building, he let out a ferocious curse. Though he had a rifle, he didn't take a shot. He turned and ran back inside the hotel. Ryan heard him yelling a warning to his comrades as he raced down the hall.

The rope under Ryan twitched, tensed and stretched. He looked past his boots and saw that he was no longer the rope's only passenger. Many stories down a stickie had grabbed the end of it and was shinnying up after him, light and quick, like a spider on a web. Even as Ryan watched, five more of the mutants caught the end of the rope and started up.

With the suckers on their fingers and the adhesive glands, he knew there was no way he could shake them off the line, so he didn't even try. Instead, he redoubled his efforts to climb the rope, moving toward the penthouse as fast as he could. His concern wasn't just that the mutants would overtake him. He knew the stickies were so stupid that more and more of them would keep jumping on the rope until their combined weight finally snapped it. He didn't want that to happen while he was still climbing.

When he reached the top-floor balcony, he caught hold of the rail and pulled himself over. The first thing he saw were the bodies of Elijah's kin. They were sprawled amid shards of glass. The patio floor was a bloody lake. Out of the corner of his eye Ryan caught a glimpse of shadows moving inside the penthouse. He couldn't do anything about them. There wasn't time to secure his back. The first stickie on the rope was already level with the twenty-second floor.

He grabbed one of the fifty-pound sandbags and laid

it on its side on the rail. The tag ends of the rope that cinched the bag closed were six inches long. Ryan quickly wrapped the ends around the rope and knotted them tight. Then he pushed the bag off the balcony. It sizzled as it slid down the main line. He saw the stick-ie's dead eyes go wide and its flabby mouth gape as it looked up and realized what was about to happen—and that there was no escape.

The sandbag sailed down the rope, gaining speed until it smashed into the head of the first stickie, knocking it loose. The mutant spiraled in space, then dropped in a headlong dive. Still looped to the rope, the bag kept on going, and once again picked up speed. The stickie below swung around on the rope to avoid getting bashed on the head. The bag missed its skull, but the impact of the sliding loop broke the sucker grip of its hands. The bag continued to slide down the rope, and like beads on a string the climbing stickies slipped away, falling off the end of the rope and crashing to the parking lot.

"Nice work," said a voice behind Ryan.

It was Baron Willie Elijah, his face nicked and bleeding from broken glass. Blobs of spattered blood clung to his coarse white chest hairs. The baron held one of the G-12s aimed at the one-eyed warrior's heart, the fire selector set on three-round bursts.

Ryan thought about going for the Redhawk's grip, but knew even if he reached it, he'd never get seven and a half inches of barrel out of the front of his pants before Elijah drilled him. He slowly raised his hands.

THE BLASTERFIRE and explosions from inside the compound gave the mutie slaves in the baron's fields their first clue that Willie ville was under assault. They stopped whatever they were doing, straightened from the rows of crops, leaned on the handles of their shovels and turned toward the sounds of the pitched battle.

The overseer stared in disbelief at the plumes of smoke and debris spiraling up from the center of the ville. Behind him the slaves in the pit jumped up and down. The overseer didn't know what to do, where to run. He should have done something; he shouldn't have just stood there flat-footed, with his back to his prisoners.

The raghead slave gripped the end of his shovel's handle and swung the side of the blade at his oppressor's head. The steel edge sliced into the flesh, shearing off a great bloody chunk.

Screaming, clutching at the back of his head with one hand, the overseer unlimbered his whip with the other. Before he could strike, another of the slaves brought its shovel's blade hard across the boss man's shins. The overseer crumpled into the pit, and the slaves closed in on him, raising and swinging down their shovels.

It was payback time, and they repaid him with interest, using the edges of their shovels to chop and hack his body to ribbons of flesh.

The slaves in the surrounding fields saw what the pit crew was doing and seized the opportunity to attack their overseers, as well. Using garden tools, sticks, hands and feet, they overpowered them and beat them to the ground. In a matter of minutes there were no more living slave masters outside the walls of Willie ville.

When the muties in the pit saw a group of stickies coming toward them from the shantytown, they whooped and cheered and waved their gory shovels in the air. Then they rushed across the river valley to meet their liberators.

As the two bands of mutants came together at the edge of the cultivated area, other slaves in distant fields moved to join them, hobbling with their young strapped on their backs.

Raghead stepped forward to greet the leader of the stickies. "Thank you, brother. We come to join Kaa in the war against the norms."

No sooner were the words out of Raghead's mouth than the muffled mutant realized something was wrong. Very wrong. Backing up as the stickie advanced, Raghead bumped into fellow shovelers.

The stickie captain sniffed the air around him, then its dead eyes caught the glint of red on the edges of their shovels. Whimpering, it smelled the fresh blood on their tools, and its tongue traced over the points of needle teeth. It started to shake, and strands of clear goo began to weep from its fingertips.

The same thing was happening to the other stickies. The pit crew had nowhere to go. They were surrounded and outnumbered.

Rogero, captain of the stickies, paladin and peer of Kaa, leaned down and grabbed hold of the chain that connected Raghead's ankles, jerking it so the mutie crashed to its back on the ground. The stickies swarmed in a flash. As they tore off the headgear, exposing the hideous, tumor-ravaged face, other stickies tripped and jumped the remaining slaves. Their agonized death screams rolled over the river plain.

The other slaves coming in from the fields stopped where they were. They stared at the mad scrambling in the dirt, the clouds of rising dust. Then they turned and ran for their lives.

Chapter Twenty

In the flickering torchlight of the bank vault, Krysty watched the huge mutant called Kaa thrash and quiver on the floor. His jaws snapped together. His norm eyelids, which were shut, fluttered and twitched. And he wasn't the only one having a fit. The quartet of stickies in the vault was shaking uncontrollably and moaning. They, too, appeared to be unconscious. The suddenness and violence of the attacks had made Krysty, Jak and the other muties stop what they were doing, which was stuffing the baron's Apocalypticon into plastic trash bags.

Of the twenty fully conscious muties in the vault, only Krysty dared to go near the piebald man. She leaned in for a closer look at the blind white eye in his forehead. Under the milky surface, she could see a tracery of fine capillaries. The lids that protected it were flabby, puckery things; they were made of the kind of skin usually associated with a scrotum, not a face. Bloody tears welled up in the sagging cup of the lower lid, then overflowed, spilling down his brows and cheeks.

Lord Kaa was caught up in a terrible internal struggle; for what and with whom, Krysty had no way of knowing. The powerful muscles of his neck and shoulders were corded. His lips curled back from tightly clenched teeth. The battle had begun the moment he had unpeeled his middle eye.

It was a conflict he didn't seem to be winning.

Krysty was confused by her own emotions as she watched him suffer the torments of an invisible hell. There was a terrible beauty to him—not just his size and massive musculature, not just his skin, not just the third eye that decorated his forehead. She sensed something inside him, something vulnerable, something pure. She couldn't even describe whatever it was to herself because she didn't have the right words, images, context. She only knew what it made her feel to be near him.

Awe.

The creature who called himself Kaa was unique. The folktales of Deathlands, which Krysty had learned by heart at her mother's knee, encompassed a wide range of mutated species, real and imaginary, with attributes and powers equally diverse, but such a being as this had never even been hinted at.

Though there had been no jack, no gain in it for him, Kaa had freed her from the captivity of the norms. He had freed all the slaves of Willie ville. It was unheard-of.

And somehow he had managed to unite the stickies and other mutie races into a cohesive fighting force, which was impossible.

"What do you think's wrong with him, Jak?" Krysty asked. "Do you think he's dying?"

"Lion says he's chilling," the teenager said, "in his sleep."

Krysty hadn't heard the lion talk, but she knew that didn't mean he couldn't. She wondered if only Jak could hear him.

"He's chilling norms out in the ville?" she asked.

"No. Can't do nothing to norms with head. Chills them with his M-60. Does things to stickies with brain, though. Look at those guys over there. Shaking them apart."

That's what it looked like to Krysty, too. The four stickies' bodies were jerking and snapping, and white foam was pouring out of their mouths.

When she glanced back at Kaa, she was relieved to see that he had stopped his thrashing. He sat up and, bracing his back against the brushed steel of the safety-deposit boxes, pinched his third eye shut. The battle was clearly done, but at a cost. Kaa let his chin sink onto his chest for a few seconds. When he raised his head, she saw there was anguish, perhaps even a touch of despair, in his face.

The first words out of his mouth formed a question, and a strange one at that.

"Have you ever chilled someone you loved?"

"No," she said, "I haven't."

"I did, just now," he told her, "with my mind. I chilled a trusted friend who betrayed me, because he couldn't overcome his nature. Because I was too weak to protect him from it. The predarks had a word for such weakness. They called it hubris. I didn't realize until now, because I was blinded by pride, that there were limits to my gifts. It never occurred to me that my control might be finite, that six thousand stickies were too many to contain when there was blood mist in the air."

"I don't understand," Krysty said.

"My paladin, Rogero," he explained, "committed the ultimate crime against the moral order of the new people. He willfully and for his own pleasure caused the death of a fellow mutant. He did this while connected to every other stickie mind in my legion. Once he started the chilling of the field slaves, I couldn't make him stop. I couldn't stop the stickies with him, either. Soon their blood lust would have infected the whole army. I had no choice but to terminate the life of one I loved, as son, brother, friend, also in full view of the others. I didn't do it to make a point, as an object lesson to my troops. Stickies don't learn through pain, their own or that of others. Pain is their sacrament, Angelica."

When Krysty looked puzzled, he said, "I know all this is strange to you. I know and I apologize. You and I have much to talk about. There is much that I do not understand myself. Much that puzzles me. I know you will be able to help me sort it out."

Kaa rose and went over to examine the four stickies. They had finally quieted down. They might have been sleeping, except for the thin trickle of blood that leaked from the noseless nostrils, the twin holes in the centers of their faces. "They were too close to me when I showed the death card to Rogero," he said ruefully. "I didn't intend to chill them, only him. Brave ones lost, for nothing."

When Kaa turned back, he caught Krysty staring at the M-60. She hadn't formed the thought of trying to grab it and use it on him until the instant their eyes met. Then it was there, as big as life. Grab the blaster and use it. And she knew that he knew what was in her mind. It was the kind of shameful idea—the opposite of the heart, the spirit—that pops up without warning sometimes, perhaps to chasten people for presuming to think they know precisely who and what they are. And what they are capable of.

Kaa picked up the autoblaster and leaned it against the wall beside her, along with yards of belted ammo, thereby demonstrating that he trusted her, even though he knew what was on her mind.

"I call it Joyeuse," he said, stroking the front sight. "It means 'joy' in a predark language. It was the name a predark baron gave to his weapon. That baron used Joyeuse to beat back a plague of darkness and evil and rebuild his land."

Outside, the sounds of battle raged on.

"Continue the packing," Kaa told the freed muties. He observed them as they took the stacks of documents from the floor and from the open safety-deposit boxes and piled them in plastic trash bags. "Don't fill the bags too full," he said. "We have to be able to carry

them. And I don't want them to break. Double-bag
them until the supply of bags runs low."

Kaa then moved closer to Krysty and, while she
worked, he spoke to her in a low, confidential voice.
"This predark baron," he said, "this hero I mentioned,
he established law, order and peace in his land during
his lifetime. But after his death, the countryside and
the people he had freed descended back into the pit.
The power that he alone possessed had held together
the wild and disobedient paladins, the competing interests of corrupt administrators and traders.

"I learned much from my study of this man's story.
I learned enough to see my life reflected in his tale. I
know that when I die, if my power dies with me, whatever I have built will fall apart. That even if we rid
Deathlands of the norms who have enslaved and butch-
ered us, the new people will have no future. That is
why you are so important."

"I don't understand."

"You will, Angelica. You will."

HOWLING, THE STICKIES ripped and clawed at the few
remaining sec men who stood between them and the
twenty-fourth floor landing. Murchisson thrust his Uzi
over the shoulder of a man in front of him and fired
full-auto into the seething mass of muties, stitching a
line of 9 mm lead across their heads. Even as he fired,
the dead-eyed bastards yanked down a sec man and
started to pull his face off. They were damn hard to

chill. Even a head shot, unless it was a brain-corer, didn't stop them.

All the way up the stairs, he and his men had battled the army of stickies. The more they chilled, the more they faced—a seemingly endless supply of needle teeth and suckered hands. Murchisson didn't know how many men he'd lost, at least half of his force, maybe more.

The stairwell was full of stickies now, and they were all climbing, pushing up to the top floors. The baron's security force had reached the end of the line. The stairs didn't access the penthouse; the twenty-fourth floor was as far up as they went.

"Inside!" he shouted to his men. "Get inside the door."

When the last man stepped back over the threshold, the sec men behind him slammed the fire door closed. Or tried.

A cluster of stickie hands and arms blocked the door from shutting.

Murchisson shoved the muzzle of his Uzi through the crack and opened fire. The clattering action spewed a cascade of spent brass as he blasted the stickies away from the door. He fired until the mag came up empty.

Before he could get the blaster back in, a stickie grabbed the barrel. For a second they played tug-of-war with the carbine, a game Murchisson realized he couldn't win. With a curse he let go of the weapon, and the sec men crashed the steel door closed.

The situation was bad.

Murchisson avoided looking into the expectant, terrified faces of the norms huddled on the couches and chairs of the hallway. They wanted to hear some words of encouragement from him. He had nothing good to tell them. The defensive plan for Willie ville was a bust. There was no way they could have foreseen having to face an army of that size. And now they had retreated as far as they could go. They had ammo stockpiled on this floor; they were committed to making their stand here.

Except for the crying of the children and women, it was eerily quiet. For the first time in many minutes, there was no shooting.

The lull seemed ominous.

Murchisson did a quick count of his men. There were fewer than he'd hoped had survived. Not fifty, but twenty. It wasn't enough to put a blaster on each of the possible entry sites for the stickies. There were so many ways they could get in: through the balconies, windows, air ducts, elevator shaft. For all he knew, they could chew through the rad-blasted walls.

The head sec man walked over to the double pair of open doors of the elevator shaft. He stuck his head in and shouted up to the penthouse. "Sir? We could use some more shooters down here. Could you send down the sec team you've got up there?"

There was no answer.

"Sir?"

"Hold out the mutie bastards," came the voice of

the baron, echoing down the shaft. "I'm counting on you."

End of conversation.

"Damn," Murchisson said. He gestured for three of his men to give him a hand. They broke into the long wooden crates stacked along the wall opposite the elevators. The boxes were full of stamped-steel, cheapo blasters. He rearmed himself with a KG-99, a giant step down from the Uzi he'd just lost.

He started going up and down the rows of chairs and couches, passing out loaded handblasters and machine pistols to the male toadies. He had no choice. He put them in position to defend the women and children from various possible angles of attack.

"Don't use them blasters unless the stickies break onto the floor," he warned them.

Which, he thought, was going to be any minute.

"MURCH IS RIGHT," Ryan said. "You're going to need every shooter you can get. How about giving me back my blaster?"

Elijah looked over at the pile of confiscated weapons. He seemed to vacillate, then his expression hardened. "Just sit there and shut up. I need to think."

The one-eyed man used the moment to survey the others trapped in the penthouse. The handful of very important toadies cowered on the couch, and nervous sec men were pacing with their blasters at the ready. Roonie-Two sat in a corner with her babe on her lap, hugging her. The eyes of the baron's granddaughter-wife were huge with fear. Across the portal of the shattered slider lay the bodies of her sisters and their children.

Ryan found it hard to feel sorry for any of them, except the girl child. The others had brought all this on themselves, especially the baron. It just went to prove that you reaped what you sowed, eventually. A few thousand stickies had reduced the baron's sphere of influence—which had, only hours before, extorted tribute from hundreds of miles of Deathlands—to two floors of a hotel. When the stickies were through with it, there'd be nothing left of Elijah's enterprise but ashes and bone chips.

It was all over for Willie ville.

He wondered if it was all over for his friends. If so, he knew that Krysty, J.B., Doc, Jak and Mildred probably suffered terribly before they died. It's what the stickies did best. Hurt people. He knew that from experience.

Ryan considered whether he should try to chill the baron, to pay him back for causing the deaths of his companions. Elijah was a stupid, greedy man, typical, really, of the feudal lords who ruled parts of Deathlands by force of arms. Across the room the Redhawk lay beside J.B.'s hat. If he was going to make a dive for a blaster, that would be the one. It was shorter than the G-12s, so it would be quicker to sight.

He weighed the pros and cons, but in the end he decided not to go for it. The stickies would make a much better job of chilling the baron than he ever could. Despite Elijah's warning to keep quiet, Ryan decided he couldn't miss this final chance to rub it in.

"Seems like we're all sort of up a tree," he said.

Sec men guarding the balcony glared at him, as if a few hard looks would make him stop talking.

"We've crawled out to the last branch and out to the very tip," he continued.

"Shut him up!" Skeen said.

Ryan regarded the toadie with contempt. "You better calm down and get your mind around what's coming," he said. "Otherwise, you won't be ready to face it."

"We still have a chance," Skeen protested.

"Yeah, that's right," Ryan said. "But only if we can learn to fly real quick."

Roonie-Two looked up at the baron. "Is he right, Poppadaddy? Are we all gonna die?"

Elijah tried to speak, but he couldn't seem to get any words out. He gently stroked her hair.

"Don't let them get us, Poppadaddy," Roonie-Two said. "At least Poonie-Two and Toonie-Two and their babies died real quick. Don't let the stickies tear me and Roonie-Three apart. Poppadaddy, promise me that before that happens you'll chill us yourself."

For the first time ever, Ryan saw defeat in the baron's eyes, crushing defeat and a terrible sadness. It wasn't a pretty sight. Elijah was coming to terms with the facts, and the facts were that everything ended here, all that he had worked for his whole life, all his dreams.

"I promise you, gal," he said as his eyes welled up with tears. "I won't let them have you."

"THEY'RE ON THE BALCONY below!" the sec man cried, drawing back from the rail. "There's a fucking million of them!"

The blasterfire on the twenty-fourth floor started up almost immediately. Ryan had never heard anything like it. It shook the floor under his feet, rattled paintings off walls, vases off tables. Under it, screams were barely audible.

"Chill them!" the baron shouted. "Chill the bastards!"

The sec men leaned out over the rail and sprayed the stickies on the balcony beneath them.

"It's coming apart, Elijah," Ryan said.

"Get your blaster," the baron told him. "One-eye, get your goddamn blaster."

As Ryan crossed the floor, bullets clawed up through it, a spray of lead that chewed chunks out of the rug and gnawed at the ceiling. Ryan dived for the corner with slugs clipping at his heels.

Chapter Twenty-One

"I believe I can carry one more," Doc said, wiggling his left index finger. The old man was laden down with round and rectangular cans. He held them not only hooked over his arms, wrists, hands and fingers, but wedged under his arms, as well.

J.B. glanced over the row of metal containers that remained along the subbasement wall, checking the labels. He selected one that was nearly full and looped the handle over the old man's extended finger.

"Can we go now?" Mildred asked. She was likewise bent under the combined weight of numerous one-gallon cans. "This stuff isn't getting any lighter."

"Go on," J.B. said as he gathered up his own burden. He followed Doc and Mildred back to the elevator. At his direction they piled the selection of solvents and thinners in front of the elevator opening, alongside the others they had brought on the previous trips.

The clatter of battle rattled down the shaft.

"Seems farther away, doesn't it?" Mildred said.

"It does," Doc agreed. "Most definitely."

"The stickies are charging up the tower," J.B. said, "driving the baron's sec men ahead of them. It looks like old Elijah's going to make his last stand on the penthouse floor, which means all those chill-crazed stickies will end up jammed butt to elbow on the floor underneath, beating on the walls and ceiling trying to get in and get at him."

J.B. led his friends back through the power-plant door. The slaves didn't look glad to see him.

"Okay, let's get that car down here," he told them.

Sullenly the muties rose to the task, bracing their arms against the steel turnstile. No one pushed, though.

"Move it," J.B. ordered.

"You got to pull that lever first," Lester said. "Take it out of gear."

When J.B. hauled back on the steel handle, something clacked in the machinery above them and a big blob of black grease dripped onto the floor. The slaves started backing up, and as they did, the overhead gears turned, unwinding thick, braided steel cables from a massive drum.

"Better get out there with the blasters," J.B. told Mildred and Doc, "in case there's stickies riding in the car."

They grabbed up the autorifles and hurried out into the corridor. Bracing themselves against opposite walls, sighting down the barrels of their weapons, they bracketed the left side of the shaft. In a few seconds the bottom of the car appeared at the top of the shaft opening. The black gap grew wider and wider. Then they saw the soles of shoes facing them, then legs. They weren't moving. They belonged to two women who had been crushed at the back of the car by their fellow norms. The elevator creaked to a halt at the bottom of the shaft.

Doc and Mildred didn't have to check the bodies to know they were dead. They left them there and rejoined J.B. in the power plant.

"How long does it take for you to pull the car up to the top floors?" J.B. asked the slaves.

"Depends on how much weight is in it," Lester said. "I'd say no more than a couple hundred pounds."

"Then four, mebbe five minutes."

"What're you gonna take up there?" the gill mutie demanded. "'Cause mebbe we don't wanna move it if it's gonna chill stickies. Ever think of that? Mebbe we want them to win. They're gonna let us free."

The other mutie slaves grunted in agreement.

"Oh, it's going to chill stickies, all right," J.B. said, taking the AK from Mildred. "If they're all packed in at the top of the hotel about now, trying to slaughter the last of the norms, the baron and his sec men, I figure to nail most all of them in one swoop."

Carried away with his own eloquence, the gill mutie pounded on the spoke with his fists. "Mebbe we'll let the sec man there do all the pushing," he said. "See how long that takes."

J.B. shouldered the AK and shot the slave once in the head, blasting its brains all over the room. Other slaves ducked behind their spokes. The gill mutie's body hung from its chains, twitching.

"Anybody else want to make a fuss?" J.B. said. "Anybody else think I'm not serious here?"

The slaves glowered at him, but there were no more objections.

J.B. passed the AK back to Mildred. Then he and Doc walked back to the elevator. With the old man's help, he dragged the women's bodies out of the car, then began to fill the floor with rows of metal cans. He was very particular about their order of placement. Certain chemicals had to go against the back wall of the car, and others right up at the front. As they set down the containers, they unscrewed and discarded the lids.

"Merciful Lord," Doc said, "these vapors are making me light-headed."

"Take it easy, Doc," J.B. said. "The fumes from this stuff can be dangerous. Why don't you step out and let me finish the job."

When he was done, J.B. took two of the open cans and poured their contents over the rest. The floor of the car was puddled with accelerant.

"How are you going to ignite it?" Doc asked.

"That's all figured out, don't worry," the Armorer said, turning back for the power plant. "Let's get this show on the road."

AN ENGINE OF DESTRUCTION roared beneath the feet of the occupants of the penthouse. On the twenty-fourth floor blasterfire raged, wilder and wilder. Flurries of unaimed slugs continued to tear up through the rug, pocking the walls and ceiling. Then the battle sounds below dwindled to nothing. The only noises were shrill, individual cries of pain.

They, too, soon stopped.

"Watch the rad-blasted windows!" Ryan shouted to the still-stunned sec men. Then he snatched up a G-12 autorifle and sprinted down the hallway to the open elevator shaft. As he had expected, the stickies were coming that way. Like pale cockroaches, they crawled up the inside of the empty shaft. Some scampered up the swaying cables, while others used their suckered fingers to gain impossible handholds on the concrete walls.

Switching the G-12 to single shot, he sighted down the shaft and picked off the stickies, one by one. The mushrooming rounds didn't kill them, but the brutal slap of impact broke their grips on cable and walls, and they dropped down the shaft, twenty-five stories to their deaths.

To Ryan's surprise the cables in the left side of the shaft suddenly began to move. One set slid down and another rose up. Someone was operating the elevator. As the cables moved, they brought more stickies into Ryan's chill zone. Four of the mutants clung to the cables, riding them up from twenty-four.

Ryan flicked the fire-selector switch to full-auto. He aimed at the bottom stickie and pressed the trigger. The recoil of automatic fire raised the aim point for him, and in the process, hosed the tightly bunched stickies from bottom to top. The spray of bullets blew them off the cables and they vanished, cartwheeling, down the shaft.

A crash behind him made Ryan whirl. The duct vent in the ceiling had dropped to the floor, and a stickie was already falling through the opening.

Where there was one of the bastards, there were many.

He raked the hallway ceiling with autofire, drawing a line in lead down the center, from just above his head to the duct vent, then down to the face of the oncoming stickie. Multiple hits shattered the mutant's skull. Its legs whipped out from under it, and it flopped, kicking furiously, onto its back.

Ryan didn't really think a few slugs would keep the stickies crawling in the ceiling at bay. From his experience with the subspecies, flesh wounds only made them crazier. He knew he had to get past the opening or risk having his avenue of retreat cut off. As he ran under the duct vent, he fired the G-12 straight up, without looking. There was a shriek above and behind him, then a heavy thud as a dead mutant dropped to the floor.

He turned and knelt at the corner of the hallway. Dead and wounded stickies were falling out of the ceiling, pushed out by the live ones coming up the duct from behind. They crashed to the floor or onto the tightly packed furniture along the walls. Some struggled to get up, despite grievous injuries, throwing off the bodies of others who would never move again.

A check of his round counter told Ryan he still had

thirty bullets in the magazine. He switched the fire selector to triburst to conserve ammo. He knew it was hopeless, of course. Even if he had a case of reloading units for the G-12, even if he could keep refilling the mag as it came up empty, even if the action didn't get so hot that the entire fifty rounds cooked off every time he slapped a fresh unit home, even if he made every shot count, he was going to lose.

Knowing that made the one-eyed warrior very angry.

So mad, in fact, that it drove him past the fury to the ice-cold realm of chilling machine. As he hunkered there, his mental focus was as sharp and as deadly as a razor. Though he wasn't back in the mayhem of his jump dream, he touched on his memory of it to find a place inside himself where there was no fear, no regret, no second thoughts, where there was only the ravening will to destroy. Just like the enemies he now faced.

Though he had them in his sights, and it was an easy 150-foot shot, he let the stickies drop from the ceiling without firing a round. They poured through the vent, landing one after another, and as soon as their feet hit the floor, they started running straight at him, screaming. That was just what Ryan wanted. He wanted as many of them as possible, as close as possible to the muzzle of the G-12.

He didn't let them have it until the first stickie was ten feet away. Aiming for its center chest, he ripped off a single triburst. The three cartridges fired so quickly, so close together, that they virtually entered and exited the same hole in the target. The lead stickie crumpled, and behind it so did the next, and the next, and the next. The stickies toppled until the three rounds ran out of steam. The slugs bounced off the last mutant they hit. They knocked it down, but it got up right away and resumed the attack.

With all the bodies clogging the hallway, all those entrapping, tripping arms and legs, the stickies were forced to move more slowly and they packed themselves more tightly together as they advanced down the corridor toward him. Ryan had what seemed like a long time to stare into the face of the first stickie in the line, who had just barely escaped death and who had to know that it wouldn't be so lucky the next time. There wasn't any fear on its face, only eagerness.

Ryan reflected it back to him, like a mirror.

If chilling was what he wanted, Ryan gave it to him, with pleasure. At a range of less than four yards, he put three slugs through its heart. The same chain reaction of death followed. One after another the stickies behind absorbed the triburst, continuing to topple until the rounds lost their velocity and lethality.

The pile of dead doubled in height, creating a much greater obstacle for the stickies still dropping from the ceiling. As Ryan waited for them to scramble over the bodies and bunch up again, a woman's scream rang out behind him. It was followed by savage bursts of fire.

Ryan abandoned his position and ducked around the corner. When he entered the room adjoining the balcony, he saw stickies swarming over the patio rail. Others already had the four sec men down on the glass-littered floor, and a mad, thrashing battle was in progress.

Elijah opened fire again, tribursting his own men in order to chill the incoming stickies. Standing just inside the room, he emptied the entire 50-round reloading unit into the melee. By the time he was done, there was no one alive on the balcony.

Elijah tossed aside the empty autorifle and picked up another from the pile of gear he had confiscated from Ryan.

"They're coming!" Skeen wailed, pointing first toward the hallway, then in the opposite direction, toward an interior door that led to the baron's bedroom suite.

They were coming from every which way by now, Ryan thought. Through the windows, up the elevator, too. The corner he and the norm survivors had been backed into, had just gotten much, much smaller. It was down to one room and the balcony.

"They're gettin' ready to rush us," Ryan said. "Get away from the doorways."

The toadies started to move back from the doors, but not quickly enough. Like a pack of wolves, stickies darted out from the hallway. They snatched hold of two of the norms and dragged them around the corner, out of sight.

Neither Elijah nor Ryan could get off a shot.

With screams of the victims and the victimizers ringing in their ears, the last three toadies ducked behind Ryan and Elijah, the men with the blasters, and stepped out on the corpse-littered patio. Roonie-Two with her baby in arms slipped between Ryan and Elijah for protection.

Before the first screams had died away, fresh ones erupted from the balcony. Ryan turned and saw that a new pair of stickies had leaped over the railing and driven two of the toadies into a corner of the patio. There was nowhere for them to run, no escape from the frenzied attack.

Skeen blundered back into the room, stumbling over the threshold as Ryan one-handed the G-12, drilling rounds into the bases of the stickies' spines. They shrieked and fell, arms flailing in the air. It was too late for the toadies, though. They lay in puddles of their own gore, their throats already torn out.

Stickies charged from the bedroom door of the penthouse, making a suicide rush for the five survivors. Elijah turned them back with a full-auto burst, but only just.

Roonie-Two put a hand on her grandfather-husband's shoulder and squeezed it hard. "It's time," she said. "Chill me and the baby, Poppadaddy. Me and Three. Do it now."

When Elijah didn't move, didn't speak, she reached out and lifted the G-12 he held, putting the hot muzzle against her own temple.

The sounds of running feet echoed from the hall. The stickies were coming once more.

"Now, do it now," she wailed, looking over her shoulder with terrified eyes.

"TRY TO THINK on the bright side," J.B. told the slaves as they struggled to turn the enormous wheel. "One way or another, this is the last time you're ever going to have to do this."

Mildred was horrified and repulsed by the scene. Though she knew it was necessary, that there was no other way, it was hard for her to watch the agonized effort of the mutie slaves, to see their rad-blasted faces twisted in pain, the muscles of their naked bodies corded, shaking with the strain. As the slaves turned the wheel, wrapping the cable around the drum, it was as if they were winding a spring tighter and tighter. The more cable that filled the drum, the wider it became, and the more difficult it was to turn. The slaves were pushing as hard as they could, but merely inching the wheel around.

Doc held the clutch lever, feathering it as the gears ticked, and somewhere invisible above them, the car rose in the shaft. In the ceiling over the old man's head, the heart of the clutch, a huge steel dog, clattered against gear teeth.

The floor indicator dial said 21 and it was swinging up to 22.

Over the sounds of the slaves, the chitter of the oppressive mechanism, they could barely hear the noise of battle. It was no longer steady, but came and went, and there were long silences between bursts of gunfire.

"I'd better get to it," J.B. said when the indicator hit 23. He picked up the AK and checked the 30-round mag. There were plenty of rounds left. "Once the car gets to twenty-four, Doc," he said, "lock up the gears. And stay clear of the machinery, just in case."

The Armorer returned to the elevator shaft. When he stuck his head inside and looked up, he couldn't see the bottom of the car, but he could hear the grinding of the machinery and see the cables moving around the pulleys. He hopped into the empty shaft and lay down on his back. Dropping the fire-selector switch to full-auto, he shouldered the weapon.

As he waited for the signal, J.B. had a moment of doubt. His plan wasn't quite the sure thing he had made it out to be to Doc and Mildred. Theoretically a steel-jacketed slug passing through the floor of the car and striking the stainless-steel wall would cause a spark. Theoretically he had about twenty chances to set off the firebomb.

"Twenty-four!" Mildred called to him from the power plant.

J.B. sighted up at the center of the shaft and let the AK rip. The hard chatter of the autofire in the enclosed concrete space obliterated the sounds of the hits one hundred yards above.

But he knew right away that he'd scored.

High above him the shaft blossomed with flame, and the whole building rattled with the power of the explosion.

Chapter Twenty-Two

"Now, Poppadaddy, do it now!" Roonie-Two cried.

The baron took his fingertip out of the G-12's trigger guard. Tears streamed down his craggy face. "I can't do it, gal," he told her. "I can't chill ya. You're all I have left in the world."

"Bastard!" she shrieked at him. "You're not thinking about us. You're just thinking about yourself. Listen to what you're saying. You're still trying to keep what you got. Me and the babe, we aren't things. We hurt. Do you want us to suffer? Don't we mean anything to you? You've got to have mercy, Poppadaddy, you've got to give us up!"

Elijah shook his head.

"Coward!" Roonie-Two yelled at him. "Think of us, you miserable coward!"

"I won't do it, gal," the baron said. "I don't have it in me to harm you or that child."

Roonie-Two's face went livid. "You think we're some kind of pets, Poppadaddy? So it doesn't matter if you lock us away and starve us or leave us for the stickies? Well, I'll show you! I'll show you what we are!"

Moving with amazing speed, she darted over and

picked up the Redhawk from the floor. Without another word she poked the muzzle at the middle of Elijah's sternum and pulled the trigger. The big blaster boomed and jumped out of her hand, flying over her shoulder. As Elijah's body leaped back, flames licked up through his mass of white chest hair. He crashed into the wall, then fell forward onto his face. He was so dead he didn't even quiver. The smoking exit wound in his back was big enough to put a boot through.

Before Ryan could stop her, Roonie-Two dashed out onto the patio with her baby in her arms. She scrambled onto a tabletop, and from there to the railing. From the railing she jumped off into space, all without a pause. As she dropped, the tips of her long, corn-silk blond hair lifted straight up by the wind. Then she was gone.

"What are we going to do now?" Skeen wailed. The man was groveling on his knees, hiding behind Ryan's legs.

The one-eyed man snatched a blanket from the couch and, into the middle of it, threw an armful of the gear Elijah had confiscated. He grabbed stuff at random and when he had as much as he figured he could safely carry, he tied all four corners together in a double knot.

"What now?" Skeen repeated, rising shakily to his feet.

The world rocked without warning. The floor under their feet lifted so violently that both men crashed to the carpet. Ryan winced at the heat of the explosion; he could feel the scorching pulse right through the floor. He instinctively raised a hand to protect his sole surviving eye. Through the floor he could hear the whoosh of fire spreading through the corridors below, the squeal and sizzle of the stickies caught in the blistering shock wave.

Ryan jumped up from the carpet at once. Tongues of orange light were flicking up through the bullet holes in the floor around him, and the foam backing of the carpet was already starting to smoke and flare. He recognized the handiwork. His first thought was that maybe the Armorer wasn't dead, after all.

"Oh, no," Skeen shrilled. "They're coming again!"

Over the escalating roar of the fire, Ryan could hear the tramp of bare feet running down the hall. The stickies on their floor had recovered from the blast. As they rounded the corner, Ryan was already on the patio and he had slipped the knotted blanket over his head and under one arm, carrying the load in a sling over his back, which left both hands free for fighting and for climbing.

"Don't leave me here!" Skeen bawled.

As Ryan took hold of the rope and hopped over the railing, he looked back and saw the man kneeling in a spreading puddle of his own piss, while dozens of stickies closed in and sheets of flames swept up the walls.

AS THE ELEVATOR CAR crept up to the twenty-fourth floor, stickies jammed the long hallway on either side of the shaft. They had already ripped all the norms within reach to tiny shreds and were eager for the fresh meat they thought the car was bringing them. They stood not only on the floor, but on the couches, the chairs, on the sprawled dead bodies of their kin. After they had opened the twenty-fourth floor's fire door, stickies from the stairwell had rushed in and filled every room to the corners. There wasn't enough space between the mutants for them to move more than a few inches in any direction. Such close confinement didn't bother the stickies. They liked to bump into one another as they danced.

And they were dancing as the top of the elevator car rose up above floor level.

Almost instantly the stickies closest to the opening caught the sharp scent of spilled accelerant. Realizing that disaster was close at hand, they signaled a warning to their assembled kin.

The problem was, there wasn't room to move, no matter how pressing the danger.

The elevator continued to rise, and stickies all around the shaft opening could see the rows of bright metal cans inside and smell the volatile fumes. The ones that could see tried to take a step back and were stopped by the wall of bodies behind them.

Linked by the psychic network of Lord Kaa, all the stickies on the top two floors realized what was about to happen and froze, holding their breath as they awaited orders from the piebald general. Kaa, far from the center of the action, at the base of the hotel, scoured his book knowledge of tactics and maneuver for some way out of the predicament. In vain.

It was a checkmate. There were no possible countermoves.

All Kaa could think of was for them to duck and cover. Because his psychic command to do so was so powerful, the stickies on both floors did just that, all at once. As it turned out, neither their ducking nor their covering did much good.

Autofire crackled from the bottom of the shaft, and heavy slugs rattled the floor of the elevator, piercing the cans, scoring the stainless-steel walls and in the process sending plumes of bright sparks shooting across the interior of the vapor-filled car.

The ignition of the fuel bomb was multiple stage, thanks to the way J.B. had stacked his cans, but it happened so quickly that it sounded like a single, horrendous blast. First the trapped fumes exploded. They blew out with such force that the stickies standing closest to the car never felt the heat; they were vaporized by the shock wave. The elevator car acted like a crude cannon, focusing the blast out its open doorway. The initial explosion sent the lidless cans of solvent flying out the door. As they flew, they tumbled, trailing flammable liquid and even-more-flammable vapor. Some cans ricocheted off the walls of the hall before exploding. None escaped the ignition temperature of the primary blast.

Fireballs swept down the hallway in both directions.

The heat was so intense that everything in its path exploded, living bodies, couches, chairs, walls.

The stickies at the ends of the hall were far enough away so they weren't instantly incinerated. They had their arms melted to the tops of their heads. The fortunate ones inhaled in order to scream, and in so doing, drew searing-hot gases into their lungs, which cooked in a heartbeat, making them instantly dead.

The mutants protected from the initial blast by the hotel's interior walls couldn't escape the raging fire that followed, even if they had wanted to. And it appeared that they didn't want to. The thousands that survived the explosion continued to dance, gibber and drool as the flames consumed those dancing right next to them.

It was so hot at the core of the blast that the metal frame of the elevator doorway began to melt. The I-beam girders of the car glowed incandescent red through the stainless-steel walls, as did the concrete lining of the elevator shaft. With a groan, the cable system on the roof of the car sheared and gave way, and the burning hulk plunged back down the shaft, this time in free-fall.

A HALF SECOND after the firebomb blew, the powerplant room rocked. The lifting cable snapped hard against the windings on the drum. The powerful jolt shook the whole apparatus; the spokes moved, driving the slaves back a step even though they had their bodies braced. Grease sprayed down on them from the meshed gears in the ceiling. Doc leaned on the clutch lever, making sure the dog stayed in place.

Mildred was looking at the quivering floor indicator when J.B. raced back into the room.

"It worked!" he said jubilantly. "Dark night, that was one sweet fireball!"

"I'm curious, John Barrymore," Doc said, "at what temperature does your petroleum-distillate cocktail burn?"

"Oh, it's hot," he said. "Rad-blasted hot. Mebbe six thousand degrees, mebbe more."

The slaves stood and dared to relax, leaning against the spokes.

"You did good work," J.B. told them. "We just fried a whole shitload of stickies."

The only one who looked happy about it was Lester.

Then they heard the groaning sound from above.

"What's that?" Mildred said.

There was no time for an answer, even if J.B. or Doc had had one—which they hadn't. The severed elevator cable came exploding back through the hole in the ceiling. The tension on the winding drum sprang loose and the gears overhead ground together. Doc tried to hold the clutch lever back only to have it jerk from his hands with such force that it snapped off at the base. The steel bar shot across the room and hit a slave square in the face, practically beheading it.

J.B. dived at Mildred, pinning her against the wall with a shoulder.

Without a clutch there was nothing to stop the great

wheel from turning. And turn it did, going from zero to one hundred revolutions per minute in the blink of an eye.

Chained to the whirling spokes, the helpless slaves were lashed and battered against floor and ceiling. And then the elevator car, which dropped from the top of the hotel, slammed into the bottom of the shaft. The impact did something to the alignment of the machinery. Sparks showered from the ceiling, then the whirling gears broke loose. They dropped like giant buzz saws into the spokes of the wheel, and the room was instantly full of shards of metal and chunked slaves.

J.B., Doc and Mildred hurriedly backed through the doorway. Flames from the crushed elevator car billowed out into the hall. Their hands shielded their faces from the intense heat.

"At least you didn't lie to those unfortunates, John Barrymore," Doc said as they searched for a staircase leading up.

"How's that?"

"You promised the poor bastards they'd never have to turn the wheel again."

RYAN LOCKED HIS ANKLES around the rope and slid down from the penthouse. Thirty or so stickies were on the balcony of the 24th floor, having a dance-in-place party. Without music. Or maybe there was music, but only they could hear it. Ryan stopped just out of their reach. They weren't paying him any mind. Wildly gyrating, waving their arms, they were watching the fire race through the floor they were on. They didn't seem to realize that the rope on which Ryan hung was their only hope of escape. Or if they did, they didn't try to jump for it.

He could see more of them inside the smoke-filled rooms, hundreds, perhaps thousands, dancing as they burned up. It was as if they were unable to break the spell of the flames.

As Ryan slid down below the level of the balcony, another explosion ripped the air just over his head. And it was suddenly raining stickies, burning stickies. The intense heat had blown out the balcony's glass slider and with it, the patio full of naked stickies. Ryan was blocked from the withering wall of flame by the building, but not from the falling mutants. He clung to the rope as their bodies bumped him on the way down, living comets hurtling to earth.

When he looked up, he saw that the heat surge between floors had been so hot that it had started his rope on fire. He loosened the grip of his ankles around the line and let himself slide faster. The friction ripped the hell out of his palms as he tried to control his fall. He dropped past balcony after balcony, but he didn't see any more stickies—any more signs of life inside, period. The mutants had swept up through the hotel, slaughtering everyone they found.

Below him, about ten stories, a couple of straggler stickies hung on to the rope. They weren't climbing; they were just hanging there, blocking his path. And tripling the amount of weight on the flaming rope.

Ryan could've drawn the Redhawk, which he'd tucked into the back of his trouser's waistband, but shooting them would've meant stopping and aiming and maybe missing what with the way the rope was swaying. So he took a page from the sandbag success earlier and just loosened the grip of his hands a bit more.

He rocketed down the rope, digging the sides of his boot heels into it to take some of the pressure off his tortured hands. When he was within fifteen feet of the stickies, he swung his boots out to shoulder width. It was an uncontrolled dead fall.

The soles of his boots crashed into the top stickie's head, and for a second the mutant's body resisted, then its suckered grip failed, and the first stickie plus Ryan—about 350 pounds of total weight—fell on top of the stickie hanging on to the rope below. Again there was a split second of resistance, then everything started sliding.

Ryan clamped his hands tightly around the rope and dug in the sides of his boot heels. He kept on sliding. He knew there was a critical speed, and once he passed it, nothing he could do would keep him from falling. He squeezed tighter, feeling the skin of his palms and the insides of his fingers rip off. And he was still sliding.

He dropped down seven stories before he got himself slowed and under control. Meanwhile the stickies beneath him had tumbled to the parking lot below. He lowered himself to the end of the rope, then dropped the ten feet to the ground.

The last pair of stickies wasn't dead. Jaws snapping, heads bloodied, limbs broken, they tried to crawl over to get him.

"Fireblast!" he said, reaching behind his back for the walnut grips of the Redhawk.

"Wait, Ryan," a familiar voice said behind him. "Let me."

J.B., Doc and Mildred were running toward him from the hotel lobby. The Armorer held an Armalite between his hands. He stepped up and fired at extreme close range, putting a round in each stickie's head.

"Look out!" Mildred cried, pushing Ryan back.

Twenty-four stories of rope dropped from the sky and landed in loose coils on top of the dead stickies. The last thirty feet of it were still burning.

They looked up at the top of the hotel, which was now engulfed in flames. Black, greasy smoke was floating east, on the hot afternoon wind.

"Nice job, J.B.," Ryan said.

"It was inspired," Doc agreed. "The work of a pyrotechnic genius, if not a pyromaniac."

Ryan extricated himself from the makeshift sling, set it on the ground and untied it. The first thing he took out was J.B.'s fedora, which he handed to his old friend. "Thought you might want that back," he said.

"Dark night, I never thought I'd see it again!" J.B. donned the hat and adjusted the rake of the brim.

Ryan looked with concern at Mildred. She was staring up at the burning hotel, as if mesmerized. He put his hand on her shoulder. "Mildred, are you okay?"

"Uh, yes. Yes, I'm okay," she said, coming out of her trance. "I was having another flashback from the jump." She closed her eyes and shuddered. When she opened them, she noticed his injuries for the first time. "Ryan, your hands!" she said. "They need immediate attention. They look like ground chuck."

"There's no time for that," he said, passing out the rest of the weapons. He tucked Krysty's Smith and Wesson pistol in his back trouser pocket. "We've got to find Krysty and Jak. They could still be alive."

"Let's go check out the zoo," J.B. suggested.

"Watch your step," Ryan told them. "These stickies might look dead, but they can fool you. Blast anything that moves."

The four companions retraced the route the stickie army had taken to the hotel. They walked along the edge of the golf course, past its still-smoking blast craters. The path was littered with broken bodies. Some of them weren't stickies. Some were muties wearing ankle chains.

Mildred knelt and looked at the lethal wounds with the trained eye of a medical doctor. "Some of these slaves were chilled by stickies," she said. "I think Kaa had some trouble making his dream of a noble brotherhood of mutants into a reality."

"Like the tower of Babel," Doc said. He didn't bother to explain the reference, and no one asked him to. They had much more important things on their minds.

"Do you think Kaa was in the top of the hotel when it went up?" J.B. asked.

"I didn't see him." Ryan said. "But then I wasn't looking real hard, either. If he was up there, he's chilled—unless he grew wings."

When they passed the bank where Elijah kept his Apocalypticon, they found the front doors open and paper litter blowing through the foyer. Doc picked up a single, torn sheet of paper that wrapped itself around his shin. He cleared his throat and read the page title aloud. "'Reserve Component 071-315-2304. Zero AN/PVS-2 to an M-16 A-1 Rifle.'" Then he said, "I think our mutant commander has made off with the baron's prized collection of predark documents."

"Then mebbe he never went up in the hotel," J.B. said. "Mebbe he's still alive."

"Could be," Ryan said as they continued on.

It was odd seeing Willie ville so devoid of life, so quiet. Except for the whistling of the wind and the crunch of their boots on the dirt, there was no sound. A half hour before, the place had been thriving, one of the few jewels of Deathlands' human civilization. Now it was just another stinking boneyard.

They came upon the trampled length of intestine as they walked up the path to the zoo entrance. The doors to the building were open, as were all the cells they could see from the doorway.

Open and empty. The place was as still as a tomb.

Ryan's faint, desperate hope of finding and rescuing his red-haired lover began to evaporate.

They walked around the ravaged corpse of the zoo-keeper, then split up to quickly check both of the long corridors. On Ryan and Doc's side of the zoo, all the cage doors were open and no one was home. J.B. and Mildred returned alone from the other side of the zoo.

"They're not here," J.B. stated.

Chapter Twenty-Three

Over her shoulder, in the distance, Krysty could see the pall of black smoke rising from the top of the Freedom City Motor Hotel and Casino. Even though the wind was blowing the smoke at right angles to the highway, the nasty, charred plastic and overroasted-meat smell of it surrounded her. Ryan was still back there at the ville, along with Mildred, J.B., and Doc, probably dead, she thought dully. Their burned flesh was probably part of the stink she smelled. Krysty felt too numbed to grieve for them. So many had died. So quickly.

Soot particles and bits of ash peppered her face, arms and hair. She shifted the awkward load she carried to her opposite shoulder. The underside of the black plastic bag was sweaty where it had rubbed against her. The bulky pile of documents inside the sack banged against her lower back on every step.

Jak walked by her side. He, too, carried a plastic bag stuffed with papers and books. All the muties who accompanied Lord Kaa on his retreat from Willie ville, twenty in all, were loaded down with the liberated treasure of the Apocalypticon. Even the mutie mountain lion had a bulging bag tied across its back. They slinked away from the burning ville, led by their pie-bald leader.

Though Lord Kaa had won the battle for Willie ville, that victory had cost him everything. Virtually his entire army had been caught in the top of the tower when the fires broke out. Though he had fallen into an even more violent foaming, thrashing fit, there was nothing he could do with his third eye to save his troops from destruction.

Because they didn't want to be saved.

The power blood and flame had over them was greater than the power of his love, his vision, his integrity. He couldn't convince his stickies to run. He couldn't make them even descend one floor to escape their horrible fate. Their instinctive drives negated every mental image he sent them. The long view, the big picture he provided, no longer mattered when there was that much gore and smoke in the air.

Kaa had taken the loss hard; it had drained him both physically and mentally. Krysty could see it in the way he held his head, his shoulders, in his gait. He really cared for his troops. He felt he had let them down terribly, that he hadn't done his job, hadn't protected them from themselves. Seeing him like that, in such internal pain and torment, made her want to cry. But she couldn't muster tears for him.

Whatever Kaa's plans had been, whatever campaign he had in mind after the victory at Willie ville, they had gone up in flames along with the top of the hotel. He no longer had an army. He had a platoon made up

of former zoo inmates, most of whom were the products of the half-baked genetic experiments of Baron
Willie Elijah. They were headed south down the highway, in the direction of the way stop and the redoubt.
No one asked any questions of their leader. They just
followed the piebald giant, a flock of sheep trailing
behind a broken-hearted shepherd.

When they came to the first collapsed overpass, Lord
Kaa led them around the obstacle. Ahead, on the dirt
path, they could see the pit trap, its limbs and branches
caved in. He stopped at the edge.

There was movement down there, and as Lord Kaa's
long shadow passed over the hole, a chorus of an-
guished cries rang out.

He removed the shoulder strap from his M-60 and
lowered it down into the pit. One by one the mutant
general lifted out a dozen naked stickies. As he did, he
passed his hand over their bald heads. Their feet and
ankles, and their legs up to the shins, were covered
with dirt-encrusted gore. When Krysty peeked over the
edge of the pit, she saw the muddy bottom and red,
raw shards of bone sticking up from the trampled
muck.

Kaa's touch seemed to calm the stickies who pressed
around his knees with lowered heads. Because of the
psychic network, they knew exactly what had happened
to their kin; they knew that they were the only survivors of the once great and glorious army. After a minute of his laying on of hands and their soft whimpering,

they drew back and stood. They stared at the group of zoo muties with their dead, unblinking eyes.

One of the stickies broke off from the pack and circled around to approach Jak and Krysty from behind. When they turned toward the stickie, it moved quickly away and hunkered down, sniffing the air in the direction of the mutie lion's backside. The stickie was curious about the huge beast, but cautious. However, when the lion didn't appear to object to being examined in this way, the stickie grew bolder and got right in its face, breathing in the rotten-meat fumes directly from its mouth.

The lion moved faster than any of their eyes could follow, swatting the stickie on the side of the head with its forepaw. The pale mutant cartwheeled across the path, landing finally on its face. It rose up, shaking its head and blinking rapidly, bruised but alive. The mutie cat grinned and licked the pad of its foot. It had struck with sheathed claws. If it had used them, the stickie would've been dead in a heap in the dirt instead of scrambling back to its agitated kin.

Kaa made the former zoo inmates put down their burdens. Then he went through the bags, dividing up the Apocalypticon so its weight could be shared among all the muties. A few loose papers blew out and fluttered across the highway. He made no attempt to recover them. Each of his people carried one half-full bag of documents. With their loads lightened, the ragtag force moved off at a faster clip to the south. From the increase in the pace he set, it appeared that Kaa had a particular destination in mind, even if he wasn't sharing it with them.

It didn't occur to Jak or Krysty that nothing was stopping them from escaping; they could have slipped to the back of the file, dropped their loads and hidden in the weeds until the others moved off. They were fascinated by Kaa, by what he had tried to do, by the hope he still offered. And by the dignity and grace with which he bore his great tragedy, the loss of his army.

RYAN DEFTLY PICKED his way up the rubble pile on the back side of the fallen overpass. He jumped from block to block until he reached the coils of hurricane wire that blocked its summit. He gripped the wire and stared down the long, straight stretch of six-lane highway. "Something's moving down the road," he said over his shoulder.

J.B. joined him at the wire. Tipping down the brim of his fedora to block the sun's glare off the roadway, he squinted at the tiny moving dots in the distance.

"Could be them," he said. "I just thought I saw a flash of white. Mebbe Jak's head in the sun."

"Ryan, my dear fellow," Doc said from behind them, "look what Mildred's found."

When Ryan looked over at the woman, she waved a couple of sheets of crumpled paper at him.

"More stuff from the Apocalypticon," she said. "It's got to be Kaa up ahead."

"Looks like they're goin' back the way they came," J.B. observed. "Mebbe all the way back to the redoubt." He stared at the dots on the horizon again. They were much smaller than they were only a moment ago. "They're really moving. We're not going to be able to catch them unless they slow down or take a rest stop."

"If Krysty and Jak are still alive," Ryan said, watching the distant figures as they vanished into the mercury lake of the heat mirage, "they're probably up there with Kaa, if that's him."

"One thing, Ryan, mebbe you hadn't thought about," J.B. said.

"What's that?"

"Mebbe they don't want to be rescued."

JAK CLIMBED through the hatch in the roof of the redoubt's only functional elevator. The mutie mountain lion, his inseparable companion, stood in the car on its rear legs. Stretching up against the wall, it was almost tall enough to stick its nose through the hatch.

Almost wasn't good enough.

It let out a baleful yowl.

When Jak lowered his head upside down, back through the hole, it stopped making the horrible noise and smiled at him.

"Can you fix it?" Lord Kaa asked.

"No problem," Jak replied. "Have to find thing J.B. disconnected." He withdrew again. After a moment he yelled down, "This it."

The car jerked as power returned to its motor.

At Kaa's direction all the plastic bags were loaded

into the back of the car. There wasn't enough room in the elevator for everyone to ride on the first trip, so he left the stickies to wait on the top floor. The zoo muties and Jak and Krysty got in with him, and they started down. The damaged car screeched and shuddered as it scraped against the shaft's wall.

Kaa caught Krysty staring at the explosive scorches and bullet holes that marred the inside of the car. He hadn't asked her or her ruby-eyed young friend about the dead stickies heaped in the elevator when it awaited them on the top level. But he wondered about them.

He also wondered why no more stickies had used the redoubt's gateway to transfer here. Though he hadn't considered the possibility of losing 99.9 percent of the army in its first day in the field, he had thought enough about casualties to be continuously breeding replacements. The plan had been for fresh troops to come through the gateway as soon as they were of a size suitable for combat.

No stickie replacements had been present on the first floor. No live ones, at least. Even if the first batch or two of new soldiers were the ones they'd found chilled in the car, more of them should have materialized. Of course, it was possible that they were trapped in the lower stories by the decommissioned elevator.

Kaa peeled open his third eye and had an internal look-see.

He quickly confirmed the fact that there were stickies in the redoubt, but no more than twenty. And as he had guessed, they were all down on the bottom floor. There should have been at least a hundred of them by now. After opening a psychic connection to his lost soldiers, he showed them where to meet him.

Then he squeezed his lids shut.

He had no way of telling whether the white-haired boy and the red-haired female were responsible for the deaths of his troops in the redoubt. By their own admission, they had been here only days before; they had admitted to nothing else yet. Under the circumstances, he didn't hold the slaughter against them. As well as anyone in Deathlands, and perhaps better, Kaa knew that stickies outside his sphere of psychic control, such as the ones who'd transferred in after he'd left, would be incredibly dangerous. The only way to deal with them would be to chill them, and quickly, before they chilled you.

When they reached the fifth floor down, the lowest level of the redoubt, a crowd of stickies was waiting in front of the elevator for them. They were most excited to see Kaa, their mighty general. They wanted to touch his piebald skin and for him to touch them.

As Kaa stepped out of the car, he glanced at the other side of the elevator shaft, at the car crushed by impact with the ground. It was sprinkled with stickies so dead and stiff they might have been cardboard cutouts. He pushed the living soldiers away from his legs and in a loud and distinct voice, ordered them to help carry the bags out of the back of the car.

They trooped in a ragged file back across the lower level of the redoubt, under the low, acoustic-tile ceiling and the banks of sputtering fluorescent lights. At Kaa's direction they deposited the bags on the floor beside the open door to the gateway.

The odor of death was thick and noxious, despite the hum of the nuke-powered air-filtration system. That was because the source of the pollution was still inside the mat-trans chamber. Kaa could see the soles of bare feet, already blackened by decay.

The chamber door was standing wide open, which, he thought, could have explained why no more reinforcements had arrived. Without a closed circuit at this end, the book had said it was very dangerous to send anything living through the system. Perhaps that's why there were so many dead inside. Had the last stickie out of the chamber forgotten to shut the door? Stickies were capable of great thickheadedness, especially when excited.

Kaa stuck his head in the chamber and saw the sprawled bodies of half a dozen stickies. He knew right away they weren't mat-trans casualties because they didn't have the telltale marks of a failed rematerialization—incomplete heads, fingers, toes. These stickies had been hacked to death, their skulls broken apart by multiple blows by a sharp, heavy weapon, a cleaver or machete. Quite violent blows, from the look of them. Two of the stickies had their arms cut off at the elbows.

"Get them out of there," Kaa said. "And get something to mop up the mess." The blood, vomit and excrement in the chamber was still in a semiliquid state. Before they used the gateway again, it needed to be completely swabbed out. Either that or they risked arriving at their destination coated head to foot with a fine film of the stuff.

The zoo muties rummaged around in the surrounding rows of desks and came up with various paper products, some more absorbent than others. They set to work inside the chamber.

"You," Kaa said to Jak, "what do you know about all this chilling?"

The white-haired teen didn't lie and he didn't beat around the bush. He looked up at the mutant giant and said, "Was us or them. They didn't give us choice." He leaned over and pulled out one of his little black throwing knives from the throat of a dead stickie. He wiped off the blade on a desk blotter. "We were just trying get out here," he said. "Stickies didn't want to let us."

Kaa looked at his Angelica, who nodded. It was the truth, and he accepted it.

"I understand," Kaa said to Jak. "You had no choice. Regrettable, but there's nothing more to be said." He watched the cleanup for a minute or two, then he said to Jak, "I want you to go up in the elevator and bring the rest of the stickies down here to me."

"Lion come, too?"

"If he wants to," Kaa said, "but don't let him smack around any more of the stickies. They don't like it."

"Can't blame 'em for that," Jak said. He trotted off for the elevator with the lion at his side.

When the teenager was gone, Kaa took Krysty's

wrist and led her away from the others. She followed willingly. "Sit, Angelica," he said, indicating one of the office chairs behind a desk. She sat, gazing up at him expectantly with her clear green eyes.

"I want to finish the conversation I started in the Apocalypticon vault," he told her. "I said that you are important to the future of the new people of Deathlands, but I didn't explain why. Now is the time for me to do so. I told you back in Willie ville about my worst fear, that I might succeed in uniting our land and its people during my lifetime, but that once I die, it will all pass into chaos again."

"I remember," Krysty said.

"Good." He smiled at her warmly. "From my study of the treasures of the Apocalypticon, I've learned one of the secrets of history. There is a single key to the forging of an empire that will outlast its creator. And that is, the siring of a true heir. In this case, one who carries Armageddon's gift of the third, all-seeing eye, one who believes in freedom and respect for all the mutant peoples. If a true heir does not appear to carry the standard, our noble cause is lost just as it begins."

"I understand," she said.

"Angelica, you and I will give our people such a prince, a prince to lead them into the future. He will be the fruit of our coupled loins."

"Does it have to be a prince?" she asked.

Kaa's brows furrowed in momentary confusion. "What?"

"Couldn't it be a princess?" Krysty said.

He laughed. "Yes, of course. External sexual characteristics don't matter in the least. It is the seeing and the believing that matters, and possessing the will to complete the task." He caught both her hands in his. They were lost between his huge palms. "I ask you, Angelica, will you bear my offspring? My prince or princess? Will you help me breathe life into my beautiful dream?"

Tears rolled down Krysty's cheeks. She was surprised to discover that she was no longer afraid of giving birth to a gaggle of monsters, needle toothed or otherwise. Monsters were long-suffering, noble, ill-used, capable of greatness, as Kaa had proved. Not degenerate, but evolving. If what he proposed was her destiny, who was she to question it?

"It would be my honor," she said, and she kissed the back of his hairless hand.

By the time Jak returned with the stickies, the zoo muties had scrubbed out the gateway chamber. Kaa ordered the plastic bags moved into the mat-trans unit and when they were inside, he said, "There's only room for four travelers this first jump. Angelica, you will of course accompany me."

"I want Jak to come with us," she said.

Kaa nodded.

"And lion?" Jak asked.

"Of course."

Kaa cracked open the chamber's control panel and made a few necessary adjustments so they could reach their intended destination. Krysty and Jak joined him inside the gateway, but the lion refused to enter the chamber with them. It stood outside, roared ferociously and swiped at the air with its paw. And when Jak wouldn't come out, the lion tried to entice him by leaping around playfully and chasing its tail.

"I don't want to leave him," Jak said.

"It'll be all right," Kaa assured him. "It'll be safe here with the others. We'll be back shortly with another group of stickies, and you can rejoin it then."

Jak stuck his head out of the chamber door, and the lion licked him from neck to forehead.

Then Lord Kaa pulled the door closed. Because the door was shut, he didn't hear the clack and whine of the elevator as it started back up for the surface.

RYAN AND HIS FRIENDS lost sight of their quarry as evening fell over the long valley. They had followed them down the highway for many, many hours. It was all they could do to dog their trail; they were unable to make up any of the ground that separated them because the muties kept up such a chiller pace. Before they lost them in the lengthening purple shadows of the slope leading to the redoubt, Ryan and the others did get a better view of the people they were tracking, a view unobstructed by haze, glare and mirage. It was pretty obvious to all of them that Jak and Krysty were in the group, and that Kaa was in the lead. He loomed so much larger than the others, they looked like children tagging along behind him.

They were too far away to be able to tell if Krysty

and Jak were being held at blasterpoint, or if they were tied or chained to the others.

Ryan figured they were at least twenty minutes behind Kaa, which translated into almost a two-mile gap at their current pace. He didn't dare drive his companions any faster; he couldn't really, since they were pushing themselves as hard as they could go. If they pressed further, they wouldn't have anything left for the fight, when it came to that. And he knew it would.

When they neared the entrance to the redoubt, they slowed. It was always possible that they had been seen and that Kaa had left an ambush behind for them. They advanced in leapfrog fashion up to the bunker that housed the redoubt's double entrance doors.

The doors were open.

Ryan went in first, his G-12 up and ready. He found the passageway empty except for the Mitsuki Meatball, which stood where they had abandoned it two nights before. Ryan closed the distance to the armored personnel vehicle on a dead run, then peered around its rear end. He saw nothing—no rear guard, no sentries. He waved for his friends to come up.

As they rounded each right-angle turn of the passage, they prepared to face the enemy. At each turn they saw only empty space leading up to the next zig in the road. They paused about three-quarters of the way down the twisting ramp to catch their breaths from the half mile of consecutive wind sprints.

"What do you think Kaa's up to?" Mildred asked.

"There's only one thing here that could interest him," Ryan said, "and that's the mat-trans chamber."

"So, he's going to take his Apocalypticon and jump the hell out of here?" J.B. asked.

"Wouldn't you?" Ryan said. "He's got no more army, so he can't go after the other barons around here. In fact he's got so few troops that he'd be pretty easy pickings for even the weakest of them. I'd say he's going back where he came from, wherever that is, to regroup, to lick his wounds. Mebbe to build up his forces again."

"It seems what you're saying," Doc said, "is that we can expect to run into the piebald man again."

"Exactly," Ryan replied. "He came real close to getting everything he wanted out of Willie ville. If it hadn't been for J.B.'s pyro cocktail, he'd be on his way to Byrum ville by now, with his army intact. Mebbe even bigger, if the slaves joined up. This Kaa's no stupe. You can bet he knows that he missed the gold ring by about a whisker and a half. Next time he won't be making the same mistakes."

"And if he raises another army of stickies," Mildred said, "we could be looking at the same trouble all over again."

"It's not 'if,' Mildred," Ryan said, "it's 'when.' Because as sure as we're standing here, he's already thinking up how he's going to pull it off."

"We got to stop him cold, then," J.B. stated.

"That's what I intend on doing," Ryan told him.

"Get our friends back safe, and then chill the rad-blasted bastard once and for all."

They moved forward again, and kept on moving down the ramp until they came to the entrance of the first level of the redoubt. Ryan gestured for them to stay back behind the edge of the opening. He poked his head out for a look-see and jerked it right back.

"Stickies," he whispered. "Lots of them. Over by the elevator. We might have to chill them to get to it."

"Shh," J.B. said. "Hear that noise? It's the elevator. They got it running again."

Ryan peeked around the corner. When the elevator doors opened with a chime sound, he was pretty sure who had got the machine going again. Jak stepped out of the car and said something to the stickies that Ryan couldn't make out. The stickies weren't looking at the teenager; they were concerned about the huge lion that stood behind him. Jak waved for the stickies to join him in the car and they did so, staying as far away from the lion as they could get. The elevator doors closed, and the arrow indicator over the lintel lit up and pointed down.

Ryan stepped out of the shadows. The first level was deserted now. There was nothing to stop them from crossing it on a run. When they arrived at the elevators, Ryan told them what he'd seen.

"Young Jak gone over to the enemy?" Doc said with dismay. "That's a development that pains me sorely."

"No doubt about it, Doc," Ryan said. "He fixed the elevator. He was running it for the stickies."

"Doesn't mean he was doing it willingly, though," J.B. said. "Dark night, Ryan, they could have Krysty downstairs, threatening to chill her if he doesn't do what Kaa says."

"That's true enough," Mildred said. "I don't think we should jump to any conclusions about anyone changing their loyalties."

"Excellent point, Dr. Wyeth," Doc said. "For all we know, the youth may be under any number of compulsions to obey the piebald man, some of them might even be unconscious. That Kaa has a hypnotic way to him."

"I think it's time we took the war to Mr. Kaa," Ryan said. He pushed the elevator's call button. Somewhere deep in the bowels of the redoubt, a powerful motor responded. The elevator began to climb.

"What if he isn't expecting more company?" Mildred said. "When the doors open, we're going to face a firing squad."

"This time we're the firing squad," Ryan said. "Just follow my lead."

The four companions had the elevator bracketed from every angle when the doors finally opened on their floor. The car was empty. They dashed into it.

"What floor?" J.B. asked, his thumb hovering over the control panel, ready to stab.

"Bottom," Ryan said. "Hit five. I'm bettin' that Kaa has made a beeline straight for the gateway."

The car descended hesitantly, amid squeakings and screechings. When it passed the fourth level down,

Ryan dropped to his belly on the floor of the car. The others did the same. He double-checked his autorifle's round counter and then flipped off the safety. J.B., Doc and Mildred did the same with their blasters.

Ryan gave them a terse word of advice as the chime toned and the doors whooshed apart.

"Don't miss," he said.

When the doors opened, there were plenty of targets to go around. Dozens of stickies scampered around the rows of desks that lay on either side of the broad strip of gray linoleum. Muties armed with the dead baron's blasters stood over by the gateway. Before the doors were all the way open, they started spraying lead across the level. Their unaimed fire pocked the walls around the shaft, spanged the back of the car, but didn't come close to hitting the belly-down foursome, which opened fire at once.

Ryan had his G-12 set on triburst. He chopped down three of the closest stickies, sending them flopping to the linoleum, spurting blood from devastating chest wounds. Then he raised his sights in order to silence the baron's machine pistols. He put the scope's cross hairs on the chest of the most active mutie and fired. The three rounds punched a single hole between its sagging, purple-tipped breasts. The scalie's arms flew back, rag-doll style. The Beretta 12-S hurtled off across the room, and the scalie slumped onto its backside on the floor.

Mildred worked her own special brand of lethal magic with her Czech target pistol. Firing single shots, she head-blasted six stickies in a row without a miss. Three of the muties died instantly, toppling as though their strings had been cut. One of the remaining three, blinded in both eyes by the crossways through-and-through of the .38-caliber slug, turned and ran in the opposite direction, slamming into the edge of a desk and skidding sideways behind it. The other two got up with blood pouring out of their heads and continued their charge at the elevator.

Doc sighted down the massive bulk of his Le Mat pistol and touched off the .63-caliber barrel. The single shot amidships blew the right-hand stickie onto its bare behind. He followed up on the survivor with three balls from the Le Mat's built-in revolver. The .44-caliber balls shattered the stickie's pelvis and hip joints. It, too, sat down suddenly on the floor. Neither of them could get up; though they tried, all they could do was flap their arms and scream.

The withering fire from the elevator made the gateway's defenders break ranks. Stickies took off across the complex in all directions. The muties with guns also deserted their posts, scattering out of sight behind the rows of gunmetal gray desks.

The one mutie who stayed behind had a bright idea.

It jumped into the mat-trans unit.

"Back me up," Ryan said. He got to his feet and raced across the complex. Somebody shot at him, but the bullets went high and wide, shattering a bank of fluorescent tubes to his right. Answering fire, single shots that had to have come from Mildred, silenced the shooter long before Ryan reached the gateway chamber.

No way was he going to let one of Kaa's men make a jump and warn his master who and what was coming down the pipe. Ryan snatched the chamber door before it could be closed to trigger a jump.

The would-be jumper, a grubby-looking swampie, held a beat-up hand-blaster in his fist. The action of the autopistol was locked back. The weapon was out of beans.

Ryan didn't shoot him. He just reached over and grabbed the little creature by the greasy roots of its hair and jerked it bodily out of the chamber. The swampie crashed to the linoleum outside.

As Doc and J.B. crossed the room to join them, something big and yellow dashed across their field of view. They both opened fire, Doc with the revolver portion of his Le Mat, J.B. with his 12-gauge scattergun. Neither man came close to hitting the great beast. With an irritated yowl it vanished behind the rows of desks.

KRYSTY FELL through darkness. Her sense of rapid, uncontrolled descent didn't come from her whizzing past anything stationary—the space she occupied was devoid of landmarks, beacons, signposts. It came from a sinking feeling in her gut, a rushing sensation against her skin, a fluttering wind against the tight coils of her hair. She was completely at the mercy of gravity, unable to make meaningful progress in any direction, except down.

She was grateful when she lost consciousness.

Then she began to dream.

The figure of a woman loomed over her, backlit by a supernova, rays of incandescent light shooting out from the tips of her writhing hair.

It was Krysty's birth mother, Sonja Wroth. She could tell by the voice.

"Come here, child," Mother Sonja said in tones both soothing and tender, arms stretched wide to take her in and comfort her.

Krysty tried to go to her waiting mother, but she could hardly move. She was connected to things behind her, things that held her back, things that rattled and clanked, things that scraped and tinkled. She looked over her shoulder. Strings were tied to her clothes, her hair, her fingers, her arms, her legs, her ankles, her toes; they stretched back for miles. There was no end to them. And knotted along their lengths every few feet along the way were objects of assorted types: tin cans, empty bottles, cartridge casings, homemade straw dolls, hubcaps, long-playing records, sunglasses. Bright bits of rubbish fanned out as far as she could see.

"Come on, child," Mother Sonja said. "You must hurry. We are late."

"Mother," Krysty sobbed, "I can't. Help me."

She stood there shaking, eyes downcast, afraid to look straight into her mother's light, light that grew brighter as Sonja descended and came closer.

"This you do not need," her mother said. "Nor this. Nor this."

At her words the strings began to break. And as they did, Krysty realized that they weren't only holding her back, but they were holding her down. She began to rise up in the air, tethered only by a few remaining lines. Behind and below her, she dragged answering machines, VCRs, candelabras, wax fruit, napkin rings, cans of paint.

At her mother's touch, these, too, broke away. And Krysty rose from the flat dark plain, hurtling faster and faster toward distant pinpoints of light.

KRYSTY AWOKE ON THE FLOOR of the gateway chamber with her stomach knotted in cramps. Fighting back the pain, she pushed up into a sitting position. Jak was dry-heaving on his hands and knees, his long white hair swaying over his face. There were many black plastic bags in the chamber. And one other person.

Krysty had thought she'd dreamed him.

He was enormous. His white skin was blotched with velvety brown patches. He was hairless and practically naked. All that covered his private parts was a knotted and filthy loincloth.

Lord Kaa rolled over on his back, still struggling against the aftereffects of the jump. His third eye was closed, but the lids had slipped apart, leaving a gap between them. She could see the glistening white surface of the blind orb.

Krysty backed as far away from the piebald mutant

as the chamber would allow. She could see things squirming just under the surface of his skin, wormlike creatures, crawling at high speed. Her first thought was that they had to be some kind of rad-mutated internal parasite. The smell of him in the enclosed space made her head spin. Not just rank and cheesy after the normal fashion of Deathlands, but fishy and putrid like the stickies he was always stroking so fondly. Krysty wasn't exactly sure what she was doing in the chamber or how she had gotten there, but she knew that she and Jak were in great danger.

"Jak! Jak!" she whispered.

The teenager had his forehead pressed to the floor and was trying to puke up meals he'd eaten a week ago. He was in no condition to help.

Then Krysty saw the neon-colored M-60 lying on the gateway floor. There were no other weapons visible in the chamber, so she grabbed it. It was very heavy, and she couldn't hope to lift it, along with the attached belt of linked 7.62 mm cartridges, without a surge of Gaia powers. She had only just found the safety and moved it from Safe to Fire and was looking for something to prop the barrel on when a huge hand gripped the barrel and gently but firmly took the machine gun away from her.

"You shouldn't play with that, Angelica," Kaa said to her. "Joyeuse bites."

Chapter Twenty-Four

Ryan stood sentry along with Doc outside the redoubt's armory. Inside, J.B. and Mildred were trying to open the vanadium safe that housed the armory's baby nuke. They had been at it for what seemed like a long time.

"Tough nut to crack, eh?" Doc said.

"Mebbe impossible," Ryan agreed.

Way down the long hallway they guarded, a shadowy, skinny-limbed figure darted from one doorway to another. The flickering of the overhead fluorescent lighting created a kind of stop-action, strobe effect. Ryan braced his caseless autorifle against the armory's doorjamb and sighted across the hall from where he had last seen the stickie. With the bad light and the short distance between the doorways, a trap lead was the only way to score consistently.

A trap lead and a triburst.

He had learned that the hard way.

When the stickie bolted from the door to his left, Ryan tightened his finger on the trigger. His smooth, steady pull ended when the trigger broke and the autorifle bucked against his shoulder. The triple shot caught the stickie high in the chest and sent it sprawling on its back in the hall. The stickie wasn't alone there. In the half hour J.B. had been sweating over the safe's security system, Doc and Ryan had dropped eight or ten stickies as they tried, rather clumsily, to sneak up on them.

"I do believe that puts you one ahead, my dear Ryan," Doc said, shaking his gun hand to loosen up the muscles.

"Bingo!" a voice said behind them. J.B. had finally sprung the safe.

"Stay on the door, Doc," Ryan said as he entered the armory. J.B. and Mildred were staring at the open door of the safe. Both of them were grinning. "How'd you do it?" Ryan said.

"Just got lucky, I guess."

"He had about a zillion connections wired up," Mildred said. "He cross-rigged the card sensors somehow."

"Feedback loop," J.B. corrected her. "It takes a while but it works every time."

"Have we got a nuke in there?" Ryan said.

J.B. reached into the half-height doorway and rolled out a fat, gleaming silver cylinder, bristling with electronic do-dads, keypads and readouts. The nuke had its own little wheeled gurney, complete with tool rack and ops manual. "This was thoughtful," J.B. said, flipping through the loose-leaf notebook. "Hey, it's a twenty-five kiloton model. Crater city."

"How much longer till we can make the jump?" Ryan asked him.

"It'll take me fifteen to twenty minutes to work through this checklist, if Mildred helps me."

"Sure," she said. "Just tell me what you need."

"Get on it, then," Ryan said.

IT TOOK PRECISELY eighteen minutes for J.B. to prep and fuse the baby nuke. When he punched in the last code sequence, the device gave off a series of high-pitched peeping noises, like an electronic chick desperate to find its mother.

"We can move it now," J.B. said. "I'm not going to arm it or punch in the time to detonation until after we've jumped and we've arrived wherever the hell we're going."

"Sounds good to me," Ryan said. "Better pick up more ammo and some grens for the trip back down to the lowest level. We still got a lot of hostiles between us and the gateway."

The trouble was, they didn't know where all the hostiles had gotten to.

Even though Ryan and the others had done a sweep of the lowest level of the complex right after securing the mat-trans chamber, they hadn't found a single mutie. They had vanished into the ventilation system like cockroaches under a baseboard. Ryan and J.B. had found a couple of duct grates torn off and some fresh blood drops inside.

The escaped muties could be anywhere in the redoubt by now.

Ryan and J.B. walked in front of the nuke-on-wheels. Doc and Mildred took turns pushing it and bringing up the rear. They saw a lot of stickies on the way to the elevator. None of them live, however.

"You sure know how to make a mess, Ryan," J.B. commented as he booted the body of a stickie out of the way so the cart could roll past.

"That was one of Doc's," Ryan said.

"Yeah, how do you know?"

"Did it have a head?"

"Not that I could tell."

"I rest my case. His Le Mat takes no prisoners."

"Hey, Doc," J.B. said, "we got to get you a neater blaster."

"My boy, neatness only counts in penmanship," the old man countered. "I assure you I am quite content with the antique blaster I have. It is a perfect match for my damnable failing eyesight and the palsied trembling of my shooting hand. A room broom."

J.B. checked the roof of the car before they entered it. He remained on top of the elevator as they rode it down to the bottom level, to make sure that no hostiles leaped on top as it crept down the shaft.

When the doors opened, the companions fanned out from the entrance, searching the broad room for targets.

"Where is everybody?" J.B. asked.

The room looked deserted, but it didn't *feel* deserted.

Mildred scratched the back of her neck.

Ryan caught her gesture, and they shared a look. "Yeah, I know," he said. "I feel it, too. I think we're going to catch it from both sides in about a minute."

J.B. started to pull stun and frag grens out of his pants pockets. He stacked them up on the gurney on either side of the nuke. "Help yourselves, when the need arises," he said.

They started moving away from the elevators, blasters at the ready. A head popped up way back in the rows of desks to the right. Autofire clattered and flashed. Bullets whined harmlessly overhead, then the figure dropped back down out of sight.

"Gone but not forgotten," J.B. said, plinking off the grip safety of a fragger. He expertly underhanded the gren between the desks where the head had disappeared.

The travelers ducked as an earsplitting explosion sent the desks flying apart and made it rain ceiling tiles. A slurry of gore splashed over the banks of overhead lights.

"Got him," J.B. said.

The grenade explosion acted like a call to arms for all the blaster-toting muties in the level. They jumped up on both sides of Ryan and company and fired at will.

None of them could shoot with any degree of accuracy.

In the blaze of full-auto blasterfire, a couple of them did manage to hit one another, but that was an accident made possible by the sheer number of rounds they expended.

Ryan and the others returned fire as slugs pinged off

the legs of the nuke's gurney. They mowed down the muties before they could duck behind the desks.

Doc had just discharged his monster barrel when the tile ceiling in front of them collapsed. For a split second the companions thought there was a connection between the two events. Then they realized there wasn't.

If they'd been wondering what had happened to the rest of the stickies, they wondered no longer. Bunches of the naked mutants dropped through the ceiling on all sides of them. There wasn't time to think, only to react. And since they had fought together as a team for some time, they knew exactly how to do that. They backed up against the cart, each taking a corner, and cut loose with everything they had.

Mildred used an H&K MP-5 A she'd picked up in the armory. It was a brutal weapon at close range. And this was very close range. She fired on full-auto inches from the stickies' chests, heads and bellies, blowing them back onto the linoleum. The backsplash of guts and brains alone would've caused a less hearty soul to faint dead away. Mildred dumped the empty mag, flipped it over and cracked in the full one she had joined to it with duct tape. She clacked the bolt and let the H&K rip some more, aiming up into the gaps in the ceiling where she could see movement.

Bodies dropped through the ceiling's metal framework, bodies already mortally wounded.

J.B. tromboned his 12-gauge and sent blast after blast of fléchettes into the oncoming muties. Before the second plastic hull had hit the floor, he had cycled through the mag. The stickies he hit with fléchettes didn't get up. At a range of four feet, all those little steel darts were still clustered in a supertight spread. It was like getting slammed by a howitzer round, and it made a big hole.

Finally the stickies stopped coming.

The rolling thunder of their blasterfire echoed deep in the building, then quickly faded. They could hear the chitter of the computer banks again.

"Watch out for the empties," J.B. said, kicking aside a welter of brass hulls that littered the floor. "You could break your rad-blasted leg."

They pushed the cart bearing the nuke over to the entrance to the gateway. It took all four of them to lift the weapon and its cart inside. They set it down on one of the hexagonal floor plates.

"Make sure your mags are full," Ryan said. "There's no way of telling what we're jumping into."

When the others had done that, he reached over and pulled the chamber door shut.

Static electricity crackled around and around the armaglass walls.

Ryan looked up and watched the fog begin to form just under the ceiling. He remembered his last jump and for a moment, just before he sat on the floor, he felt a twinge of nameless dread.

His jump dream started out better than most.

He appeared quite suddenly in the middle of a scene of domestic bliss in a Swiss-chalet-type farmhouse,

Ryan, the daddy dirt picker, and Krysty, the vastly pregnant dirt picker's wife. Mildred was there, acting as midwife because an infant Cawdor was due to make its Deathlands debut.

On a rustic, wood-framed bed, dressed in a long cotton nightshirt, Krysty lay back and prepared to give birth. Her face was flushed and beaded with sweat, her breathing hard and quick.

"That's it," Mildred said. "Push now. I can almost see the top of the head."

Ryan could see nothing because Mildred was in the way. He moved closer to her and looked over her shoulder. The woman was right. There, peeking out between his lover's splayed labia, was the crest of his child's head. It appeared to have no hair.

"Push harder," Mildred urged.

Krysty panted and pushed, gritting her teeth as she strained.

"It's coming," Ryan told her. "It's coming."

The head popped out into the light of day, face up. It had no nose to speak of, just a pair of holes in the middle of its face. Its eyes were black and dead, like a doll's. And when it opened its mouth, it had rows of little needle teeth.

Ryan choked back a gasp. With his left hand he reached over Mildred's shoulder and went for the hairless head; with his right, he grabbed the leather-wrapped handle of his eighteen-inch panga, which was sheathed to the back of his calf.

Before he could catch hold of it, the half-born stickie

sank its teeth into its own mother's crotch. Krysty screamed and started pounding between her legs with her fists. Blood sprayed all over the bed.

"Back!" Ryan said, shoving Mildred aside.

Everything moved in slow motion, everything except the little stickie's jaws.

Ryan grabbed the thing by the head and jerked it out of Krysty's body. Its neck was stronger than it looked and it didn't break. He flipped the stickie around and held it by its ankles. Still connected to Krysty by the umbilical cord, it growled at him and snapped.

He swung the panga down in a tight arc, severing the cord in the middle. While Mildred tried to stop Krysty's bleeding, Ryan left the chalet, carrying the stickie infant by its heels. He took it across the farm-yard, under snow-capped mountains and a bright blue sky. He carried it to the pigpen, where his hogs awaited their slops.

And threw it in.

RYAN CAME TO ON HIS KNEES. His head was spinning, but he knew he had to get up and get ready to fight. The lapis-lazuli-colored armaglass wall was no help when it came to standing. It was slicker than slick. He bit the tip of his tongue until he tasted blood. The sharp pain cleared his head, driving back the tendrils of jump fog.

Mildred was already up and trying to rouse Doc. J.B. appeared to be awake, but just barely. Ryan gripped him under an armpit and helped him to his feet.

"Bad jump?" J.B. asked.

"Is there any other kind?"

"Yeah, dumb question."

Doc stood up on his own and brushed at the front of his frock coat's lapels. It was a fruitless gesture. What was on those lapels had been there for a very long time, and it was never coming off.

"I don't see anyone outside," Mildred said as she turned back from the chamber door's small window. "We'd better move while we can."

They gathered up their weapons and slipped out the gateway door.

The room outside could have been transplanted from most of the redoubts they had visited over the years. It was standardized, government issue: low ceiling, fluorescent lights, computer banks, linoleum floor, rows of metal desks. The only thing different about this place were the piles of black plastic garbage bags lying along the outside of the chamber.

Ryan untied one of the bags and poked around inside. When he drew his hand back, it was full of papers. "The Apocalypticon," he said. "It's all right here where Kaa dumped it."

"The glory that was Greece, the grandeur that was, et cetera, et cetera," Doc intoned.

"Help me get the nuke out of the chamber," Ryan said.

When they had lifted the device and its gurney onto the floor of the complex, Ryan lifted the plastic bag he had opened and dumped the contents out on the tile.

He grabbed one of the handholds built into the side of the nuke's casing and nodded at J.B. "Give me a hand here," he said.

The two of them muscled the bomb into the center of the opened plastic bag.

"Set the timer but don't engage it yet," Ryan instructed.

J.B. leaned over the nuke and tapped a nine-digit access code into its keypad. "Okay, how much time should we give them?"

"Five minutes ought to do it."

J.B. input the numbers. "To engage the timer you just hit this button once."

"Got it," Ryan said. He started pouring the papers on top of the nuke. He didn't tie the top closed, but left it folded over. "Now let's find a way out of here," he said.

Chapter Twenty-Five

It was hard for Krysty to maintain her composure with Kaa sitting so close to her on the settee, discussing his plans for their imminent marriage. The veil of illusion had been lifted from her eyes. Whatever the mat-trans system had given to her in terms of psychic simpatico with Kaa and members of the stickie race, it had subsequently taken it away. She remembered what she'd felt before her last jump, but she couldn't remember why. In retrospect it all seemed like one of those fever-inspired nightmares in which the internal logic is perfect, if demonic, and when you wake up, you recall that while you slept, you acted against all your waking principles and, to your shame, had a great time doing so.

Krysty had been taught by Mother Sonja to respect all life, and to judge beings by their actions, not their genetics. Mother Sonja had taught her to judge quickly, and be right. Deathlands was no place for a universal do-gooder, even one with the power of Gaia. Do-gooderism wasn't a survival trait in the place Krysty called home.

What had seemed so attractive to her before her recent jump, Kaa's unification of all the mutie races against the norms, now seemed utterly wrong to her. For a time she had been ready to spill the blood of every norm, if necessary, to free "her people." Now she wasn't. Now she was able to measure Kaa's philosophy through her own perspective.

Sure, mutants had been getting the wrong end of the stick from norms for a long, long time. Sure, mutants outnumbered them. Sure, mutants weren't inherently evil. But neither were norms. Some of the norms she'd met were capable of compassion, gentleness, decency, honor. In a world peopled by far too few honorable beings, it seemed a criminal waste to chill every norm. After all, mutants decidedly weren't inherently good, either. Not only that, but there was something twisted in most of them, though not each and every one. In a way they were a danger to the human species and she knew that was the root of the way many norm humans reacted to them. Krysty knew that from her own experience. So why should the bad mutants live while the good norms died?

It made no sense.

In some other situation, in some other place, she might have raised these questions to Kaa. She might have even debated with him, point by point. But here, trapped in his lair, far from her friends if they still lived, sitting so close to him, she had no intention of risking an argument. This despite the fact that he had shown no tendency to temper. In fact he seemed quite gentle. Except when he was lost in the throes of a third-eye fit.

His politeness and reserve only made the whole situation more confusing for her. If he had been violent and threatening, she could have written him off as just another Deathlands thug. But clearly he wasn't. She could see how that genteel part of him might have been attractive to her, but she couldn't understand how she could have overlooked the repulsiveness of his physical appearance, how she could have agreed, without a second thought, to mate with him. She deeply regretted that decision now.

"Angelica, you seem distant," he said. "Are you all right?"

She managed to smile up at him. She was less successful in her attempt to avoid staring at the wiry little creature that was wriggling under the skin of his cheek. "I'm fine," she said, shifting her gaze to the mossy green shadows that framed his front teeth.

"Good," he said, "then let's go. Everything is ready downstairs. I can't stand to wait any longer."

Offering a hand, he helped her to her feet, then guided her out of the room and down the second-story corridor.

"I wish my friend and sponsor, the owner of this place, was here to witness our wedding," Kaa said. "Pressing business called him away to another part of Deathlands. I know he'll be disappointed."

Krysty wasn't listening. She walked like a pull toy on a string. As they descended the wide, carpeted staircase, the woman saw the audience Kaa had assembled for their wedding. Standing in front of the great windows of the house were a few dozen stickies, mostly immature ones, some still suckling, and Jak Lauren.

Krysty wanted to break away from Kaa's grasp, but she didn't. It was so strange. She was reluctant to hurt his feelings, but ready to chill him if given half the chance.

Jak looked apprehensive as she took her place by the window.

The ceremony was brief and to the point. Kaa asked her to be his wife and bear his offspring. She said she would, though she didn't intend on doing anything of the kind. There was no public kissing to seal the deal; for that, Krysty was thankful. Kaa scooped her up in his massive arms and carried her back up the stairs.

"I know we will be content," he was saying.

Again she wasn't listening. She was trying to think of a way to escape before the marriage was consummated.

He carried her into a lavish bedroom suite and gently set her down on the edge of the bed. She noticed that his huge hands were trembling, and that there was a great bulge stretching out the front of his loincloth.

"I've waited for this moment for such a long time," he told her. "I've never been with a female before. Not ever. I've saved myself, I've saved all my seed for you."

With that, Kaa ungirded his loins, and his turgid member sprang up from its confinement. "For you," he said, stroking himself to full erection. "All for you."

His cock wasn't only big, it was too big. And the

hairless scrotum beneath it looked bloated and swollen, and it was drawn up tight like the bag of an aroused bull.

He moved closer to her so she could touch it.

Krysty didn't want to be anywhere near it, but she needed to buy some time. Though she tried, she couldn't get her fingers all the way around it. And as she tried, she could feel the wire worms wiggling under the tightly stretched skin. She steeled herself to the task and caressed him once, from root to tip, then she said, "Wash first. Please."

He stepped back at once. "Of course, I'm sorry," he said. "I'll do it now. I'll be right back."

The moment he shut the hallway door, she was up and running. When she tried the handle, she found it was locked.

"Krysty?" a voice on the other side said. "You in there?"

"Jak! Get me out of here!"

"Can't do it," he said. "Door not open. No key out here. He be back any minute."

Krysty closed her eyes and called on her Gaia power. As she emptied her mind, the Earth Mother force swept into her body, filling her with incredible strength. She gripped the knob with both hands and turned it. It snapped off with a crack. Tossing the knob aside, she poked her finger into the hole and clicked over the latch. She had the door open in a flash. Strangely, using the power didn't sap her strength.

"Back to the redoubt!" she said to Jak as she dashed past him.

They sprinted down the stairs and across the great hall's entry room. They were out the door and down the path toward the steam shadow when they heard a voice boom from the mansion behind them.

"Angelica! Angelica! Wait!"

Waiting was what they had no intention of doing.

It was a downhill run all the way to the redoubt's entrance. The path was in better shape than most they'd seen. The asphalt was still intact, with no gaping holes to stumble on. Muggy clouds hung low over the road, shrouding the tropical trees, vines and flowers from the sun. Krysty's and Jak's backs and heads were instantly dripping with condensed moisture.

Neither one of them spoke as they ran, not wanting to waste their breath. They knew that Kaa would be close behind, and that he wouldn't be pleased. When they came to the redoubt's vanadium-steel entry doors, Jak punched in the entry code. The doors swung back and they entered. On the way past the inside control panel, he tapped in the close code. Then he raced to catch up with Krysty.

The ramp they followed zigzagged down to the top floor of the redoubt. Unlike the complex near Willie ville, it didn't have a fleet of vehicles in cold storage. The upper floor was given over to rows of large crates and boxes, which were stacked to the ceiling in places. Krysty and Jak ran down an aisle between the rows, heading for the double doors of the redoubt's elevators.

As they skidded to a stop in front of them, a bell chimed and the right-hand set of doors started to slide apart.

"Go for it," Jak shouted, prepared to throw himself at whoever was inside the car.

Krysty was ready, too, but when the doors opened she found herself looking into the face of her lover.

"Ryan! You're alive!" she cried, throwing her arms around him.

He hugged her briefly. "Sure am."

"Good to see you safe, my dear boy," Doc told the ruby-eyed teenager.

"Same here," Jak said impatiently. "Hate rush things, Kaa two minutes behind."

"Step in," Ryan told him. When the boy got in the car, Ryan hit the Down button. The doors slid shut, and the elevator descended smoothly.

"Are you all okay?" Krysty asked as she accepted her handblaster from Ryan.

"Everybody's fine," Mildred said. "Funny, but all that stickie dream stuff seems like it happened to someone else. The last jump seems to have cleared my head."

"Mine, too," Krysty said. "I feel like my old self again." As she looked around the group, the others nodded, as well. "I wonder what happened?"

"DEEP," Doc muttered.

"What's that, Doc?" Ryan said.

"I do not know," he admitted. "It just popped into my head. D.E.E.P is an acronym for Download Error

Elimination Protocol, I think. I seem to recall that it is part of the gateway software package. It could be a replication checker."

"Dark night, Doc, could you put it a little plainer?"

"I seem to recall there was a program that shifted through the gateway's information on you before you were actually rematerialized by the system. It checked to make sure that no mistakes were made, that everything was in sync with your DNA code. On the other hand, if it is disabled for some reason, then I suspect errors can creep in."

"So, when we went back through the mat-trans system," Krysty said, "it automatically removed the stuff we got from the stickies?"

"I do believe that was what happened. Are we still going to nuke this place?"

"Nuke it?" Krysty repeated.

Ryan nodded. "J.B. busted into the nuke-safe at the other redoubt. We got a live baby-nuke screamer waiting down by the gateway chamber. We know how dangerous it is." He gave her an intense look. "Do you have a problem with that?"

Krysty didn't have to think twice. "No. No problem. It's something that has to be done. It's just that with all the rad poison that's already all over Deathlands, I hate to add more. That madness was supposed to have ended a hundred years ago."

As soon as they stepped out of the car on the lowest level, the elevator chimed and the doors closed. They

could hear the motor engage and the car start back up
to the top.

"He's here already," J.B. said. "We'd better get a
move on."

They ran under the low ceiling, across the gray, in-
stitutional linoleum to the piles of plastic bags beside
the gateway chamber.

"It's the Apocalypticon," Krysty said.

"More than that," Ryan told her. He folded down
the top of one of the bags, exposing the armed nuke.
"Is this the button here?" he asked J.B.

"Hit it."

Ryan pressed the keypad, and the device started to
cheep. It cheeped about a dozen times in rapid succes-
sion, then a set of numbers appeared in the LED readout: 5:00, 4:59, 4:58. Ryan pulled up the sides of the
bag and tied it closed.

"What about all this stuff?" Mildred asked, gestur-
ing at the piles of bags. "Shouldn't we take some of it
with us?"

"No time for that," Ryan said. "We've got to be out
of here before Kaa reaches the mat-trans unit."

They scrambled into the chamber, and J.B. punched
the LD button, which would send them back to the
Willie ville redoubt. Ryan pulled the door closed. The
moment the lock clacked, they heard the rapidly building whine of the system's electronics. The scent of
ozone trickled through the chamber.

Ryan watched the elevators through the clear armaglass window. He saw the doors open and Lord Kaa

rush out. The mutant was naked except for his combat boots, and he carried an M-60 machine gun.

That was the image Ryan carried as he fell into unconsciousness.

Chapter Twenty-Six

Lord Kaa sprinted across the redoubt's lower level, heading straight for the gateway chamber. As he neared the door, the system was still cycling down; he could hear the shrill whine of its electronics. The whine died away as his finger closed around the door handle. He jerked open the door.

There was nothing inside. Only a few wisps of mist remained.

"Angelica!" he cried. "Angelica, why did you do this to me?"

He slumped to the floor of the chamber, dropping Joyeuse by his side. He had read of females who betrayed and teased. The legends were full of them, beautiful women with wiles that mesmerized and vanquished even the most valiant and steadfast of Charlemagne's heroes. Had Angelica in reality been one of those deceptive, cunning creatures? If so, why hadn't he sensed it? Up until the moment she had made her escape, he had been certain that she shared his feelings and his dreams.

He put his head between his hands. What was he to do now? he asked himself. To pursue her to the ends of the earth? That's what the heroes of the legends had done. They had put aside all other concerns and chased after the ladyloves who had rejected them.

It seemed an empty quest, more suited to willful and wild paladins than to their wise and respected leader.

That, too, he had learned from his study of Charlemagne's life.

But he couldn't deny the pain in his heart. It was exactly as he had imagined it, and as hurtful as what he had felt at the death of his loyal troops, at the loss of his army. It was hard for him to reconcile the equality of pain. Though no one had died just now, his sense of loss was no less. Twice in a single day, a victory that he had longed for had been snatched from his grasp.

He wanted revenge against the impostor Angelica for deceiving him, but only on his terms. He wouldn't spend time and energy chasing her down now. To do that would mean giving up his plans for the rebuilding of his army. No, he would wait to taste vengeance. Once he had his troop strength up, much wiser for the mistakes he had made, he would resume his campaign against the eastern barons. Eventually his path and hers would cross again. And then he would make her pay.

Kaa got up and looked at the gateway chamber's control panel. The LD button was still clicked in. She and the boy had jumped back to Willie ville. So much the better, he thought. They might still be in the vicinity when he returned in a week or two with fresh troops.

As he stepped out of the chamber, he regarded the stickies who had followed him down from the mansion.

They were the nucleus of his new army. He reached up to open his third eye and converse with them, but a sound nearby made him stop.

It was a cheeping noise, harsh, electronic.

It seemed to be coming from the pile of trash bags.

Kaa knelt over the heap and quickly located the source of the sound. He ripped open the bag and stared dumbfounded at the domed top of a mininuke. The cheeping abruptly stopped. It was meant to draw attention to the countdown timer, and it had.

The numbers had fallen to sixty seconds, fifty-nine, fifty-eight.

The piebald man leaped to his feet. There was no time to explain the situation to the stickies, no time to peel back his lid and show them the kind of help he required. Kaa began to grab the black plastic bags and throw them over his shoulder into the gateway chamber.

There were a lot of bags, and he didn't have much time to work.

He tried not to think about how Angelica had sabotaged him, the extent of her treachery, how she had to have conspired with others to plant the nuke under his nose. In a fury he moved the Apocalypticon from the floor to the heart of the chamber. The stickies huddled together uneasily out under the lights. They didn't understand his agitation, and it alarmed them.

Twenty-two seconds.

Twenty-one.

He had to stop, even though there were still precious

documents outside the chamber. He knew it would take time to reprogram the controls and for the system to cycle up for transfer.

Without a word to his stickies, Kaa jumped back through the chamber entry. He couldn't risk just hitting the LD button again. There was no telling what kind of welcoming committee Angelica and her friends would have waiting for him. He wasn't an expert at running the gateways yet, but he knew how to switch the system to automatic, which meant that once the chamber powered up, he would be sent at random to the nearest available mat-trans unit, and that meant he could end up well away from ground zero.

He tripped the automatic sequencer, and the chamber began to hum. As he reached for the door handle, he looked at his stickies, clustered there with the remaining plastic bags. How could he turn his back on them?

Ten.

Nine.

Kaa opened his third eye, and the stickies jerked. He sent one image into their mutant brains, a moving picture of them running, diving through the chamber door.

Seven.

Six.

By the time the counter dropped to five, the last stickie had hurled itself over the portal. Kaa slammed the door shut. He glared out the window at the device that stood only a few yards away. It was close enough that he could see the readout.

Four.

Three.

Fog tendrils caressed the top of his head, numbing it.

He turned away from the chamber door's window, knowing he had waited too long.

THE SECOND JUMP in such a short time took its toll on Ryan and the others. It left them shaky and disoriented. No one vomited, but they all tried, dry-heaving in chorus. Gradually the retching subsided, and they sat on the hexagonal floor plates with their backs pressed against the armaglass wall, trying to catch their breath.

"Do you think we got him?" Dix asked.

"If the nuke detonated," Ryan replied. "I saw him come running out of the elevator right before everything went black. If it detonated, there's nothing left of that redoubt. Probably took out half the mountainside with it."

Mildred opened the chamber door. She had her ZKR 551 target revolver out in front of her. "Don't see any more stickies," she said. "It looks all clear to me."

They exited the gateway and, once outside, stretched and loosened their cramped muscles.

"See a big mutie mountain lion here?" Jak asked the others.

"Yeah, we saw it," J.B. said. "It was a blur going that way."

"You didn't chill it?"

"We tried, my dear boy," Doc said, "but we missed by more than a mile."

"If you're thinking about getting reacquainted with it," Krysty said, "mebbe you'd better think again."

Jak frowned at her.

"Because you aren't the same critter it licked up and down a few hours ago," Krysty went on. "You've lost something you were never supposed to have. It might not find you such a good companion anymore."

"Might find it likes you more as lunch," J.B. said, laughing.

"Not afraid of him."

"Seriously, Jak," Krysty said, "you'd be taking a big risk if you let that cat get close to you again."

"Not around here, so not a problem."

"Probably took off up the ventilation system," Ryan said. "He's out there, roaming Deathlands by now."

"Fine with me," Jak said. "Deserves to be free."

They checked their weapons, then moved for the elevator, which was still where they had left it. It didn't look as if they had any new hostiles to worry about.

When they reached the redoubt's top level, J.B. once again disconnected the elevator from its power source. Then they walked up the ramp and through the double doors.

It was night outside. The moon was already high in the sky, a disk of polished bone. A soft, warm breeze ruffled their clothes.

"Smells good out here," J.B. commented.

"Yeah, clean," Jak said.

"Did you ever in your life see so many stars?" Doc asked, tipping his head back.

Ryan put his arm around Krysty's slender waist, his fingers finding the rounded curve of her hip. She leaned against him, and as she did, strands of her hair uncoiled to softly brush his cheek.

"Where to now?" Mildred asked him.

"Don't know. Mebbe we should take a hike over to Byrum ville."

"Why would we want to go there?" J.B. asked.

"I'm just thinking that we don't know if we chilled Kaa. Nuke could've been a dud. Mebbe we should head on up the baron's road and have a talk with Blackheart Hutton. Then mebbe go on and visit the other barons around here."

"Ryan, we practically got ourselves chilled the last time we tried to warn them."

"Yeah," Jak said. "Didn't believe us then. Why would they believe us now?"

"Because of that," Ryan said. He pointed way down the valley, under the glittering field of stars. Almost on the horizon line, something glowed red-orange.

"That's Willie ville?"

"Still burning," Ryan said. "Everybody within fifty miles of that tower is going to know something bad went down. We don't have to prove anything this time."

"I think it's a good idea," Mildred said. "If Kaa isn't dead, he's going to be back this way sooner or later."

"I don't think it's a good idea, but I'll go along with it because I'm too tired to argue," J.B. said.

"Count me in, as well," Doc said.

"Then it's settled," Ryan said. With that, he and Krysty started down the ruined road.

A FEW HOURS LATER, when the company stopped to rest, Ryan and Krysty slipped away from the others. Until they kissed, there was still a strangeness between them. Once their lips touched, however, the old magic returned in a rush.

"I missed doing that," she said huskily. Her palm was already pressed flat against the bulge of his crotch, gently but insistently rubbing him to life. "Missed this, too."

"Wait a minute," he said, lifting her hand from him. He kissed the center of her palm. "I want to talk to you about something first. It's something I should've told you about a long time ago."

Haltingly at first, but then with rapidly growing confidence, Ryan gave her the whole story on his participation in the Mutie War and the battle of Coupe ville. He didn't sugarcoat it for her. He didn't underplay his role in the massacre. He didn't try to excuse his actions because he was young and wild, or because he had lost friends to the mutie rebels' blasters and blades. He laid it all out for her to see, and when he was done, he told her why he hadn't explained any of that part of his history to her before.

"How could I tell you about it when I couldn't face up to it myself?" he said. "Until that real bad jump we had with the stickies in the chamber, I couldn't make myself look at what I'd done. I guess because I was afraid that I might do it again."

"That won't ever happen," Krysty said. "You're too strong to let it."

"I think you're right. I know I'm not worried about it anymore."

"Come here, lover," she said, putting her hands on his shoulders and pulling him close. She unzipped the front of her jumpsuit and put his hand inside.

Ryan brushed her nipples with the backs of his knuckles, gently bumping them over the rising tips.

Krysty stood still for this teasing caress only for a moment. Then she was climbing out of her jumpsuit and unzipping his fly. She drew him out with her hand, then wrapped her arms around his neck and jumped up, locking her long, slender legs around his waist. Her tongue pushed into his mouth as she reached for him under her buttocks. Her fingers guided him into her blazing warmth.

Her wild squirming, coupled with an unseen fallen branch, sent them both toppling to the ground. Laughing, she remounted him. Krysty finished first, then using the amazing interior muscles that were part of her Gaia gift, drew him to sudden, violent climax, as well.

Under the stars they lay exhausted in each other's arms. Secure in the knowledge that J.B. was on watch, they drifted off to sleep.

KAA FELT NEITHER the heat nor the flash of the nuke. That was because, technically speaking, he was no longer inside the mat-trans chamber when the device detonated. A few nanoseconds before the explosion, his molecules—as well as the molecules of all the living and inanimate contents of the gateway—had been mapped and deconstructed, and the information necessary for reconstruction prepared for transmission.

At the instant of thermonuclear ignition, the data was already cycling through a back-loop on the planet-straddling, mat-trans pathway; it was in a holding pattern until the computer selected its random final destination. The automatic system had been designed to operate that way so it could accommodate thousands of nearly simultaneous transmissions without rematerialization overlay. A final electronic handshake between destination and departure point was required before the transfer was effected.

Therein lay the glitch.

A nanosecond postblast, there was no longer a departure point for any one of the hundreds of possible destination gateways to connect to. Encoded and perpetually en route, Kaa's DNA sequence, his brain-wave pattern, the three-dimensional structure of his every cell, surfed the Cerberus network, going nowhere in particular at the speed of light.

And as it hurtled around and around, Kaa's digitized simulacra dreamed a dream that had no discernible beginning or end.

He appeared to tumble through a black void, and as he fell, thin objects fluttered all around him, like leaves, only rectangular. And white. There was an endless supply of them. And they flicked past him so quickly that he couldn't tell one from another. There was no pattern to their coming and going, no repeating shifts in their density or direction. It was all perfectly, horribly random, which was why he couldn't tell the past from the present or the present from the past.

No end.

No beginning.

In other words, a loop.

Out of desperation, he fumbled for the flaps of his third eye and peeled them back. He looked inward, hoping for a glimpse of something he recognized. Even his worst nightmare was preferable to this.

But the view inside was the same as the view outside: a timeless black waste, millions of sheets of paper whipped by a silent whirlwind, and Kaa, falling.

The Destroyer takes on a plague of
invisible insects—as the exterminator

THE

Destroyer

#107 Feast or Famine

Created by
WARREN MURPHY
and RICHARD SAPIR

Is the insect kingdom mobilizing to reclaim the planet...or
is something entirely different behind it all? Unless the
Destroyer can combat this disaster, a whole nation may
start dropping like flies.

Look for it in April wherever Gold Eagle books are sold.

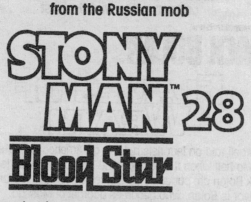

Don't miss out on the action in these titles!

**Don't miss out on the action in these titles featuring
THE EXECUTIONER®, STONY MAN™ and SUPERBOLAN®!**

The Red Dragon Trilogy

#64210	FIRE LASH	$3.75 U.S.	☐
		$4.25 CAN.	☐
#64211	STEEL CLAWS	$3.75 U.S.	☐
		$4.25 CAN.	☐
#64212	RIDE THE BEAST	$3.75 U.S.	☐
		$4.25 CAN.	☐

Stony Man™

#61907	THE PERISHING GAME	$5.50 U.S.	☐
		$6.50 CAN.	☐
#61908	BIRD OF PREY	$5.50 U.S.	☐
		$6.50 CAN.	☐
#61909	SKYLANCE	$5.50 U.S.	☐
		$6.50 CAN.	☐

SuperBolan®

#61448	DEAD CENTER	$5.50 U.S.	☐
		$6.50 CAN.	☐
#61449	TOOTH AND CLAW	$5.50 U.S.	☐
		$6.50 CAN.	☐
#61450	RED HEAT	$5.50 U.S.	☐
		$6.50 CAN.	☐

(limited quantities available on certain titles)

TOTAL AMOUNT	$
POSTAGE & HANDLING	$
($1.00 for one book, 50¢ for each additional)	
APPLICABLE TAXES*	$_____
TOTAL PAYABLE	$_____
(check or money order—please do not send cash)	

To order, complete this form and send it, along with a check or money order for the total above, payable to Gold Eagle Books, to: **In the U.S.:** 3010 Walden Avenue, P.O. Box 9077, Buffalo, NY 14269-9077; **In Canada:** P.O. Box 636, Fort Erie, Ontario, L2A 5X3.

Name:_____

Address:_____ City:_____

State/Prov.:_____ Zip/Postal Code: _____

*New York residents remit applicable sales taxes.
 Canadian residents remit applicable GST and provincial taxes.

GEBACK17